QUARTET E

A POSTHUMOUS CONFESSION

Marcellus Emants created, in the uniquely solitary character of Termeer, who has plotted and coldly carried out his
wife's murder, the embodiment of his beliefs about the
character of modern man. Termeer is unremarkable, or so it
seems until he gradually reveals the sad childhood and
youth that have turned him into an emotional cipher.
Obviously disappointed in him from earliest childhood, his
parents seized upon every opportunity to strengthen his
conviction of his own worthlessness. This subtle brutaliza-
tion had its inevitable effect, and he fulfilled their dismal
prophecies, until, to his own amazement, he successfully
courted a beautiful, accomplished woman.

The marriage could not withstand Termeer's coldness.
Incapable of joy, he relentlessly persecuted his wife and
even took satisfaction in the death of their infant daughter.

Locked out of his wife's bedroom, Termeer began an
affair, an association which was the turning point of his life
because it was, in a ghastly way, his emotional awakening.
At last he is motivated by desire. In order to enjoy his
increasingly demanding mistress without the encumbrance
of his wife, he tries to force her to agree to a separation but
finally decides that only her death will permit him to enjoy
his new-found pleasure.

After the funeral, Termeer sits safely in his study and
meticulously examines the events that led him to poison
his wife. As he recites his litany of self-justification, he
begins to experience other new varieties of feeling. Fear,
guilt, and an overwhelming desire to unburden himself, to
confess, grow within him.

MARCELLUS EMANTS

Marcellus Emants was born in 1848, and became one of the most important figures in the reorientation of Dutch literary life. He started as a poet and dramatist, but his fiction is his best work. Fiercely criticized by the literary establishment for transgressing prevailing ethical and religious principles, he earned the reputation of a trail-blazing pioneer among the younger generation. He was especially instrumental in spreading the fame and influence of Zola throughout the Netherlands. After the disappointment of his initial idealism, however, he became profoundly pessimistic, and always remained a solitary figure in Dutch letters. He died in 1923.

MARCELLUS EMANTS

A Posthumous Confession

Translated from the Dutch
and with an Introduction by
J.M. COETZEE

QUARTET ENCOUNTERS

Quartet Books   London Melbourne New York

First published in Great Britain
by Quartet Books Limited 1986
A member of the Namara Group
27/29 Goodge Street, London W1P 1FD

Translation copyright © 1986 by J.M. Coetzee
Introduction copyright © 1986 by J.M. Coetzee

British Library Cataloguing in Publication Data

Emants, Marcellus
  A posthumous confession.
  I. Title   II. Een nagelaten bekentenis. *English*
  839.3'135[F]   PT5833

ISBN 0–7043–0023–0

Reproduced, printed and bound in Great Britain
by Nene Litho and Woolnough Bookbinding
both of Wellingborough, Northants

INTRODUCTION

The Netherlands of the mid-nineteenth century was one of the cultural backwaters of Europe. The great current of the Romantic movement had barely stirred its complacent materialism. It had produced only a single literary work of stature, Eduard Douwes Dekker's novel *Max Havelaar* (1860), an attack on abuses in the colonial East Indies.

In the last quarter of the century, however, the new waves of Impressionism, Wagnerism and Naturalism began to wash Dutch shores, and by the 1880s a full literary awakening, the Movement of Eighty, was under way. Among the prophets claimed for them-selves by the young men of the movement was the writer Marcellus Emants. It was a role Emants de-clined, as he was to decline affiliation to any group or school.

Born in 1848 into a patrician family from The Hague, Marcellus Emants was intended for a career in the law. But he detested the joyless drinking and promiscuity of Leiden student life, and abandoned his studies as soon as his father died. Thereafter he lived as a writer of independent means, travelling abroad to avoid the Dutch winters. He made three marriages, the last of them singularly wretched. After the world war, fearing Socialist government and high taxes, he removed to Switzerland, where he died in 1923.

Though Emants thought of himself as a playwright first and foremost, it is his novels and stories that have kept his name alive, principally *Een nagelaten beken-*

tenis (*A Posthumous Confession*, 1894), *Inwijding* (*Initiation*, 1900), *Waan* (*Delusion*, 1905), *Liefdesleven* (*Love-life*, 1916) and *Mensen* (*People*, 1920). Their principal subject is love and marriage: deluded love, unhappy marriage. Emants is one of a line of European novelists who, in dissecting the intimate discords of modern marriage, have also explored the discontents of modern Western civilization: Flaubert, Tolstoy, Ford Madox Ford, Lawrence.

In the literary handbooks Emants is usually classed among the Naturalists. He seems to belong there because (like the Goncourt brothers) he is interested in the sexual under-life of the bourgeoisie and because (like Zola) he uses the language of the new sciences of heredity and psychopathology to explain human motivation.

But, though Emants was influenced by the patron thinkers of Naturalism – Taine, Spencer, Charcot – he differs from the Naturalists in important respects. His pessimism is far removed from Zola's faith in the power of the novelist to guide man towards a better future. Nor is there in Emants much of the painstaking and systematic description of milieu characteristic of Naturalism. His interest is in pyschological processes, his style analytic rather than descriptive. Where the committed Naturalist gathers a corpus of data on which to base his *roman expérimental*, Emants comes to his material in the traditional way, via chance, memory and introspection. His true sympathies lie with the older generation of European Realists, in particular with Flaubert and Turgenev.

In 1880 Emants published an essay on Turgenev which describes his own philosophy rather better than it does Turgenev's. In youth, he writes, we create a fantasy ideal of the self we hope to be. The pattern our life takes, however, is determined not by any ideal but by unconscious forces within us. These forces impel us to acts; and in our acts it is revealed to us who we truly are. The transition from living in terms of fantasy ideals to living in self-knowledge always entails dis-illusionment and pain. Such pain becomes acutest when we recognize how unbridgeably vast the gap is between the ideal and the true self.

There is a dual emphasis in this account: on the powerlessness of the individual before unconscious inner forces, and on the painful disillusionment of coming to maturity. If we turn to Willem Termeer, the narrator of *A Posthumous Confession*, we find both aspects present: a helpless drifting in a sea of passions, fears and envies; and an agonized twisting and turning to escape confrontation with the true self his life-history reveals to him: impotent, cowardly, ridiculous.

Yet in terms of his own view of life, Termeer cannot be blamed for being what he is. The son of a cold, spiteful mother and a sickly, irascible father with a taste for pornography who ends his life in a mental asylum — a 'degenerate', in the language of the day — Termeer is doomed (or at least feels himself to be doomed) by his birthright to repeat the past: to become a voluptuary and crypto-sado-masochist terrified of women, to choose a cold, dutiful spouse with whom to re-create his parents' loveless marriage, and at last to descend into madness.

As for social relations, the first memory Termeer has is of being taken to school and abandoned there like a rabbit in a cage of wild beasts. All around him he senses antagonism: people know there is something wrong with him, and for the good of the species want to put an end to him. His fellow-men are savage beasts, and society itself a gigantic system of cogs and wheels in which ineffectual creatures like himself are doomed to be crushed.

From the beginning of his life-story, Termeer thus presents himself as a victim, a victim of heredity, of the Darwinian jungle of life, of the impersonal social machinery. Quite as much as it is a piece of self-rending analysis and sly exhibitionism, his confession is an agonized plea for pity.

But is Termeer simply a victim? His self-fulfilling conviction that everyone hates him can equally well be read as a projection of his own malevolence. Before he commits his murder, he experiences episodes of blind rage during which he barely deflects himself from assaulting his wife, whom he has already contemplated raping. When he eventually kills her, the act is directed not only against a woman who denies him both love (the mothering love he craves) and, in the name of her duty to the institution of marriage, freedom, but against the society on whose behalf she stands like a wardress barring his way to what he wants: bliss. (Like Emma Bovary, Willem Termeer has read of bliss and is convinced it exists, somewhere.) Indeed, the agitated leaping and darting of his language is indication enough of the violence within him.

Termeer resorts to action in his war against society only when words fail him. The document he bequeaths us, we should remember, is his *second* confession. The first, 'an unadorned revelation of my most secret feelings', has been offered for publication and turned down as 'trivial'. In his failure to become a writer – an occupation for which he feels eminently qualified, being 'sick, highly complex, neurasthenic, in some respects of unsound mind, in other respects perverse' – we detect what is perhaps Termeer's deepest crisis. If there is no symbolic avenue by which he can claim a value for his life, then the only recourse left is action. Since revelation of his inner self, no matter how bizarre and wretched that self, is not enough to win him currency, he must create something outside himself and display that to the world, to give himself substance.

From this point of view we can see Termeer, and perhaps Emants too, as children of Rousseau, who in his *Confessions* inaugurated the literary mode of the exhaustive secular confession. Since the time of Rousseau we have seen the growth of the genre of the *confessional novel*, of which *A Posthumous Confes-*

sion is a singularly pure example. Termeer, claiming to be unable to keep his dreadful secret, records his confession and leaves it behind as a monument to himself, thereby turning a worthless life into art. As for his author, in the name of investigating the inner life of this 'superfluous man', this marginal member of the upper bourgeoisie, he is doing – what?

Some twenty years after *A Posthumous Confession*, in the heyday of Freud, Emants was to defend his interest in psychopathology by claiming scientific goals. The deviant, he suggested, is characterized above all by an inability to censor and repress the forces at work within him. By documenting the self-expression of the deviant psyche, can we not expect to uncover fragments of what is kept so carefully hidden in the 'normal' inner life?

I would not deny the importance of the aims Emants claims here. Artists have told us as much about our inner life as psychologists ever have. But are the artist's motives ever as clear-cut and dispassionate as Emants would have us believe? Marcellus Emants is not disjunct from Willem Termeer: the author is implicated in his creature's devious project to transmute the base metal of his self into gold.

The gabble of Willem Termeer, so frank, so perceptive, yet so mad, is not new. We have heard these accents at least once before, in 1864, from the nameless 'underground man' of Dostoevsky's story. Both he and Termeer tell their woes and pick their sores in the name of the truth; both acknowledge the exhibitionism of their performance, despise themselves for it, yet go on nevertheless. The difference between Dostoevsky and Emants is that, after *Notes from Underground*, Dostoevsky, with deeper insight into the motives behind and inherent demands of the confessional mode, was to go on to write *The Idiot* and *The Possessed*, in which he would destroy the pretensions of Rousseau and his heirs to arrive at true self-knowledge, uncovering the worm of ambition at the heart of the feigned disinterestedness of secular confession. Emants, a lesser thinker, a lesser artist, a lesser psychologist (and who is not?), remains bound in Rousseau's toils.

J.M. Coetzee
1986

A Posthumous
Confession

My wife is dead and buried.

I am alone at home, alone with the two maids.

So I am free again. Yet what good is it to me, this freedom? I am within reach of what I have wanted for the last twenty years (I am thirty-five), but I have not the courage to grasp it, and would anyhow no longer enjoy it very much.

I am too frightened of anything that excites me, too frightened of a glass of wine, too frightened of music, too frightened of women; for only in my matter-of-fact morning mood am I in control of myself, sure that I will keep silent about my deed.

Yet it is precisely this morning mood that is intolerable.

To feel no interest—no interest in any person, any work, even any book—to roam without aim or will through an empty house in which only the indifferent guarded whispering of two maids drifts about like the far-off talk of warders around the cell of a sequestered madman, to be able to think, with the last snatch of desire in an extinct nervous life, about only one thing, and to tremble before that one thing like a squirrel in the hypnotic gaze of a snake—how can I persevere to the end, day in, day out, in such an abominable existence?

Whenever I look in the mirror—still a habit of mine—I am astounded that such a pale, delicate, insignificant little man with dull gaze and weak, slack mouth (a nasty piece of work, some people would say) should have been capable of murdering his wife, a wife whom, after all, in his own way, he had loved.

Yet it is true. What is more, I have listened with the greatest amusement to the lamentations of my parents-in-law; I have sat quite calmly next to her father, facing my brother-in-law, and driven behind Anna's dead body through the crowded streets to the cemetery; dry-eyed I have seen her coffin sink into the grave and her broken father go back to his mourning wife; and now I roam about the house again, this house in which everything still speaks of her, roam without pain, without remorse, but also without joy, without hope, feeling only fear, fear of the slightest noise, fear above all of my own voice.

Sometimes—at night, for example, or when I imagine that someone is eavesdropping on me from behind the door—I cannot help calling out aloud, "I murdered her!" Whereupon, shivering with fear and chilled suddenly to the bone, I open all the doors and search all the cupboards to make sure that my secret is still undisclosed.

Do I then find my own deed so extraordinary, so unheard of, so terrible? Alas, I am afraid not; one thing followed from another far too gradually.

When I close my eyes and go through my life once more in my thoughts, it becomes perfectly clear to me how step by step I came to where I am. I have such a compulsive desire to come out with the story that simply for safety's sake I am going to put it down on paper.

It *must* come out! Perhaps then I will be better able to keep quiet about it; and perhaps there are people, or perhaps one day there will be people, interested in the course of my life's development. Who knows how many there are who are just like me, yet will realize it only when they have seen themselves mirrored in me.

To make the reader understand how different I seem to myself from the vast majority of people, it is not enough that my confession begin with the day on which I made the acquaintance of my late wife. I must work my way back to the first experiences that unveiled my shadowy inmost self to me.

My memory has never been very good. So I no longer see my youth before me as a continuous series of events, but remember only the isolated moments when I received strong—and generally unpleasant—impressions.

One of my first and most painful experiences was of entering grade school. My only memory of the scene itself is of a vast gray space in which sits a mass of tittering children guarded by a surly teacher. In front of the class stands a gigantic blackboard; against the gray walls hang outline maps in pale tints. More clearly I remember the feeling of being something small, something

8

weak, something negligible, abandoned and lost in a hostile crowd—the rabbit in one of my picture books being thrown alive into a cage full of wild beasts. I saw at once that all those eyes were looking at me with enmity, and though more than twenty-five years have passed by, nothing has been able to erase that impression of hostility. Even today it is into a cage with wild animals that I must step whenever I want to move among people. No amount of reasoning has ever been strong enough to overcome the mistrust with which I approach my so-called brothers.

My first fight followed soon afterwards, or more accurately my first clash, which ought to have ended in a fight but in fact ended in flight.

For some time I had known with instinctive timidity that I should avoid all bigger and stronger boys; but finally I was taunted by one of them to such an extent that in a surge of temper I gave him a punch.

"You'll pay for that!" he shouted; and when, after school, I heard his conceited, bragging voice behind me on the stairs, I saw that I was in for it. The thought of standing my ground did occur to me, but ah! so feebly.

Once I was downstairs I looked around wildly for a moment. By the time his tanned, foursquare face had appeared above several smaller boys in the doorway, I had spied a policeman on his beat some distance away. I made off and without a word attached myself to the policeman. He glanced down at me but said nothing. The jeering group of boys followed us at a fair distance... and it grew clear to me that I was a coward.

How often have I not heard the remark that a person who knows his faults can eliminate them too. How little self-knowledge people must have who speak that way!

Suppose that a miser, ashamed of his vice (which means that he knows his vice well), doles out handfuls of money. He seems to have become generous; but are we faced here with anything but a sham? Will he not always in his heart go on feeling an aversion to giving away, and is that not the hallmark of greed? Even if a deaf-mute learns to understand what one is saying, it does not mean that he can hear it!

My cowardice had not in the least been overcome when in later

9

life, armed with the knowledge that no one noticed me, I occasionally dared to enter a crowded room. Faced with the new, the unknown, I have always shrunk back. Yet I have always yearned for it. My soul is rich in such contradictions. I thirst, for example, for emotional excitement, yet shun whatever might disturb my peace of mind.

A confession of cowardice must immediately set all readers against me. That I am aware of. But are they so unfair that they do not see I would much rather have been brave? How senseless, after all, to condemn a person for physical and spiritual failings for which he is not at all responsible! Does anyone think he enjoys being the way he is? Is it so pleasant to know you are despised?

Cowardice has remained the indestructible worm gnawing at the fulfillment of all my wishes. My most terrified nights have always been those during which in my dreams I again go to school for the first time, or take to my heels before a stronger, braver individual.

Of course as a boy I did not think that my timidity would turn out to be invincible. On the contrary, I convinced myself that it would inevitably disappear of its own accord in the face of a growing acquaintance with people and the ways of the world. I counted on experience breaking down my timidity, when in fact timidity would prevent me from gaining experience. My way of seeing things was reasonable enough, insofar as even experience that was forced upon me could perhaps have reshaped me a little. Suppose there had been no policeman in the vicinity, or that the boys had surrounded me and prevented me from fleeing. Then I would surely have been forced to defend myself, and if my first antagonist had been vanquished by a lucky punch, who knows how much courage self-conceit might then have bred in me?

So with a little judicious coercion my parents might have given a better twist to my unhappy existence. But who asks himself before marrying whether he is capable of exercising that kind of judicious coercion? It is not for his own sake but because his father and mother long for a pretty little doll that a child has the labor of life imposed on him.

Meanwhile as a boy I conjured up for myself the ideal of a

10

man always certain of his cause, and, sensing that I would never become such a man, did my best to copy at least his externals.

This was—as far as I remember—my first attempt to hide my true nature under an assumed role. Later on I became so absorbed in this playacting that, no matter how badly I acted, it became impossible to ever simply be myself again. When I tried to be myself it seemed that I no longer had any self, that I was nothing but a soulless organism without a single like, dislike, opinion, impulse. As a rule, however, my likes and dislikes, my opinions and impulses shouted out to me, "Shut us up in your heart, we don't conform to fashion, we are taboo in human society." And the better I learned to hide my true self under the right face for the occasion, the more indifferent I became to the perversity of my impulses or deeds, as long as they remained unnoticed. It is only acts of clumsiness that have ever caused me grief.

Lying may have been a necessary consequence of role-playing, but I lied even when it was not necessary, yes, utterly without cause. When a boy who has been up to mischief takes some liberties with the truth, who is surprised? But why should I have claimed I had come from Scheveningen when I had been walking in the park? Why did I volunteer, "We were looking at pictures," when my friend and I had been playing with tin soldiers? Nowadays this compulsion to tell something other than the truth in the simplest day-to-day situations has lost much of its urgency, but I am still loath to give a truthful account when I can cook up a story. I once even took the trouble of trying to find out whether my parents had been liars, but my efforts yielded no result. Those who had known them denied it. However, their declarations inspired no confidence in me.

Stealing without lying is unthinkable. What of lying without stealing?

Only in my very early years did stealing hold much temptation for me: a marble doubled its value to me if it was stolen, and before I had the courage to smoke I was stealing cigars from my father's writing table. Unless memory deceives me I seldom or never took anything out of greed. What enticed me was the stimulation I got from sudden illogical aggrandizement.

Nor does my gross egoism spring from strong attachment to

11

my possessions. It is much more the product of my constantly inward-directed gaze, which ignores the existence and the sorrows of others. My acquaintances—friends I have never had—did not find it easy to ask me a favor, but if they did I seldom refused. This was not kindness on my part—they never mattered enough to me for that. I suppose I did it out of vanity, gratified by the unusual request.

I have always ascribed the failure of my vanity to make me seek distinction to physical weakness. Every attempt to push myself told so heavily on me that overcoming obstacles left me not satisfied but exhausted. Few things surprised me more during my boyhood years than the ambition of my fellow scholars to outdo one another. When I heard them discussing plans for coming first in class, when I saw the nervousness with which they compared the marks in their quarterly reports, when I observed their spells of self-denying industriousness, it felt as if I, with my bland indifference to official signs of distinction, my total lack of interest in my teachers' judgment, and my unquenchable thirst for all kinds of fun, was a being of a quite different (and, I conceded, worse) quality from all the others. The words "excel" and "become famous" exerted not the slightest power of attraction upon me. I certainly understood that if one is poor one has to study so that later on one can earn a living by means of one's knowledge; but the boys had told me that my father was well-off, and the fact that he no longer did anything seemed to confirm this—so why should I drudge over such unpleasant things as algebra, cosmography, or weights and measures? If Papa was rich enough to have all the fun he wanted without earning anything, then such would also be the case for me, his only son. Of course I made up my mind to search out other more interesting, more adventurous pleasures than those favored by Papa, who seemed to want only ways of relaxing his highly strung nerves and rare spices or wines for his poor appetite; but for the realization of my still very vague ideals it was certainly not necessary that I have any particular ability to calculate or name the stars at night. I learned exclusively what appealed to me in some degree, like history, or what I thought I would need later on, like geography and foreign languages; and no punishments, no promises of future reward,

12

no admonitions, friendly or formal, could tempt me into exertions the utility of which remained unclear to me. I considered all my activities as coolly as possible, and the arguments in favor of doing something had to be really powerful to triumph over my innate sluggishness, which steered me toward inaction. This cautious pondering, this detachment from my energetic schoolmates, this skeptical reluctance to give in to an impulse of the moment, naturally gave me the reputation of being secretive, underhand, shifty. I found out about this only in later life; but even as a boy I had the feeling that no one could bear me.

As against so many shortcomings there stood to my credit the fact that I was certainly not jealously inclined. Yet seen from closer quarters this was a purely negative virtue. Though I have never coveted anyone's means, anyone's position, my hatred for so-called normal people nevertheless ultimately stemmed from envy. As a child I envied them because they had more fun, as a youth because they had a greater variety of feeling available to them, as a man because they were able to be happy.

I had far less contact than other boys with people I knew or with my elders. At school I was bored, incapable of keeping my attention on the lessons; outside school I preferred solitude, for fear of clashes with rougher schoolmates; at home a sickly father and a grumpy mother left me entirely to myself.

Nevertheless I was sometimes invited out, and then social obligations had to be met. Such festive days were days of martyrdom to me. I had to listen to the other boys talking about their rivalries, which left me cold, or about the jokes they played, in which I did not dare take part: never did I feel more lonely, more rejected than in the company of my peers and contemporaries. I stood on the fringe, and, imagining that I had left the circle after my first botched fight, saw no chance of ever entering it again.

The result was of course that the others taunted me, despised me, and sometimes attacked me in a body. Then I really had to defend myself, and did so either in a blind frenzy of despair or with whatever little dodges and shams restore something of a balance against such odds. None of which prevented me from regularly having the worst of it. Out of this continually nourished realization of inferiority there evolved a powerless embitterment.

13

Of this embitterment, not counterbalanced by any love, I was by the age of twelve already clearly aware, but it has taken many years of continual self-scrutiny and self-analysis to bring me to realize how it developed and why it necessarily turned out to be ineradicable.

Meanwhile I was approaching the age at which woman begins to exert her influence on our thoughts and actions. I should prefer to write, "I became a man"; but it seems to me that I have really always remained a shy, clumsy boy. The vital sense of power that so often degenerates into arrogance has never been mine to know. For me the transition limited itself to a shift in my solitary meditations, which became strongly tinged with eroticism, and a change in my secret hobbies, which had previously consisted of petty thefts and other acts of mischief. My playacting also acquired a new character, for I now preferred trying to imitate the idiosyncrasies of great, mysterious criminals or melancholic heroes of novels. In this fantasizing of ideal models I noticed for the first time that each different influence can arouse a totally different person within me.

If I am generally cold, indifferent, bent on sensual pleasure, beyond the reach of altruism, nevertheless a few bars of Wagner, a glass of champagne, a beautiful painting, the echo of church music, can—or rather could—fill me with enthusiastic, voluble friendliness, cerebral reverence, self-denying love. At such times I feel as if my sluggish blood suddenly begins to flow faster, a tension arises in my slack nerves, and it becomes light, colorful, lively in my exhausted, gray, drowsy brain. I feel a revulsion for my ordinary sober self, with its indifference toward what interests people, what holds them together, and its singular desire some day to cause pain, particularly to women; and as the yearning to offer some great sacrifice makes my soul glow with somber enthusiasm, there arises before my misty eyes the immaculately beautiful form in chastely girded attire of her whom I kneeling adore but never shall possess.

Even a change in the weather—the first mild touch of spring after a biting winter, sunshine after a gray, rainy day, thunder or a storm after oppressive stillness—in fact, even the rising and setting of the sun and moon, are capable of uplifting me to a

14

heightened, a more intense life, and for that reason I hate the unvarying summer- or wintertime no less than the severe middle hours of the day or night. I am never happy—that is, contented, cheerful, sanguine, healthy—for if in one of my better moments the longing for an unknown, overwhelming happiness should lift me out of my dull stupor, then at the same time a painful sense of dejection awakens in me, and, without my knowing why, a "never, never,..." without cease wells to my lips.

Thus whichever phase I found myself in, woman became the dominant image in my daydreams, and the more violently I desired her the more bashfully I avoided her. In my calm morning mood this issued from the fear that in my eyes she would read my desire, which I considered forbidden, vile; in my rare moments of excitement it issued from the dread that I would look ridiculous in her presence.

Oh how hotly I desired, how fervently I adored in those days! Just as a single drop of rose attar, once escaped, can permeate a whole room with exquisite fragrance, so my whole being would have been spread through with a vitalizing aroma if in those years I could have enjoyed a single moment of satisfaction! What is the point of growing rich if there is no longer anything we want? What does it help to have sources of pleasure at our fingertips when our nerves are blunted?

My schoolmaster had a pretty daughter who naturally made a daily appearance before the few boarders, but who became visible to me only twice a week at the drawing lesson. She would stand at the big table next to me, and behind the lattice screen against which our models hung I could cast surreptitious glances at her creamy throat, her milk-white temples, and her plump little hands. If I make the effort to recall her image, I think I would now have to say that her complexion was pasty and her curvaceousness not to be ascribed to sound development. Whatever the case, in a tightly fitting sweater her full arms, her heavy bosom, and above all her soft little hands attracted me irresistibly. Those hands were so white, so small; I imagined they must be velvety soft too. Often the left hand lay there next to me throughout the lesson, and I would be incapable of getting anything done, so fiercely did my desire to touch it struggle with my fear of a commotion.

15

It was impossible to turn my eyes from it. I did not hear the questions addressed to me and sometimes behaved as if I were not all there. In this particular case my shyness was intensified by the rumor that a boarder from the Indies whom I carefully avoided because of his giant strength and his militant bearing was on a most intimate footing with the girl. This unsatisfied desire, this battle with paralyzing fear, sent me every Wednesday and Saturday into such a state of feverish nervous tension, with ensuing exhaustion, that I myself did not know whether I longed for the drawing lesson or abhorred it.

One Tuesday the colonial boy fell ill, and the whole night I immersed myself in the question, would I now dare? In the morning class-periods the next day I gave nonsensical answers to every question; when the drawing lesson began I was standing flushed, staring at my model, yawning and trembling with nervousness, unable to concentrate, with no control over my hands and feet. The two hours passed; but I had neither drawn a single true line nor made any attempt to appease my burning desires.

The colonial boy got worse rather than better; so by the following Saturday it was again a case of: would I dare? Until halfway through the afternoon there was no improvement at all. My cheeks glowed, my sight failed, my lips trembled, and though I seemed ceaselessly busy, in truth I was accomplishing nothing.

Then something happened to give me the boldness I needed. The band of a passing regiment struck up a stirring march in the street, and it was as if these blaring chords tautened my lax nerves. I felt a wave of strength course through my veins, and all at once fancied that I could do anything, would venture anything. I laid my hand on the pretty white fingers from which my eyes had not moved for one second during the past hour. And it happened as I knew it would happen and yet thought impossible—she did not pull away.

I can still see the brown table behind the hanging model that shielded us from indiscreet glances; I can still hear the march which fired my blood like strong wine; and sometimes, particularly at dusk on clear spring days, when the roar of the city grows fainter and a bell tolls in the distance, then, among other pallid sensations, the glory of this contact comes to life again within me:

16

the presentiment of a voluptuousness such as has never been granted me to enjoy.

A few days later it was our teacher's birthday (of course we called him the old man). Aside from the obligatory present, we celebrated the occasion each year at our own expense. Usually we had a conjuring show; this year the wealthy parents of dull twins had made one of their farms available to us for an outdoor party. At first the excursion did not appeal to me. If I played robbers or soldiers, leapfrog or puss-in-the-corner, there would be all kinds of clashes with stronger boys to dread. But when I heard that *she* was coming too and that the colonial boy was still having to stay at home, the affair took on quite a different look.

By pushing, twisting, and sneaking cautiously and silently, I managed to secure a place next to her in the carriage. In itself this ensured that I would be her neighbor for at least an hour and a half, and in the depths of the vehicle I was easily able to enfold her enticing little hand under her cloak. This time too she made no attempt to withdraw from my grasp, and she succeeded at the same time in carrying on her conversation with the other boys so casually that I could give myself over to my pleasure undisturbed. I imagined that I now knew what love was. A longing to be allowed to die at her feet as a sacrifice toward her happiness filled my soul with melancholy and my eyes with tears, while my hostility toward the other boys grew to brutal contempt.

When we alighted at the farm she had still not said a word to me. She even acted as if the prolonged contact of our hands had not penetrated her consciousness. This self-control seemed all too strong to me. There was nothing I wanted more dearly than a secret understanding in which no third party would ever participate; but now the question occurred to me of whether she had not perhaps simply let *the child* have his way. Racked by the fear that my enjoyment might suddenly become a mirage, I hesitated in the initial bustle and confusion between on the one hand boldly and confidently leaping, dashing about, wrestling, and fighting with the raucous band that surrounded her, and on the other maintaining a theatrical aloofness to demonstrate to the boys that I considered myself far above their amusements and to give Mina the feeling that she failed to appreciate my love. Without really

17

knowing why, I ended up by joining a group climbing onto a hayrick filled almost to its thatched roof, and, snug in the hay, had already begun to absorb myself in the sudden destruction of my castle in the air when to my surprise I saw her brown hair, her heavy eyebrows, and her large, dark eyes pop up over the edge. She approached, regarded me briefly, then proceeded to lie down in silence beside me. I had neither words to say nor the courage to stir.

For a while the boys went on wrestling and shouting around us. Then one of the band had the sudden idea of going to a lower rick to look for eggs. They slid down the steep side, and under the low, dark roof it grew still and lonely.

Put at ease and encouraged by Mina's arrival of her own accord, I wanted to stretch out my hand again, but she now sat up till she was leaning half-upright on her left elbow. Running the fingers of her right hand like a comb through my hair, she began to talk.

"Why haven't you said anything to me all this time?"

For this question I was not in the least prepared, yet it was perfectly natural that Mina should ask it. All the boys spoke to her, only I dared not, feeling on the contrary deeply aggrieved that the first word did not come from her side. I clearly saw how foolishly I was behaving, yet in later life have often run aground on the same reef. In just those cases where I hope for a friendly, trusting relationship, a mysterious, insuperable resistance prevents me from entering into it with friendliness and trust from my side. So I pretend to myself that I do not want to force my company on the other person; but actually this explanation is meant to give a pretty complexion to an ugly affair.

My response to Mina was as stupid as could be. "Well...I had nothing to say."

"But you did want to look at me, didn't you—at my hands most of all. Don't deny it. I saw it, you couldn't take your eyes off them!"

That she had noticed my admiration did not surprise me; but I found the frankness with which she acknowledged it somewhat shocking. Anyhow, she had not taken my impolite staring amiss. This gave me the courage to press on.

"That's because I've never seen such pretty hands before.... You're so pretty—all of you...Mina."

18

I felt myself flush a glowing red; but she pretended not to notice, said only, "Is that so," and went on gazing at me through a long silence.

Finally with a sigh she sank back again in the hay. After we had lain stretched out next to each other in silence for a while, she suddenly asked, "Tell me, Termeer, do you like me?"

I felt my shyness give way, perhaps because she was no longer looking at me. Staring fixedly into the dark brown thatch, I replied almost smartly, "I've liked you for such a long time; but I thought you preferred that yellow Chinese."

"Jan Bronte?"

"Yes."

"Don't be a fool! I'd get sick myself from that endless coughing."

She half rose again, to be able to run her fingers through my hair. I grabbed at her hand. To defend herself she began to tickle me, something I cannot bear at all, and wrestling we rolled back and forth in the hay for a while, jumped up, fell again, and began to laugh more and more nervously. Then, panting suddenly from the heat, she called out that we should lie still again, and threw herself down. At once I slumped down beside her.

I felt like pressing myself tightly against her and repeating in whispers that I was wild about her, more than ready to die for her. But at this moment she pulled up her sleeve as far as the shoulder and stretched out her naked arm under my head.

"Why not lie down—or don't you want to?"

As if blinded by a dazzling vision, I could barely distinguish form and color. I saw only something gloriously white. Everything spun before my eyes; my head sank down, and, as I felt the velvety softness of her tender skin against my neck, it struck me that it was all over with my ethereal self-sacrificial love. The warmth of the hay filled my veins with desire and through all my nerves ran a sensual shudder. I heard a far-off hubbub from the boys, the sun seemed to darken fitfully, and a lust to tear the clothes off all the whiteness I still sensed beside me churned like fever through my blood, tingling in my fingertips.

Yet I did not dare.

For a long while I lay powerless, prey to the battle being fought between my violent desire and my paralyzing cowardice. But the upshot was that cowardice again triumphed and the precious moments sped past empty.

Perhaps I should have said my better self won. But does this better self still have any right to its name when, in place of the self-fulfillment and peace of mind that are said to follow on such victories, it affords only self-contempt and regret?

Did I ever, later on, in my sincere attempts to be a good person, enjoy anything on which I can linger with contentment equal to the bitter dissatisfaction with which I now think back to that hour of cowardice in which I remained a "gentleman"?

"But you would have been plunging yourself into a sea of nastiness."

Selfish argument! At least I would then have tasted pleasure out of the ordinary, whereas now I can only look back on wretched little debauches, which have turned the sea of nastiness into a revolting morass.

The intensity with which I have envied so-called virtuous, normal, good people (socially speaking) is enough to prove that I have been sincere in wishing to be counted among them. Since this wish has not been fulfilled, its fulfillment being impossible, since I have neither suffered the permissible pangs nor tasted the permissible pleasures, now I ask why it should not have been granted me to know, besides a misery all my own, a pleasure all my own.

It no longer surprises me that to preserve itself society brands beings like myself and at the first suitable opportunity locks them up or puts them in custody of the courts. So is it surprising that I should feel regret about every meager satisfaction that slips away after I have stalked it with the wariness of a hunted beast of prey?

"You should have taken it upon yourself to improve yourself, to develop a taste for nobler gratifications."

Have I not wanted that, have I not tried, fruitlessly?

Many animals can be tamed by force, that is, mistreated under duress, but only after many generations of breeding can old appetites die out and new ones take their place.

As for Mina, was she likewise disappointed?

At the time I still believed that women all want to be respected. She certainly gave no sign of disappointment, while a platonic

20

love between the two of us—after the departure of the colonial boy, who could not stand the climate—took on a durable character. Besides meeting at the drawing lessons, we often met in the street. I suppose we talked about love; but though I still sometimes succeed in recalling her image to mind and faintly reexperiencing the emotions she stirred up in me at the time, I cannot at all remember what we discussed. The totally inward life that diverted my attention more and more from the outside world had already taken root in me. I made no attempt to fathom her, but immersed myself exclusively in the emotions aroused in my heart by the sight of her, by her touch, her words, her kisses. *I enjoyed myself*: in other words, I endured the gnawing of my sensual desires or the strain of my self-denying worship. Sometimes Mina enchanted me as a seductive female body that I wanted to kiss and bite, sometimes even pinch and beat; at other times I would gladly have covered her hands, her throat, her very mouth, with a veil, in order simply to stare into her eyes, to love, and to die.

In this latter emotional state I found it totally incomprehensible that only a short while before I had seen Mina with such wholly different eyes, and imagined I would never be able to revert to down-to-earth animality; but the excitement abated quickly enough, and then I found it just as puzzling that the beatific feeling had vanished without so much as a trace.

Still, in an alternation between moods there was life, strong enough to make me believe in an alternation between selves within the same husk. But when the time came for one of the vacations which Mina regularly spent with her family in the country, my feelings all paled at the same time, and in my soul there remained only an unbearable barrenness. Nothing appealed to me any more. The freedom which—to my mind—everyone else enjoyed yielded me only drab tedium; and when I saw Mina on her return I not only reexperienced the paralyzing action of my usual shyness, but found that at first she even awoke in me an odd repulsion. I avoided her as systematically as I did my comrades: it was a long time before the old feelings returned and the old trust revived.

Of course she then asked for a clarification of my strange behavior, and I had to invent all kinds of fantastic lies so as to seem to explain what I myself did not understand. So many authors

21

have described how terrible it is to see oneself deceived in another. Why is it that no writer has ever told how much worse it is to be deceived in yourself? What disquieted me the most was the painful conviction that I had not the slightest aptitude for one of the heroic roles I sometimes intended to play in the future. For a Don Juan I lacked the audacity, for a Ritter von Toggenburg the steadfastness, for a Raimundo Lullio the perseverance in renunciation. I was prey to every fleeting and contradictory impulse, for no serious aspiration could take root in my soul. I was not even capable of remaining true to the ideal of pleasure, for my apathy overwhelmed everything, discoloring and smothering it. Before I knew what life was, I felt myself slowly dying, and now—not yet forty—it is only in my imagination that I am still alive.

Meanwhile I had passed the high-school entrance examination.

Accustomed as I was to underestimating myself, or rather to overestimating everyone else as well as every difficulty I met, I was not a little taken aback at this result. At the same time I was saddened, for I felt that a change of school would entail being estranged from Mina. We did set up all kinds of dates and kept them for a while; but by degrees our intimacy dwindled, leaving me nothing but the feeling of incompleteness that is still bound up with my memory of her. My love disappeared like a raindrop in hot sand: all that was left was a dirty brown spot.

My high-school years were marked by ever-increasing timidity toward the feminine sex coupled with a growing distaste for male company. I became shyer and shyer, feeling at ease only by myself yet well aware that in such solitude I would never be able to quench my thirst for pleasure of every description. My vitality was strong enough to arouse a multitude of desires, yet seemed to be too weak to satisfy any of them. Every night I resolved to be braver the next day, and every next morning I fell into the same old routine as if paralyzed. No matter how many stories reached my ears of the escapades of other boys, the fear of failing and being laughed at was a shackle around my ankle curtailing my freedom of action.

Nevertheless I kept dreaming of a better future which would dawn as soon as I was wholly my own master; and with the help

22

of wine or liquor I even succeeded in equipping my fantasies with the ideal woman, to possess whom would satiate both the clear-headed pleasure-lover of the mornings and the overwrought romantic soul of the nights.

Thus I underwent moments of pleasurable exaltation, reading poems in winter, roaming about outdoors in summer, enjoying every modulation of love in my imagination; but an oppressive premonition that reality would never answer to my expectations and that I would always remain the same awkward coward drew across this sunny inner life the black cloud-shadows of melancholy. And that would be the end of my intoxication. Once more I would see everything coated in the loathsome gray of the everyday. With a dull head I would drag myself to bed and not infrequently, even in those days, shut my eyes with the longing to awaken nevermore.

In my studies I was neither very quick nor very backward. Generally I picked up a good lead in each new subject, only to slow down gradually and finally drop behind slightly. That nearly every field of study soon came to bore me was perhaps a result rather than a cause of this phenomenon. Even in such favorite subjects of mine as chemistry, physics, and literature I soon lost my way, and then cut such a sorry figure compared with less advanced students that my lack of ambition could not safeguard me against disheartenment. For me the upper limit of intellectual development seemed to lie very low. So it mattered not at all whether I reached it by creeping slowly or in one swift leap: I would never pass it.

Of course, after such a good beginning full of diligent progress, no one saw the true reason for this dawdling and slacking. It was all put down to recalcitrance; and because in those days I did not know myself as well as I do now, yet saw I was being treated unjustly, I endured their reproaches in silence and entrenched myself in inaccessible stubbornness. In this way my hostility toward comrades and teachers continually increased, extending to the school authorities, my parents, and everyone of any consequence with whom I came in contact. It was as if I read in every face my sentence of judgment, and I felt that the judges did not know me. If I had only been able to see then that the harshness of others is as a rule considerably blunted by indifference!

Incapable of improving my lot by my own exertions, I went on pinning my hopes to the changes I was being forced to undergo. To every boy changes of school and promotions to higher classes are turning points in his existence: *I* hoped in vain that they would also lead to revolutions in my inner being. Though I might resolve firmly not to be shy of new schoolmates, not to be mistrustful of new masters, my new surroundings had the contrary effect of making me yet more timorous, more suspicious, more vacillating, more self-effacing. To feel at ease with people, with my surroundings, with my situation, I would have to win a great victory over myself. And when I saw that what cost me such a tremendous effort came easily to other people, despair overwhelmed me and I did not even enter the struggle. No matter how indecisive I was about my future career, I still thought I would play the (to me) interesting role of a Mephistophelian Don Juan in society; but whenever it caught my attention that other young men already knew how to move around with assurance in public, while *I* wandered through the city of my birth like a traveler in a strange land, I despaired of ever bringing that future into being. Only a first step was needed, but I was unable to take it. I went on roaming the streets alone, meeting no one I knew; I left school by myself, while neighbors to whom I had just spoken joined a dense throng of boys among whom there seemed no place for me; I sat alone at home working or ruminating, and neither father nor mother gave me a glance, no friend called.

In this isolation in the midst of hundreds of thousands of fellow citizens whom I saw walking around, whose bustle I heard, who brushed past me in the crowded streets, who spoke to me at school, I led a life consisting purely of feeling, founded solely on my imagination. My fantasies were usually grossly sensual. Sometimes I had visions of ethereal purity. On such occasions I felt myself becoming a good person, and to make this shining warm softness—which subsided so swiftly—last as long as possible, I tried to prolong my nervous excitement by drinking.

When I now think back to those years, it seems as if I slept them away in a restless slumber full of bizarre dream visions.

Quite often the urge came upon me to emerge from my isolation, join in what pastimes appealed to me, grow carefree and simple

24

like other people. But if ever a favorable opportunity presented itself, I hesitated just long enough to let it pass. Of course my inborn timidity was at work; but in addition I felt—or rather fancied—that everyone found me unpleasant, boring, insignificant, and my pride revolted against the thought of being merely tolerated.

It happened that I was invited to join a literary circle with limited membership. For a moment I was flattered and inclined to accept the offer; but then the suspicion crept over me that I had been asked only after everyone else had declined. Fear of difficulties to which I should perhaps not be equal conspired with my offended self-esteem, and I refused, despite my conviction that I was becoming more and more of an outsider.

Some time later a couple of acquaintances were talking about taking horse-riding lessons, and in a surge of daring I joined them uninvited. My parents had nothing against it, I was eager enough, and a touch of nervousness did not cripple my courage, for I imagined the others were on the same footing. It transpired, however, that though it was true that none of us had ever taken a lesson in the subject, I was the only one who had never mounted a donkey or a horse. This was sufficient to dishearten me again. When the time for the first lessons came I sent word that I was indisposed, and later gave up the whole project under some other pretext.

Toward young girls I behaved even more bashfully, and after I had disposed of several invitations to dance parties with weak excuses, after it had become plain to me that my diffidence was an insuperable impediment to paying a visit anywhere, invitations stopped coming. I saw perfectly well that the world was slipping away from me, yet was incapable of clinging fast to it. An atmosphere that repelled in every direction, a kind of insulating magic circle, seemed to envelop me, and I began to see that my high-school comrades would let slip at most a surprised "Really!" if they suddenly heard, "Termeer is dead."

Thus while everything worked in concert to make me more and more averse to action, and while the continuing struggle between this inertia and the desire at last to possess myself of real pleasure often sent me chasing through the crowded evening streets in feverish excitement, I saw with mounting anxiety that the time was approaching when I would have to play my part in a serious life, a life of business and duties, of earning money and meeting tiresome responsibilities.

I was deathly scared of the world. For the most part it impressed me as being a kind of bare, dark penal colony in which chained criminals are kept working under the lash of pitiless overseers. Sometimes it seemed to be a gigantic, mysterious system of cogs which shatters the limbs of its operators at the slightest carelessness or wrong move. I was sure that I would never be at home in it, indeed that I would never have the courage to cross the threshold of this gloomy, oppressive realm.

And even if the high school should not deliver me straight to that feared house of correction, the Polytechnic looked to me like a world in miniature—a somber prelude to the great drama.

The prospect of being a freshman and attending lectures, and in general all the activities in which I could not follow a line of conduct laid down in advance from A to Z but had to set about my work under my own impetus according to the demands of the moment, looked to me like a Chimborazo of difficulties. I stayed in high school six years.

Finally the great day came: the day of the entrance examination for the technical college. That day my fearfulness climbed to such heights that like a horse bridling before a shimmering puddle I lurched back from the unknown danger with all the strength in me. Quite shamelessly I did my best to fail—and was indeed turned down.

The sentence of judgment echoed within me like a cry of victory. At home I had difficulty keeping my joy hidden.

I will not easily forget the reception I had from my father.

He summoned me to what he called his office, where whatever can please the eye and busy the mind had by now lost its power to absorb him for more than half an hour at a time. The harmony of color between the dark red curtains, the Smyrna carpet, and the walnut furniture evoked no mood whatsoever in him; his collection of spicy books, works of philosophy, and belles-lettres left him wholly indifferent; the terra-cotta statuettes, the majolica vases, the bronze reliefs failed to divert him. Always agitated and yet bored, he paced through the house every half hour with a peevish face, sighing, never rightly knowing what he expected from these tours of inspection. Three times a day he went aimlessly outdoors, grumbling always about wind or rain or tiresome sunshine. In his youth he had led such a gay life that for a long time people called him and his friends "the black gang." But of this gaiety there remained nothing but an occasional nervous outburst of laughter caused by a smutty story or by contemptuous astonishment at some human stupidity.

At the age of thirty-five he had declared his youth closed and had married. Actually it would have been more sensible to have taken on a housekeeper, since he wanted nothing more; but in spite of his emancipated morality he heeded social forms.

One day he asked a good friend (from whose son I later learned the story) whether he did not perhaps know of a good wife for him, someone not too young who would bring with her a little money and some few remains of beauty and who would above all demand nothing of life. While they were out walking the friend pointed out to him a spinster who had had an unhappy home life with a gouty father, and he proposed to this stranger almost on the spot.

So as not to be too bored, he then set about looking for an occupation. He began by becoming secretary of a couple of associations, treasurer of some foundations, president of several societies, and eventually woke up one fine day a member of the municipal council. In this last-named assembly he cut rather a pompous figure; but it was not long before he had to resign to take care of his health. His nerves were upset, and from this time on he would journey first to Switzerland for the air, then to a coastal resort for a plunge in the briny waves, then again to a doctor who specialized in patching up undermined constitutions. Nothing helped.

He grew more and more irritable and spoke less and less. I do not believe that he ever addressed a friendly or even an interested word to his only son. On the contrary, he always made it quite clear that my presence was particularly annoying to him. Either I spoke too loudly or he could not bear my continual silence, while minor bad habits of mine like biting my nails or coughing needlessly sometimes made him burst into curses. And then without fail my mother would add to the scolding, in her scornful

27

way, a prophecy of all the troubles I would yet bring down on my parents' heads and all the sorrows I was laying in store for myself.

When it came to money my father was generous enough, both for my schooling and my own spending, but this was all he did toward my education. In *his* way he felt affection for his son, but what is affection worth when one is worn out, spent? Am *I* still capable of affection?

From my mother's side I encountered little more warmth. As long as I had been a sweet little doll to be dressed up prettily and shown off, she had played with me all the time; but when in the course of my development I became dour, introverted, ugly, and no longer gave her a chance to show off with me, her coldness increased daily. Vanity was her only striking character trait. To be able to gratify this already half-disappointed vanity she had accepted my father; but his sickliness, cutting her off again from the world, quite spoiled her gratification, besides burying her under tiresome cares.

So my father summoned me to his office and, while he took a spoonful of bromide, asked the result of the examination.

Despite a strong urge to tell a lie and shunt the matter aside for the moment, I admitted I had failed.

My father did not immediately fly into a rage—as I had expected—nor did he show surprise.

"I see.... Well ... it was to be expected. As for me, I didn't fool myself. I knew perfectly well I'd never get any satisfaction from you. That surprises you, doesn't it? You think I don't know what's going on because I don't spend all day keeping an eye on you! But I do know a thing or two, as you see. The only surprising thing is that you don't lie about it. That would fit in nicely with it!"

I said nothing because I did not know how to respond. I felt that my silence would irritate him, yet I could not utter a word.

"Is it beneath your dignity to say one word of apology?"

I kept silent, beginning to bite my nails involuntarily.

"Can't you leave your nails alone for once? You know that kind of thing makes me nervous!"

Rising, he paced up and down the room a couple of times; then

28

he sat down again. I had a mind to leave without saying anything, but he turned back to me and resumed.

"Are you aware that no one is satisfied with you, neither the school authorities nor the teachers, nor the headmaster, nor I myself? Your brain is good enough—you get it from your father—but you act as if that were absolutely irrelevant. Work also seems to be beneath your dignity. Year after year you begin by doing your best; but as soon as you see you are ahead of most of the class you think, 'Now I know more than enough about that, now I'm going to rest on my laurels.' Other students are not so silly and go on working. And they have probably passed, while you have failed disgracefully. Just what you deserve!"

I clearly remember feeling, at that moment, an unaccustomed need to tell the truth for once and prove to this man, who thought he knew everything, that he did not understand me at all. Yet I kept silent.

I saw his beardless, hollow cheeks turn dull red as he began to shift restlessly to and fro in his chair. His half-closed black eyes threw me quick, cross glances; his fingers were restlessly occupied in shifting all the little objects on his desk from right to left and back again. If I wished to make him understand me, I would have to admit I had failed on purpose...yet I remained silent.

Eventually he went on: "It goes without saying that you regard yourself as the victim of a great injustice. All the examiners are biased, not so? They had it in for you in particular! Isn't that so?...Well, say something: isn't that so?"

"If you say so, it must be true."

This answer sent him into a rage.

"Do you know what you are? A conceited fool! That's what your schoolmates think of you, and they are right! You look down on everyone as if you were something exceptional! You talk to no one, as if your words would be pearls before the swine! You keep to yourself as if going around with other people might taint you! In itself that's simply ridiculous, ridiculous and stupid; but one day it's going to be your ruin! You are on your way to becoming intolerable. Whatever you take on you will fail at. As people we need one another, so we must adjust to one another. Even if you were descended from Alexander the Great, even if I could leave you Rothschild's fortune, the sensible thing would still be to be friendly and accommodating. So, considering that you belong to a good but simple middle-class family and will have only just enough after my death to be able to live decently on, you really appear to be out of your mind when you alienate people and don't take the trouble to establish good relations while there is time. If you think you are wiser than your father, who is so much older than you, well, go your own way—it won't be my concern any more. I have done what I could for you—from now on it's your own affair. If you won't learn, the hard school of life will teach you! We've had as little love from you as we've had trust. But if you're still open to good advice, think about what I've told you.... One thing I will admit: I just can't make out a boy like you! If the coming generation has many specimens like you, things look bleak for the world!"

Hearing these words I could not suppress a smile which must have had something very cutting in it. I can still see my father start up in a paroxysm of rage, hurl curses at my head, then raise his clenched fists, stutter some broken, incoherent, abusive phrases, and finally, upon my mother's entry, storm out of the room screaming, "A creature like that is enough to give one a stroke! And you're supposed to be thankful when you have a child! That boy will be the death of me! You'll see, that boy will be the death of me!"

He had barely gone when my mother began in her peculiar tone of calm, sorrowful disparagement: "It's a nice sight to see you treat your sick father like that. If he dies tomorrow it will be on your conscience. But that wouldn't matter to you, would it? Nothing matters to you. You just keep quiet and think your own thoughts!"

For a long, a nerve-rackingly long time she went on talking, dwelling on parental love and the ingratitude of children, repeating herself, heaving sighs, shedding tears, growing resentful too of my continued silence, and finally crying out, "You're the most unfeeling, listless child I've ever seen! And a sneak into the bargain! What's to become of you God only knows! What's going to happen when the girls see you coming with that sour face? If

30

you were only an attractive boy! But whoever takes you will only be doing so for our little bit of money, that I'm sure of!"

Again the urge came over me to reveal what was going on inside me; again I said nothing, for the words would not pass my lips. I hesitated briefly, then ran away and locked myself in my room upstairs.

I have seldom shed tears except when listening to music. After that interview, however, I remember crying long and bitterly.

Oh, I knew perfectly well that people understood me just as little as I understood them, but did that really hold for my father and mother as well? I knew that a good deal of the blame was certainly mine, but had I no right to expect at least a little indulgence, a little sympathy from him who asserted that it was not to myself I owed my keen brain?

I had failed the examination on purpose, and my failure had not surprised them! They had never exchanged a word of intimacy with me, yet they thought they knew me! They promptly accepted the judgment of one or two teachers, without it even occurring to them that a father and a mother are surely in a better position to judge their child than strangers! And these were supposed to be my natural and best friends! These were the people from whom I was supposed to seek advice and comfort, for whom I was supposed to feel respect and love! They had asked third parties, "What is the boy really like—we don't understand him"; and when the answer had been, "He begins well but slows down, *therefore* he is unwilling; he keeps to himself, *therefore* he despises other people; he says little, *therefore* he is swollen-headed"—then without hesitation they too had come out with their verdict, sentencing me without asking what my defense might be.

I, who found myself so little, so insignificant, so despised, so rejected—swollen-headed!

It was cold and gloomy in my little room behind the bolted door. But I stayed there, for only there did I feel safe.

I had never felt any love for my parents. They had not given cause to be loved, nor had they given me the urge to love them. But now even everyday matter-of-course friendliness had turned into silent enmity. Certainly I would have done better to speak,

31

to defend myself, but was it not up to them to understand how hard I found that?

I felt deeply wronged, and could not dismiss this rankling scene from my thoughts. Leaning out of the window I ran time after time through my father's hard, stupid accusations, and mentally rehearsed endless rebuttals, convinced that my lips would never utter one word of them. For hours I looked down into the street at the restless passage of people sauntering, promenading, walking, hurrying. They all looked happy, content with their lot, capable of bettering it, longing for nothing unattainable. It was as if they formed a great brotherhood in which all members knew, trusted, loved, and helped one another, and into which I alone would not be accepted. It was then that I felt for the first time the urge welling up in me to run away, far, far away, no matter where, as long as it was to a place where I had no past and where no one knew me. Thinking of such a place, I was sure that there I would be quite a different person. As if a new environment could have changed me! As if, in the continual flux of all his constituent elements, a person did not carry with him everywhere the immutable kernel out of which he constantly renews himself!

Eventually my mother's words recurred to me, and despite myself I went over to the mirror.

She was right. My thin face with its dull, pimply skin, its pale blue eyes, its gray-blond, lank hair, was decidedly—ugly. I found my big slack mouth with its thick lips repulsive, my thin, crooked nose ridiculous. I noticed that when I shifted my gaze suddenly my right eye did not turn in unison quickly enough, making me seem momentarily squint-eyed. My small frame had also turned out rather poorly. Drooping shoulders strengthened the impression of weakness that the face already gave. My thin fingers and wrists were very knobby, and I walked bowlegged.

And so pathetic a creature as this hankered after women, saw them day and night before its eyes, viewed work and study as only a way of filling up empty time! Was it possible to be worse equipped for the life-goal toward which nature presses? My reflection irritated me, and I felt an impulse to smash the mirror to pieces. A senseless fury, a destructive despair raged through my soul until it seemed like a churning sea with white-peaked wave crests skirting

32

glassy black depths. Like one distraught I paced up and down my room. Into each chair in turn I fell, only to leap up at once. I wept and swore, moaned and raged, until I was so overwrought as to be almost drunk. In my excitement I felt myself now capable of anything. All of a sudden I was sure that for a man outward appearance makes no difference whatsoever. Courage and tact were all, and I would have the courage if only I willed it; as for the tact, I could pick it up if only I dared! Everything would be transformed once I could spread my wings in freedom. These wings were more to me than an allegorical figure. It was as if I felt them on my shoulders. Who knows what I might have done had I been entirely my own master that night!

For the time being, all I could manage was to slink down the street to a house of ill repute in order to buy, with what little nerve remained from my flagging sense of excitement, a pleasure for which I had first to overcome my loathing. At last I could bear my faintheartedness no longer: if mankind was really so hostile to me that no man could offer me friendship, no woman love, then I was no longer prepared to bow before its morality but would defy it and, for a price at least, abate the gnawings of my lust.

Enervated and dejected, revolted by all existence and fearing the dawn of the morrow, I turned homeward late that night.

We spent much of the summer in the Swiss uplands.

The next winter I would have to stay on at school; but, convinced that I did not need to exert myself, I took few textbooks along on our trip. Since mountain-climbing constituted the principal attraction of the place, and since I was thought too weak to take part, all that was left for me was to be bored.

At first the mountain air agreed very well with my father. But suddenly he was overcome with such homesickness that the resort doctor advised my mother to give the invalid his way: his restless longings, coupled with deep melancholy, were doing him more harm than the ozone-laden air could do him good. The doctor's advice hastened our return, and it was soon to become evident how lucky that was. One evening only a few weeks later

33

I heard my father fly into a tremendous rage. The next morning he did not come downstairs, and the following day I was told that the doctor had committed him to a mental institution.

Of course I did not doubt the possibility of his recovery. Nevertheless, the unexpected disappearance of the man whom I had always had to take into account in conducting my life, coupled with the certainty that he sat like a prisoner behind bars, perhaps even in a straitjacket, made a painful impression on me. For a whole day I could not erase the dismal vision from my mind, and I lay awake a whole night shuddering at what my dreams might hold. Thereafter, however, I underwent the same experience that I had known during the school vacations with respect to Mina: the intensity of my feelings flagged unbelievably swiftly and my thoughts wandered elsewhere. It seriously disturbed me that I forgot so soon, and thus, it would seem, had only such superficial feelings. But though I did my best to recall that original horrible vision of my father, it was in vain. I tried to immerse myself in the possibility of seeing him no more; but the memories materialized more and more faintly, more and more grudgingly, and when after several months news of his death came, I sought fruitlessly in my heart for any trace of feeling.

So, I decided, people were probably right to despise and shun me. Even if their understanding of me did not proceed from reasoned analysis, they perceived instinctively the chilly emptiness of my soul.

Even on those we know only by sight we presume to express a judgment, and often this judgment is much more accurate than its source would lead one to think. On the basis of a tremor about my mouth, a glance from my eyes, or the sound of my voice, the schoolmate who avoided me, the teacher who mistrusted me, the passerby who preferred to stop someone else for information unconsciously came to an unfavorable conclusion about my friendliness, my sincerity, my helpfulness; and even if they went on to infer a totally erroneous characterization of me as a person, their antipathy nevertheless had grounds.

In just this way a cat and dog feel at first sight that they are each other's enemy. And no one who has observed the furtive, selfish sensuality of the former and the gallant, faithful affection

34

of the latter is surprised at the irrational hatred with which these two animals approach each other.

Without knowing how, the normal individual recognized that I lacked all the properties that a society requires if it is to retain the capacity to survive the inevitable struggle of everyone against everyone else. Without knowing how, I saw clearly that in such an individual lived all the beautiful, noble feelings of which I knew what I knew only from books and which were therefore only empty sounds to me. Both of us felt that *he* constituted the rule, the conserving force, while *I* was the exception, the offspring of degeneracy.

What I had begun to see at this early stage became perfectly clear to me afterwards, when I had read more and analyzed myself more deeply.

After the death of my father my thoughts were at first diverted from this point, for soon my mother too died of pneumonia. So all at once I stood alone in the world, with an income of about nine thousand guilders at my disposal.

I was not yet of age, so a guardian was appointed over me. However, to this distant cousin and old friend of my father's, Mr. Bloemendael, city treasurer of Utrecht, I made it so clear that I intended to terminate all my studies at once and give up for good any thought of looking for a job, that he quickly called together my few and very distant relatives and proposed that I be declared of age. For once there really seemed to have been something decisive in my bearing: in any event, my good-natured guardian, who did not know me, suspected me of firmness of character.

Later I explained it to myself thus: when it comes to being firm in a negative sense—not doing something, not wanting something—I can display so much stubbornness that I even begin to believe in a belated development of manhood in me. As soon as I have to act, of course, I wake up out of this fantasy; but since initially nothing more than contrariness is called for, other people have no reason to doubt my inflexibility.

So with the permission of the family and the Supreme Court my guardian quit the field. At my request, however, he retained administration of my capital. What, after all, did I know about money!

Now at last I was altogether free, now I could spread my wings untrammeled. No longer was there anything to prevent me from leaving the clime in which I had grown up, from breaking with my acquaintances and my past, even from beginning a new life under foreign skies, in another society, amid people who spoke another language and had different customs and habits. Despite my timidity toward the unknown I hesitated not a moment in making a clean sweep of everything that reminded me of my first ill-fated period.

Life was good, said people—and indeed I saw them enjoying themselves, each in his own way in accordance with his individual taste. So why did I meet with nothing but disappointment? Because only the wicked, illicit sort of pleasure attracted me? But why, I asked myself, is the pleasure that attracts me wicked? Why does what is permissible not attract me? In those crystal-clear, sober moments when I discerned my past stretching out behind me like a series of links forged together by necessity, and saw this chain run onward to the furthest horizon of my future, I began to understand that my awkwardness, my lack of courage and perseverance, my want of feeling, my bent toward the forbidden, were nothing but the poisonous blossoms of seeds germinating in my ancestors. The roots stretched beyond me into closed-off lives, therefore I would never be able to eradicate them. All I might perhaps do would be to conceal certain character traits by acting a role, and this would be possible only on new ground, where no one suspected beneath the ruddy health of the greasepaint the actor's sickly pallor.

Whereas someone else might travel the world out of an interest in every manifestation of life, I was interested in things only to the extent that they might arouse me from my torpor to some variety of mood. I longed for sensation, and meant to seek it in a separate community—the dream-vision of my quest for pleasure— evidence of whose existence I thought I found in a whole host of French novels.

Just as in all layers of society there seem to be offshoots of the small Society of Freemasons, I believed in the existence of a secret *monde* which cultivated the emotions and savored forbidden pleasures. No doubt it too had established signs whereby people could recognize one another. Once a person had been accepted into it, he surely had little trouble finding companions in pleasure answering to his desires. This world was held together by the unquenchable urge to feel alive, while society at large abominated it like a plague because it would acknowledge nothing to be lasting.

I did not have a clear picture of this peculiar freemasonry, but supposed that in a city like Paris its highest orders celebrated great saturnalia. I saw its meanest representatives slinking around every city along lonely nocturnal roads; as for its middle orders, I presumed that they crisscrossed the civilized world and were to be found in hotels and gaming houses, at horse races and bathing resorts.

I shrouded this world in a romantic haze. It seemed to me the never-empty stage for the sweetest games of courtship and the most moving tragedies, the ever-bubbling fountainhead of soaring exultation and scathing pangs, the glowing, liquid core of a society that had cooled and hardened. In this world money was of minor concern, study a diversion, and the poetry of life not confined to the brief introduction to a long prosaic tale. Day and night the nerves tingled with changing sensations. Side by side with an overblown love there already blossomed a new one, nor did deference to sobering formalities delay consummation until desire had faded. Seldom was it gay there, for both desire and loss go hand in hand with deep melancholy; but this melancholy was always intoxicating as heady wine, and the soul, unendingly drunk, was protected by it from the leaden pressure of routine. Whenever I thought of this world I heard a waltz by Strauss or Waldteufel: for me, nothing evoked such feelings as I sought better than this sensual, somber yet playful music. All that remained was to penetrate this world and get to know its various signs and usages, which had gradually, tacitly grown into a secret language and etiquette.

While I was still at home thinking about all of this, there was much in it that attracted me powerfully, and I had no misgivings about the joys that awaited me. But as soon as I crossed the border my wretched pusillanimity stood again like a mocking imp in my path and shook its head, after which I endured long, empty days,

37

walking around as if through a dark forest in search of the entrance to an enchanted castle.

Where should I now look for adventures that might quicken my feelings? To the first-class restaurants, where everything was so hushed that I dared not even whisper to my neighbor for the salt? Down dirty, ill-lit streets, to be accosted by one of those hungry, dolled-up, consumptive creatures that I loathed? To the crowded theaters, where I did not know how to pick out the unaccompanied women and where—so it seemed to me—one spoke only to people one knew?

Not without nervous expectancy, I went late one night to a nightclub. But having seen the women attach themselves to regular patrons, leaving me alone behind my glass of grog, I felt that even here a magic circle of isolation surrounded me, and I left with nothing achieved, almost certain that I was being laughed at behind my back.

What was to be done?

Back in my little hotel room I saw clearly that I had not the power to take a single step to bring myself nearer the realization of my dream visions.

So my hopes rested on luck.

The world in which I wanted to live existed—that I did not doubt for a moment. I had money enough to move about in it, even if only for a while; but the art of penetrating into it I did not grasp. Other people embarked on liaisons, had exciting times; *my* existence was noticed only by the waiter, who in return for a tip gave me poor service.

For days on end I wandered around Brussels, in the mornings through the museums and churches and their environs, in the evenings through the streets, cafés, and theaters. And every night I fell into bed a little more disheartened, feeling as if I were sinking deeper and deeper into a black, chill pit.

Eventually in the course of my wanderings I chanced upon a house of prostitution, and with the pleasures offered me there solaced myself for several hours. I was less revolted than previously, but when in the pitiless dawn light I left this paltry imitation of oriental luxury, my timorousness had gained bitter justification: in the field of sex too I was feeble. The weak eyes, the pale cheeks,

38

the thin arms—they had not lied. After a night of meagerly doled out gratification I was as haggard of gaze, as light of head, as wrung of loin as if I had taken part in the grossest excesses.

I have always lacked the courage to talk about such things, but I had read a certain amount about them, and was now sure that I would be an object of ridicule to any woman in a position to compare me with other men.

Feeling my life shrink to a dreadful insignificance, I did perhaps stick my head in the sand; but could one persist in such self-deception? It was little consolation to see people, equally miserable but full of dull unself-consciousness, give rein to their disgusting little passions and boastfully squander their modicum of life-force. After all, theirs was an example I could not follow. My gaze inward soon cleared again: in myself I had my severest, most pitiless judge.

I left Brussels for Paris. There too I commanded only the kind of pleasure that is pressed upon one in return for a consideration. But now at least I saw the representatives of my imagined world in the flesh before me. I saw them in their theater boxes, lost in soft whisperings, while around them the common mass was engrossed in flat jokes, childish music, and gaudy stage sets. I saw them in restaurants, stirring one another up with fiery wine and lively talk till in their blissful intoxication they were insensible to the hum of the multitude. I saw them riding through the Bois de Boulogne, smiling at a charming memory or a fascinating image, indifferent to the glowering envy and contemptuous admiration of an inquisitive plebs.

Ah, I too wanted to live—to live as they did, gloriously, intensely, briefly!

After making no further progress in Paris, I persuaded myself that smaller towns offered me more scope, and so roamed for several months through the South of France, meeting with no adventures other than a few encounters with seemingly worldly-wise commercial travelers. As yet unacquainted with the art of boasting, in which such gentlemen delight, I began by believing their fantastic tales of erotic adventures in which they had played the role of Don Juan. Through various civilities I even tried to insinuate myself among them, if not in the hope that they might

39

know the entrance to my enchanted castle then at least with the idea of picking up some polish, acquiring a little dash. But they did no more than widen my knowledge slightly, for, even as it grew clear that their stories were lies, I found myself tending to match my own fantasies with theirs. Whatever I had dreamed up as a possibility I dished up to them as really having happened. In fact, in the process of inventing a host of details to lend more veracity to the action, I succeeded in experiencing a pale reflection of the emotion I depicted.

Seen objectively, this was only a new manifestation of my penchant for lying; but it gave me the idea that there was perhaps an artist hidden in me. Thus the search for adventure, the desire for variety of feeling, temporarily gained some kind of justification, which prevented me from collapse after my first disappointments.

Now, suppose I made for Switzerland, a country in which every year thousands of strangers congregate in search of pleasure pure and simple: would it not be surprising if there, in the hotels or on climbing trips, I did not get a chance to meet young persons looking for something more than the ascetic contemplation of beautiful scenery.

The ideal of my passivity was to meet a woman who in the presence of others would remain formal and polite toward me, yet at night would slip into my room, throw her arms around my neck, and plead, "Love me, love me!" But I imagined I would be ready to take a more active hand as well, once I had read in a glance or gesture some faint encouragement.

The days went by, linking up in the past into weeks and months, yet my existence remained empty and my need for excitement unsatisfied. Sometimes I enjoyed nature, sometimes a concert, sometimes a novel; the impressions they created on my soul were like stage sets, with meaning and value only to the drama which must be held in relief and framed by them. They gave me fiction where I longed for reality, and the time was already past when fiction stirred me deeply enough.

In my oppressive low spirits, I succumbed to spending whole days in bed, not knowing any reason why I should get up, dress, bestir myself.

40

Then it happened that, at table in a hotel at Interlaken, I sat down opposite a remarkably pretty girl. Looking at her photograph—which I was not given, but bought—I can still summon up clearly within me my first ravishing impression of that delicately pale face with its flashing eyes and that almost silver-blond hair. I liked big, well-built women: this one was extremely slight. But this did not detract from her: on the contrary, its effect was to awake a singular mixture of emotions in me. Her glittering whiteness of throat and wrist aroused my senses to the highest degree, sometimes filling me with brutal desire, while the graceful but oh so fragile little body with the great blue eyes shadowed with long, silky lashes had an ethereal quality which at other moments I longed to kneel to and worship in secret.

What struck me as decidedly unattractive were her broad though white hands. They spoiled the total effect, yet I could not keep my eyes off them.

Beside her sat an old, fat, sagging woman with a pudgy, pale face, half comedy stepmother, half dry-nurse, who ate greedily all the time while the lovely girl seemed to fast. After I had made out that they were speaking Swedish to each other, it cost me a long and unwonted effort before I could bring a word—not in Swedish, which I did not know, but in German—to pass my lips. I thought that the whole table would stare at me, and only the certainty that I was surrounded by quite unfamiliar faces finally gave me the courage to break the ice with some polite words. When these were amiably received (and barely noticed by other people), I went on more calmly. Soon the conversation went smoothly.

Of course we spoke at table about nothing but Interlaken, its surroundings, and the weather; but I succeeded, after dinner, in forcing my company upon them in the salon. The ladies seemed not yet to know anyone, and we sat down in a dark corner far from the other tourists, who formed a noisy group around the center table.

Soon the conversation turned to music, my favorite among the arts, and since I was at home in this field—at least had heard a lot and could repeat many of the melodies—it was not long before I felt remarkably at ease. I offered the ladies coffee and liqueur—

41

which was not turned down—and ventured to ask whether they were traveling for pleasure.

"Oh no, sir! Have you never seen my picture on display anywhere?"

I had to reply in the negative, and now the mother broke in. "My daughter is an artist, sir. She plays the piano. In Sweden she had an outstanding reputation; but as ill luck will have it, her health is not proof against the harsh climate of our country. The professors have advised her to come and spend a few winters in Italy and a few summers in Switzerland. That costs more money than we have, therefore she is obliged to give a concert now and again. In addition she gives a few lessons.

"May I give you a program? The next concert will take place on Monday.

"The seats are three francs."

I immediately took twenty-five seats, an act which earned me a glance from the girl in which I thought I detected both astonishment and joy. My confidence increased, and when the mother went out to fetch the tickets, I fancied I was capable of touching the pretty little creature, perhaps of quickly kissing her pale throat. But the broad hands once more caught my eye: I hesitated, stumbled over the answer to an unintelligible question, debated within myself the possible consequences of my action, and had not yet made a move when the old woman was back again. She looked closely at me, and I fancied I read suspicion in the sly, deep-set little eyes.

After we had settled our accounts, the daughter asked my nationality.

"Dutch, miss."

The answer seemed to please her. "In Holland there are quite a few millionaires, aren't there?"

"There is quite a lot of money in our country; but that money is broken up into a large number of middle-sized fortunes rather than being stacked in a few hands."

For a moment she looked at me searchingly and thoughtfully. Then her thin lips quivered in mockery, and she said coolly, "Don't you know a millionaire who would want to marry me?"

The cynicism of the question spurred me to recklessness. I

42

immediately decided to fill the role of millionaire myself—that is to say, up to the point of marrying her. "Certainly I know millionaires who would be ready this minute to lay their wealth at your feet. In fact, I am a most intimate friend of one of them. But surely you do not want to sacrifice the freedom of your illustrious artist's life?"

I read in her eyes that she caught my meaning; but now the mother again interrupted. "Ah, sir, freedom and the life of an artist are very nice things for a strong man; but to a delicate girl (though my daughter is otherwise healthy) they are worth woefully little. You are rich..." (here she paused for a moment), "so you do not know what it means to have to earn your daily bread. I assure you that all the fame and applause and eulogies in the newspapers count for little beside the tranquil pleasures of a good situation in life. Art is a nice way of passing the time, but if you have to make a living by it—"

A gesture ended the sentence, and, as if they were performing together in a rehearsed routine, the girl intervened: "You must remember that I was not brought up to be an artist. My father was rich, and my mother was born a baroness."

"And if," resumed the older woman, "after the death of my husband, our lawyer had not absconded with our entire fortune, my daughter would not be giving a concert here—of that I can assure you."

I could not get in a word.

"Do you know what my ideal is? To have a husband who loves music and to play for him only."

"But let *me* tell you something: for most men an artist is not much better than a nightclub singer. They are prepared to make love to her, but you mustn't mention marriage!"

"Now, now, Mama: there are exceptions, I'm sure."

The drift of things left little to be desired in clarity. Yet I did not despair. On the contrary, I went to bed that night in buoyant spirits. Was this merely self-satisfaction because at last I had persisted and made straight for my goal? Or did I think a conquest was still possible—even for a nonmillionaire—without the sacrifice of my freedom? While I lay unable to sleep, I went through these questions in my mind and came to the conclusion that self-satisfaction was certainly involved. I nevertheless held mother and daughter to be cunning intriguers rather than trustworthy people. Presumably they wanted to snare me, and while this troubled me coming from the beautiful young girl with the shining eyes and the enchanting mouth, it gave me both the resolution and the callousness that were indispensable to my role as seducer. That I was not in the least in love was attested by my undeniable distaste for her coarse fingers, a distaste which had made the parting handclasp an unpleasant contact for me. But precisely because of this I was not lapsing into my sentimental spirit of renunciation, and would perhaps succeed in taking advantage of her accommodating attitude without putting my head in the noose.

So at last I had an adventure in my grasp, at last I would be able to rid myself of the humiliating, intimidating feeling of being the perennial loutish adolescent. Now it was only a matter of taking judicious advantage of circumstances, whereupon all the sensations—those of winning, enjoying, triumphing, losing, despairing, parting—would follow of their own accord with preordained certainty. At last I would have a chance to taste the fullness of life, to feel every nerve thrill with excitement, every vein throb. In my inner self the gray haze cleared, the deathly silence turned to music: in a few days I would be many years older.

I began the next morning by spending a long time in front of the mirror—which was gradually becoming a habit of mine—once more asking myself anxiously how my eyes looked, whether the thin mustache had grown a little—in a word, what the total effect would be today, in daylight. As usual, the answer was, "A dreary one." But surely women do not pay attention to externals. For a man, does it not all come down to worldliness?

Taking heart I completed my toilet and descended to the breakfast room, feeling not entirely free of pompousness in bearing and tone.

I spent the whole day in the company of the Swedish girl, but without risking an attempt to touch her. I told myself that that did not yet fit in with the role of serious suitor.

We took a walk. I treated her to candy, listened to her playing, and tried to make myself interesting by once again relating as fact one of the love dramas I sometimes dreamed up for my future.

44

Finally I invited the ladies out on a climbing trip, for which we ordered the horses and guides together.

Did I simply bore her with all these attempts to please? I never found out. On that outing she certainly presented her cold, indifferent, stiff side.

It was an exceptionally lovely day, and I felt happy as I rarely did in the mornings. The fresh mountain air worked like sparkling champagne on my nervous system and spurred my heartbeat. It was as if life had gained in intensity everywhere this morning, and I felt myself raised high upon this all-pervading flood of energy, carried onward in blissful giddiness. Every shining snow-peak with its blue shadows filled my gaze with rapture, every Alpenhorn, every cowbell echoed in my ears like ravishing music. An intoxicating harmony seemed to vibrate through these immense spaces, and my soul became a chord floating away and dissolving into the All.

We rode in single file. She very seldom looked around and barely spoke. Because one's clothes get creased and dirty on a mountain pony, she had put on her simplest dress. It still showed off her slender figure; but combined with a crumpled hat and all too visibly rough shoes, her shabby clothes gave her a common touch that disturbed me whenever it caught my attention. To add to this, I lost her entirely from sight for whole periods of time when Mama, who rode in the middle, stopped because she had to change position, or because her saddle was shifting, or because she was getting dizzy, forcing me to dismount. As soon as we reached the top, Mama went into the little hostel. *She,* however, grasped my arm in order to look around at the narrow crest below us. At this I experienced a few glorious moments of triumphant joy.

She asked me the names of the snow-peaks, made fruitless attempts to catch a glimpse of Interlaken, and pressed herself tight against me as the steep slopes came into view.

It was as if I were nearing my goal of my own accord.

All at once she took it into her head to go and pick the Alpine roses that we saw blooming a short distance away in a cleft, and laughing and jumping we descended. As ill luck would have it, however, a faint air current blew constantly through the gorge.

45

No sooner had she felt it than she hastily turned back, fled indoors, and would not step outside again. At the same time she became quiet, apathetic, boring again. I offered her champagne, but she would not drink champagne in such a miserable bar; I invited her to play us something on the piano, but she could not get anywhere on such an old clinker; I wanted to talk, but with a yawn she engrossed herself in the bad drawings and silly verses in the visitors' book. Eventually mother and daughter fell asleep, and when they awoke it was almost time to leave, and it was hard to decide who was the grumpier of the two. They no longer had any eye for nature. They complained incessantly about the cold, the jolting of the horses, the discomfort of the saddles, and, back at Interlaken, I received, instead of thanks, lamentations about inflamed cheeks, tortured limbs, and burning eyes. They said hardly a word at table and vanished into their bedrooms earlier than usual.

Resentful, angered, and sorrowful, I was sitting in the salon paging through some German illustrated magazines when all at once the door was roughly thrown open and two young men came in, talking noisily. They were Americans, strong of build, healthy of color: strapping, fresh, attractive boys.

"What drivel that porter talks! There's nobody here!"

The porter, coming in their wake, observed that the ladies must already have gone upstairs.

"I'm sure they'll come along! Let's fix the surprise without saying anything!"

These last words came from the taller of the two, who was apparently also older and the leader. A premonition warned me that I had a rival before me. I inspected him again, and felt weaker, uglier, more insignificant than ever.

Sinking down in a sofa, he began to talk about a woman whom the other had not yet met. From his depiction I was sure I could recognize my Swede in the model, and a practiced libertine in the painter. Certainly he praised her flashing eyes, her fair complexion, her general charm; but he did so in the words of one who in the course of his life has made many comparisons, in the tone of one who, after the inflated estimates of his youthful years, has settled on a fixed scale for his assessments. From turns of speech, gestures, bearing, and a thousand points too fine to describe, I inferred the presence of the deft, unscrupulous professional who succeeds with all women, makes extensive use of his success, and nonchalantly tosses aside the oranges once they have been squeezed.

How I envied such a man, who both outwardly and inwardly possessed everything that I lacked!

He had met my Swede elsewhere, but the presence of his parents had prevented him from pursuing the acquaintance. Now he had come here to make up for his missed chances. Oh, they would have fun enough in boring Interlaken!

Behind my *Fliegende Blätter* I heard further that he wanted to strike hard the next day while the iron was hot. Then he rose and left the room, ignoring me.

I had understood more or less that they wanted to arrange a trip with a small group of friends. I thought it would be another mountain trip, so I decided to foil their plan by getting in first. As soon as they were gone I hunted up my guide and ordered three horses for a morning outing. Then I went to my room, wrote an invitation, and had the maid deliver it to the ladies that same evening.

Next morning I went downstairs early, breakfasted in nervous haste, and waited to see what would happen, half sure of my cause, half convinced that this stranger would yet prove the better man—how, I was not sure.

The ladies did not appear at their usual time. I walked outside, then again inside, from the dining room to the reading room and back again. No ladies, no Americans.

The guide with the horses was announced, and I did not even know whether my invitation had been accepted.

The porter wanted to go and notify the ladies, but I kept him back.

The servant said he believed they were planning to go riding, and I did not dare ask with whom.

I saw that at this moment any path of action was preferable to indecisiveness, yet I did not know what to say, what to do.

Then I heard the tinkle of bells, the crack of a whip, the crunch of wheels on gravel, and a faint noise of voices. I walked

47

toward the front again, encountering the two friends in the hall. Talking loudly, they shot past me and up the stairs. They took as little notice of my presence as they had yesterday evening. I understood perfectly clearly that it was up to me to follow them; I wanted to turn back—yet went outside.

In the distance stood my dozing horses with the dozing guide— a dreary, colorless group. Right in front of the hotel porch stood two proud, festively adorned open carriages, with four caparisoned steeds harnessed to each. Four more young Americans were sauntering about. Above the lowered hoods of the carriages the Swedish and American flags mingled their yellow and blue, white and red; each horse bore in its gleaming harness two tiny flags sticking out at an angle, stiffened with silver paste, and in addition both the headdresses of the horses and the hats and whips of the coachmen were decorated with colorful ribbons.

Some hotel servants brought out two baskets, each holding four bottles of champagne. The baskets were placed under the box, followed by eight glasses, which were carefully packed among the bottles.

What bustle and excitement! Heads appeared at all the hotel windows.

The plan was clearly and incontrovertibly better than mine.

Now the lovely girl would surely put on her prettiest dress, *now* she would surely drink champagne, *now* she would surely have to show some excitement. And besides, the organizer of the surprise was certain to have her alone with him, for Mama would simply be put into the other carriage.

But ... would *she* go along? *My* invitation had been the first— there could be no doubt about that—and yet ...

Oh, I should go to her! A single word could tip the scales in my favor. Now was my chance to show that I too could act deftly and with enterprise. Yes, I should. But ... my feet stood there as if riveted to the floor, and the world began to reel in front of my eyes.

I might still have overcome my hesitation through my own efforts if a maid had not thrust a carelessly folded though perfumed note into my hand.

My trembling fingers were barely capable of opening it.

48

I imagined that everyone was staring at me.

Of course it contained the tidings of my defeat. In a few sentences of German, full of the quaintest mistakes, the lovely girl informed me that it was impossible for her to avail herself of my courteous invitation. Her excuse was that she had already accepted another one.

At once the blood rushed to my head. What a lie! I thought I was capable of confronting all the Americans in the world. For a moment everything spun in circles about me as if moved by a whirlwind. Then I too raced down the hall and up the stairs.

My heart was thumping, my legs trembling, I felt my throat growing hoarse.

But I had not even reached the topmost stair when a laughing couple, arm in arm, came around the corner and rushed past me downstairs. I barely had time to press myself against the wall, so hastily did they shoot past; there was no question of either of them noticing me, engrossed as they were in their conversation as they skipped down the stairs.

That *she* looked twice as enchanting in elegant clothes had not escaped me. When every sound—the hum of voices, the peals of laughter, the echo of footsteps, the rustle of dresses, the crack of whips, the tinkle of bells—had died away in the distance, I still stood on the steps, humiliated, beaten, held up to the ridicule of the whole hotel as a fumbling boy.

Thus ended my millionaire act. Thus were my self-confidence and spirit unceremoniously nipped in the bud.

Back in my room I locked the door and fell down on my bed, to reappear no more that day. It was as if all my power to see, to hope, to touch, to think, to feel were shriveling within me to a ponderous, leaden, inert mass. Until late that evening I lay, my gaze fixed, immobile. Then the longing came over me to pack my bags and leave at once.

Why run away, however, when the most intense, the most agonizing emotions had yet to come? To stay on would be to suffer, that was certain; but any form of suffering was surely better than nothing at all. Just as the most pleasant sensation has always had for me a nucleus of sadness, so the most painful yet held a sensual pleasure. Therefore I stayed, spending a sleepless night. While I waited impatiently to see her again, the slight desire I had felt for the lovely girl flamed up into an acute passion, and I felt as if my senses were increasing in sensitivity from hour to hour. I shuddered at the impressions that awaited me, but would not evade them at any price. And when they arrived the next morning, I received them with an anguished, motionless tensing of my finest nerve fibers. I felt them lance through my chest, through my head, gnawing lethally into my soul, and I said to myself, "Here, this is what you were seeking after, this is ... living!"

Day after day I saw her frisking about with the American, and there was luxurious pleasure in watching her unobserved, in being able, every now and then, to revive the pain of irreparable loss.

At table we continued to sit opposite each other, without exchanging another word. In the salon I spied upon her from a distance. The more deeply I felt I had been hurt, ridiculed, insulted, the more sharply did I feel my trampled yet living love gnaw at my wounded heart; until finally at the concert her piano playing again whipped up all my excruciating feelings to their highest pitch and concentrated them to their utmost acuity. Only then did I really desire her with all my body and soul, and that night in my dreams I saw her come to me, bend down her dear blond head, press a kiss on my lips, and go away ... go away for ever.

Undoubtedly the emotions for which I have here tried to find words were—seen objectively—meaningless, inflated, half products of my own fancy. Perhaps they will even irritate strong, thoroughly healthy personalities. What, after all, is there to get excited about in a failed love affair with a cynical little piano strummer? The truly normal person—if I understand him—has not experienced such dulling apathy that he needs to play on his own feelings to put life into himself. It is his nature to be pierced to the depths of his ever-receptive soul by everything great and beautiful and worthy of his sympathy. But to the sick man whose palate craves the exotic caress of swallow's nests, what use is it to know that a healthy stomach is happy to feed on stew? Does it enable him to follow the good example and hanker after more nourishing food, or is it still advisable to dish up the outlandish foods which give him at least moments of satisfaction?

"Yet such cravings are neurotic: heavy, strenuous work might

50

well have cured you of them!" I know the lesson and have repeated it to myself hundreds of times! But what kind of work?...Where? ...How?...For whom? Could I, the feeble plaything of thousands of tiny accidents within and without myself which a normal personality does not even notice—I, who shrank in terror from the gigantic black machinery that calls itself society—I, every inch of whom trembled upon even most tranquil contact with another human being—I, who am capable only of neglecting, of giving up, of not wanting—could I declare myself fit for this or that task, ask someone for work, assume responsibilities?

Whoever has seen a man, apparently healthy but afflicted with agoraphobia, grow pale and dizzy and fall down simply because he wanted to cross a square and thereby achieve something that most people, from the weakest and most dull-witted to the strongest and the most highly educated, accomplish repeatedly day after day without thinking twice—such a person knows the power of the "You cannot!" which wells up from the mysterious depths of our nervous life and from which all argument rebounds helplessly.

I could not! I could not! He who condemns me for this as a sad specimen of humanity only repeats what I have told myself countless times. Yet the bitter truth still stands: I could not, I could not!

So I had not even been able to make use of my freedom to provide myself a little physical satisfaction. In the calm of everyday existence I had, yearning for an inner life, sought turbulence and variety. Now quiet monotony attracted me again, and like one exhausted I longed for rest and permanence. All the majesty of the imposing Alps was of no avail against the enchantment of the Dutch village scene that had risen before my soul. I saw myself on a clear summer evening in a beautiful garden by the side of a quiet brook, and imagined that I had been through enough during the past days to be able to live henceforth entirely on my memories, armored against all temptation. I felt old, disillusioned, worn out. It seemed that I had finished with the world, and seclusion attracted me powerfully.

I took three days over the return journey, and these three days were enough to reduce all the sensations that had brought a little

51

sound and color to my heart to a blurred, inert mass. When I boarded the train, my gaze, intoxicated with emotion, had still been turned inward, where every nerve still thrilled, every memory still sparkled; her enchanting image was still in my eyes, her clear voice in my ears, her soft touch on my palm. But when I finally arrived in Holland I was empty of head and heart, exhausted and drowsy as if after the excitement of a night of wild festivities, looking forward with undisguised craving to "something different." The monotonous rattle of train wheels had drowned the music in my heart, and the soughing hollowness there was filled with alternating longings for liberation from my bodily prison, for the alleviation of my hunger and thirst, and for relief from the fatigue of rail travel. I no longer understoood what had moved me to hasten back to a country where I was bound to feel lonelier than anywhere else. It seemed to me that I was giving up my airy freedom and a world full of sunshine to move into a deathly, somber, musty monastery cell.

Still, I forced myself on with my journey, overpowered by the knowledge that the blame for everything lay within me, that no new surroundings could set right what was wrong with me. Why seek elsewhere what I would find nowhere? I had beheld my ideal world and felt how impotent I was to enter it.

If only I had been transformed by the experience I had acquired, as ignorant people claim can happen! But no! At best I had learned to want more from a woman than the gratification of a sensual need. I imagined that for the first time I was now capable of appreciating the glowing enchantment of a glance, the velvety caress of a handclasp, the sweet intoxication of a breath—in a word, the full radiant, fragrant, tender, magical, ravishing delight of being with a beautiful, soft, ardently desired being; and I was racked more intensely than ever by the question of where she could be found, the woman who would captivate me physically and intellectually, who like me would seek after intense feelings and would want to share her feelings with me, and who would want to part from me as soon as the enchantment began to fade.

Once I was within the borders of Holland, seclusion by the side of a quiet brook no longer attracted me at all. My shyness had never caused me to fall in love with solitude for long: a dislike

52

of people and a need for company have always been bound in-
separably in my soul. So I moved to Scheveningen, put up at the
Baths, and there walked about on the terrace like a stranger,
aimless, friendless, interested in nothing.

Though I had busied myself little with other people during
my travels, I had nevertheless acquired more social ease. Sometimes
at table I ventured to open a conversation, and so gradually acquired
a few mealtime acquaintances. I did not get any further, however,
still lacking the courage to speak to these same people in the
reading room or the music room. At the same time I imagined
they were laughing at me behind my back precisely because I
lacked such courage.

I used to spend almost the entire morning half-asleep in a cane
chair on the beach, hypnotized by the restlessly foaming sea, the
monotonously glittering sand, the immeasurably great shining void.
I dreamed my way through the evenings listening to the band,
usually still drowsy from the morning I had slept away, on rare
occasions roused from my stupor by a catchy composition or one
that moved me.

It was in one of these moments when life flickered up inside
me that it occurred to me to make a short story out of my distasteful
adventure. I had often asked myself whether the many abormalities
I had seen in myself could not be the sign of an artistic nature.
Times when artists were the healthiest, the simplest, the strongest,
the most intelligent, the noblest children of a nation and an age
are—assuming they ever existed—long past. Nowadays every artist
is to some extent sick, highly complex, neurasthenic, in some
respects of unsound mind, in other respects perverse. His striving
after truth and life, his search for what lies at the heart of all
things, for what connects them, his will to make one see, make
one feel, make one understand the finest shades, rather serve to
set him apart from the conventional, conformist product of a long
hereditary civilization who, with resigned contentment, mindlessly
does his most obvious little duty.

Was I, with my leaning toward self-analysis, with my feeling
for art, perhaps a born artist? Only my work could answer this
question. I decided to put myself to the test.

Of course I would have to make the facts of my shoddy little
53

history much more interesting, but that did not seem too difficult. The plot of an engagement which is broken because the flighty girl is beguiled by the cool skill of a rich, handsome young man seemed to me a most suitable framework, which I could clothe in the flesh of my observations and arouse to life with the vibrancy of my sensations. In its outline I felt the work at once so clearly within me that I was sure I needed only a pen and some paper and ink to be able to write it down from A to Z. Composing the particulars was not nearly so simple. How was I to describe rooms I had never seen, render conversations I had never heard, set people in action whom I did not know, put into words feelings which I perceived only as an inner music? My experience was so extremely limited that I felt handicapped all the time. In moments of excitement I would perhaps succeed in thinking up something or other; but rereading what I had written, I could hardly conceal from myself the fact that such contrived scenes made a wretched impression beside fragments in which I tried to express in words what I had really seen, unaffectedly felt, honestly experienced. Yet even this last had not flowed easily! Every word represented the spoils of a victory over my apathy—only under a clear sky did I feel clarity within my soul. Without a doubt I would have torn up my work at once if the few good fragments had not become so profoundly dear to me. For their sake I resisted my shoulder-shrugging, wrestled with my depressions, whipped up my imagination, and finished the work.

Carefully packaged, the story left for the editors of a journal. Three months later, after repeated requests for some kind of response, I got it back, badly packaged, with a chilly rejection on the grounds of "triviality."

It was autumn, and by this time I was living in Amsterdam in a hotel. Accustomed to rating my talents low, I had not flattered myself with thoughts of a better outcome. Yet the accompanying letter affected me much as, I believe, a sentence of life imprisonment will affect a criminal who has taken heart after an eloquent plea from his lawyer.

Under the illusion that all the peculiarities setting me apart from the great multitude, and everything inexpressible which I felt so painfully within me, would eventually be revealed as the

54

finer impressionability of an artist, I had made my hero a faithful counterfeit of myself. The story had become an unadorned revelation of my most secret feelings. I had, as it were, subjected my soul to a trial by fire, and now it seemed not to be proof against the heat. Like imitations of noble metal, my impressions and my feelings had corroded and decayed under the agency of art, and I saw the rejection of my story on the grounds of triviality as a condemnation of my whole inner life. I stood lower than the public, while an artist should stand higher. Everyone else had deeper feelings than I had.

During the wait for sentencing I had accomplished nothing; my idleness had been filled with the tension of waiting. After it came I decided that, justly or unjustly, I had been put on a level with those ridiculous weaklings distinguished from the true idiot only by a glimmering of cerebral life. Lacking the firmness to resist, I bowed my head beneath this verdict and felt myself becoming what people seemed to say I already was.

No trace was left of my little spurt of energy. I only got up when I could not endure it in bed any longer, and I fell back into bed as soon as I no longer knew where I could hang about or loiter unobserved. For hours on end I lay on a sofa as if stupefied, staring in front of me; if the mists that shrouded my thoughts lifted for an occasional moment, I saw life in the light of my cold jealousy of everything and everyone, and was conscious only of an all-embracing hatred. Horrible empty days! Not a spark of interest in anything at all!

I read my story through and found the thing simply insufferable: flat, silly, and at the same time arrogant. No: I was no artist.

I spent many an evening drinking in my room so that, excited for half an hour, I would once more be able to project a romantic plan of the future. I knew it would never be put into operation, but at least it provided me with a dull foretaste of glorious emotions, a shudder of imaginary life.

What eventually roused me out of my torpor was fear of the servants.

I have always disliked meeting acquaintances on my walks. This can partly be explained by my fear of greeting people who might not recognize me; in particular it grew out of my suspicion that they would turn behind my back to stare at me, disparage me, perhaps ridicule me. The same suspicion crept over me regarding the hotel maids, who must have found my slovenly idleness most unpleasant. I was sure they were laughing at me; what if they also started spreading the story that I was not well in the head! This possibility drove me out of bed quite early one day to go and eat at the table d'hôte again. It so happened that, with a series of questions, my neighbor managed to lure me into a conversation. At first I cursed the tiresome fellow and even thought of leaving the table; but little by little I allowed myself to be carried along, and next morning I was looking forward to the breakfast hour.

The man apparently belonged among those half-artistic souls who have the shamelessness, the talent, and the need to turn other people inside out. In my case he again and again drew a blank through my dogged taciturnity and my bland lying. Nevertheless, I saw that he was gradually beginning to make me out.

The longer this went on, the more careful it made me; yet at the same time it attracted me. Sometimes I felt a powerful urge to bare my heart to him; but it never went as far as that. He was the state-appointed mayor of a village in the Achterhoek district and full of admiration for his occupation. According to him, a mayor with a little diplomacy and money could easily become the idol of his municipality; there existed no better post for young people with good heads who, for lack of energy or for other reasons, had not found a foothold in the social mechanism. He managed to paint the job so appetizingly that in the end I believed I had found the remedy for what ailed me, the refuge from my misery, the salvation of my future.

Yet I would have quailed before all the difficulties, like taking lessons, searching for a municipal secretaryship, and putting myself in competition, if my dinnertime friend had not turned out to be eager to take on a number of my burdens. The more he spoke about the project the more he extolled it, praising small-town life too, with its enforced sociability. Finally he triumphed over my indecisiveness.

Not many weeks later I was ensconced in a little town hall, full of the best of intentions, flattering myself that I would now become an ordinary person, prepared to be happy in a quiet way, as I thought other people were.

For a while this folly held out under its own power; then it led a forced existence for a while; then it disappeared without a trace.

The first thing I reacted against was precisely the sociability for which I had had such high hopes. At the moment I write these pages I no longer doubt that only the innate mistrust with which I have always approached people was to blame for this new disappointment. At that time, however, I imagined that they all remained as surly as they had seemed when I first met them, and to explain this phenomenon I supposed that they held me to be a conceited, blasé city person. I surmised that the men thought, "You look down on us villagers because you have been a little further afield than we who know only the Rhine, and because you fancy you've picked up worldly wisdom in theaters, clubs, and cafés; but in our opinion you're still a nobody." And in the eyes of the women I thought I read: "You are probably used to going about with loose hussies; perhaps you are laughing at our dresses, which are several fashions behind the times; but don't get the idea that because of that we see any more in you than a clumsy narrow-minded person who at the bottom of his heart feels ill at ease with us."

By turns shy to the point of clumsiness, then almost offensive in my boldness, I did my best to force both others and myself into familiarity; but the feeling that I was tolerated but not liked, seen through too much and understood not enough, grew stronger every day. In addition the work—like all work— soon grew distasteful to me, which did not escape the mayor. My apathy increased, what willpower I had became paralyzed. It happened quite often, particularly on warm afternoons, that I fell asleep over my papers, and the host of good intentions that came to ripeness during my evening hours had always, by the following morning, become colorless, shrunken, withered.

Yet I held out for two years in this office, and would perhaps out of inertia have hung on even longer, had I not met a young man who was preparing for the University of Amsterdam.

57

Although his parents were highly respected in the town, no one liked him. People found him shifty, stiff, egotistical, and young and old avoided his company as far as is feasible in a small place. On me too he made a most unfavorable impression; yet it struck me that we were very much alike. In itself this would have been no reason for me to seek his company; but it happened that the comparison was in my favor. I was a little less shy, a little less immature, and this gave me a singularly comfortable feeling of self-confidence. In fact we only became friends—as far as people like us can be friends—at a wedding, when he fastened on to me like a shadow and I could feel myself grow in self-confidence merely by poking fun at his anxiety.

From that day on he clung to me with his remarkable helplessness, and the consciousness of being a pillar of support so captivated me that I myself put forward the plan of following him to Amsterdam.

"And then in the evenings we'll go out for a bit of fun, won't we?"

I can still hear myself saying these words in the tone of someone with quite some experience in the field. At that moment I thought myself really capable of carrying through in the role of man-about-town.

Desire and fear gleamed in the shy look with which Van Dregten wordlessly received the announcement. A subdued smile played for a moment about his thin lips; for a long while he rubbed his ever-clammy hand over his receding chin, then a faint but rapturous "Yes" welled up like a sigh hot from his heart. He wanted it so very much, but without me he would never have dared. Once more I began fabricating stories of clandestine love, and worked myself up so much in the telling that I grew convinced that in Amsterdam I would find such adventures simply for the plucking.

So the lesson I had learned had had no effect: my predisposition—however weak—triumphed through its resilience. I knew very well that when it came to the test my diffidence would not have diminished by much, yet it was impossible to suppress the thought that I had become older and *therefore* more experienced, more adept. The *therefore* was irrational, but who dares say he is not afflicted with a similar *therefore*?

Beneath the rusty crudities of our old age lie the shining errors of our youth, yet most people seem to labor under the delusion that their life is a development, a progress.

It is true that the more at home a person is in his time, particularly in the conventions of his time, the less he gets into unpleasant collisions, and so the less he is compelled to reflect on the true impulses behind human actions, and therefore the more readily he ascribes to other people all kinds of nice features that he thinks he observes in himself, and consequently the more contented he is in his blindness and the more favorably he must think of life. In contrast to this, it seems that in spite of the nice or at least defensible motives for their acts which people think they find in themselves—and often, in spite of their acts, want to have ascribed to them—they only too often assume bad or at least indefensible motives in other people—except on the stage and in books—for acts of the same kind.

To gain knowledge of others and to acquire self-knowledge are however two very different ways of growing wise, very seldom practiced by one and the same person. Now that I no longer think the number of normal people so high, and therefore the normality of most people so enviably pure, it seems to me that self-knowledge probably always leads to pessimism, while knowledge of others does so only when one does not consider oneself and one's own experiences a shining exception to an ugly rule.

When we arrived in Amsterdam we rented rooms in the same house. I was struck with a fancy to take up my own course of study during the mornings, which I had to spend alone. Perhaps this was the consequence of an unreasonable fear that my ascendancy over Van Dregten would slip from me if I could not assert myself in the intellectual sphere. I decided to start writing again, but differently this time. I wanted to make a serious study of recent philosophy and physiology. Here the motive force was my need for self-knowledge. The nature and origin of things interested me only to the extent that I wanted to know to what Willem Termeer owed his peculiarities and what place was due to *him* among his fellowmen. Was I really in one or more respects an exception, an abnormality, and if so, to what extent were the

59

thoughts, feelings, endeavors, achievements of normal people greater or less than mine? To solve this problem I read both scholarly works and fiction, always dominated by the questions, "Am *I* like this?" "Do *I* fall under this heading?" "Is this *my* case?" "Would *I* be able to do that?" The answers were always as humiliating as they were paralyzing; but the bleakness of this outcome did not bring me to doubt its correctness. I held and hold myself to be a degenerate.

If perhaps I suffer less than the ordinary, healthy person, I am surely also less able to enjoy myself. My interest in the vicissitudes of other people is seldom anything more than curiosity, and unfeigned sympathy hardly ever rises up in me. Everything that breathes seeks pleasure; but the normal individual, the good individual, finds satisfaction in a life that benefits others. *My* nature craves for pleasure at the expense of others, and in place of joyous fulfillment derives listless fatigue. In heredity I thought I would find the explanation for this.

It was not love that had brought my parents together: hence the chilly, matter-of-fact egotism of my inner life. Exhausted by a wild youth, my father had managed to bequeath me his overwrought desires but not the strength to curb or satisfy them. Finding myself unequal to the life-struggle, I had become a coward upon my first clash with another person, and vanity, my mother's legacy, had compelled me to nourish this weakness so well that it necessarily sank ineradicable roots in the depths of my soul.

Such were my reflections on myself, nor have I ever yet retreated from this appraisal.

Meanwhile I led a miserable existence. Sometimes, waking up tired and congested, ridden by anxiety about my health, I might make up my mind that if it was impossible to become a good man I would at least aspire to live like a good man. Yet toward evening I would stray of my own accord toward the paths I always followed, and instead of letting my excitement lead me to pleasure, I sought for pleasure in excitement. And what pitiful pleasure, what pitiful excitement!

Sometimes I would revive and think again of running away, of entering the world in search of glorious, intense emotions. Generally, however, my soul remained asleep, sleeping the dull sleep of exhaustion, and the sole desire that welled up in me at such times was to force my inner self in its full rottenness on the world. How often have I not said to myself, "Come on, shame is nothing but shyness!" On such nights, with loathsome women and yet more loathsome comrades, I played the role of a hypochondriac, bragging decadent.

Every night I drank a little more, every morning it took a little longer before calm returned to my heated blood, clarity to my befogged brain; even so, my debaucheries were only the petty excesses of someone who cannot take much and cannot get the real thing. Van Dregten was wholly satisfied. With his limited powers of thought he had the advantage over me of total lack of self-criticism. Neither of us felt the attraction of good, the repulsion of evil; but I understood—or at least thought I understood—that good *can* attract, while to him normal people were nothing but a band of tedious hypocrites.

Who knows how long I would have persisted in this kind of life if I had not by chance met two young men from Amsterdam whose way of life closely matched ours. These two differed from us insofar as, moving rather more in fashionable circles, they deemed it important to maintain decorum until late at night. Utterly lacking in artistic sense, they found it boring to select a concert hall or theater for this purpose. They managed to get Van Dregten to give over his evenings to whist, and I, who had never liked cards, was weak enough to yield yet again.

But in the long run I could not stand these fellows, as stupid as they were affected. It offended me badly enough that they were capable of carrying off the poor joke of appearing at the card table in dress suits and white ties, addressing each other as *monsieur le duc, monsieur le marquis, monsieur le comte, monsieur le baron*; but the situation became unendurable when, rightly or wrongly, I began to suspect that they had come to an agreement with Van Dregten to draw our collective expenses from *my* purse alone. I had a certain amount of money and had to give reckoning to no one. So to pay for Van Dregten, who required much more than he received, seemed natural to me. But to find myself being chiseled by a pair of fops who, identifying a certain level of routine facility with worldly wisdom, conceitedly looked down on me—

that went too far. Their presence became intolerable to me. Nevertheless, something exceptional was still needed to bring me to the decision to end it all and go away.

Finally that something exceptional came; it came in the night.

I had turned thirty. My birthday had been a day like any other, only a little drearier because it had rained since early morning. We had been out late and drunk much. Almost home, I had slipped and fallen in the mud.

I had not been in bed for more than two hours when suddenly I woke up with a violent start. What had frightened me I did not know; but I had barely lit the candle before a terrible fear, like an internal cold shudder, spread through my whole glowing body. I could not think clearly; I only felt that I was scared, dead scared of the consequences of my acts. These consequences would be disorders, incurable disorders of all kinds. Already they were creeping around like snakes in my heart, in my brain, in my back, in my eyes, in my chest, in my liver, in my stomach, in my kidneys, in my arms, in my legs, and I felt that they were sapping me, that they would make me old before my time, crippled, hideous, an object of ridicule and loathing to everyone. I saw myself worn, tormented, growing thinner, losing color, decaying from day to day, languishing away from hour to hour and finally ...dying.

O death, death—how frightened I have always been of it! Yet I have so often asked myself, "Were you unhappy *before* you were born?" And my unattainable wish never to have been born has always been so sincere!

No more thought of sleep. My heart thumped so strenuously that I could see my nightshirt go up and down. Surges of heat rose to my head, and I was no longer able to move hand or foot. I simply sat upright in bed, staring, staring...and imagined that I could distinguish every organ in my body, above all feel the burning of the affected spot from which proceeded the corruption that would rampage further and further. My forehead was soaked with sweat; dark vapors passed before my eyes. What should I do, what should I do?

Only toward morning, as chilly gray streaks of light began to cut through the dark brown of the curtains, did exhaustion blur the harshly glittering terror in my brain to the lumpy grayness of a bad dream.

Waking from this dream, my first glance fell on my muddied clothes, and my soul was overcome with a longing for rest and freshness, just as in the morning a longing for ice-cold water comes over the tongue that has drunk too much. Calm and health, that was all I desired. Already thirty years old! What would become of me if I grew sickly and needed help and no one but a paid nurse would show any concern for me? For the first time the thought of marriage occurred to me, and I imagined I saw the haven where my wretched little ship could anchor.

The aspect that attracted me was not any need for the affection of a wife or of children: I saw only a sunny dwelling in which I would be comfortable and safe from people. Just as a simple walk appeals to a recuperating invalid, the prospect of routine home life without any excitement appealed to me.

But...where would I find the wife? I had no married friends. Admittedly I had heard of approaching girls in a shop or restaurant; but I would certainly never dare to do that!

Not knowing how I would ever again penetrate the world of society, from which I had now twice fled, the first idea I had was of paying quick court to a pretty little shopgirl, the daughter of a cigar-seller. Perhaps, I thought, she will feel honored by the proposal of a "gentleman" and will look up to me.

The joke was of short duration.

The girl acted friendly enough, and, strengthened both by the thought of my social superiority and by an awareness of the propriety of my intentions, I quite soon conquered my diffidence; but just as soon it became clear that for once I had grossly over-estimated my powers! It was probably she herself who one day told her parents about my advances. When I entered the shop again that afternoon, I found father and daughter there together. The former politely but pressingly requested me in future to buy my cigars elsewhere, and when, at these words, the girl burst out laughing, courage to protest against his unspoken suspicion deserted me. So I simply slunk away in shame, wounded less by my treatment from the shopgirl than by the proof I had had of my utter lack of finesse.

Then one day it occurred to me that there still existed one family to which access would surely not be made difficult for me. This was the family of my former guardian Bloemendael in Utrecht. Husband and wife were still alive. They had two daughters, of whom the elder, married to a high civil servant, lived in The Hague. Perhaps these folks knew people, perhaps I would be able to reenter the civilized world via their house. So I wrote: that is to say, I asked my ex-guardian in writing for permission to pay him a visit. His reply ran: "You will be welcome here, the guest room stands ready for you."

Of course feelings of diffidence toward the respectable and perhaps formal company in which I would find myself immediately made me regret sending the letter; but seeing that it could not go on like this gave me the strength to persevere and write a second time: "I am coming on such-and-such a day at five-thirty." The choice of dinnertime was made in the hope that a glass of wine would quickly put me at ease.

As soon as the die was cast I began preparations to present as good a front as possible.

This expression can give rise to a misunderstanding. I was not thinking of trying to make an immediate favorable impression on the girl I had never met. All I wanted was not to be unsightly, since the slightest mistake in my toilet or the smallest pimple on my face made my embarrassment mount until it was unbearable. I always had the feeling of being carefully surveyed and usually also . . . condemned.

My reception was as hearty as it was long-winded. Guests were apparently rare birds in this quiet coop. Two maids and a manservant came forward in order to assist the coachman in unloading my solitary piece of baggage. Bloemendael waited, emitting nervous sounds, behind the swing door, to relieve me of coat and hat, and his wife called instructions down the stairwell about how the trunk should be held and handled and where it should be put down. It was a long time before my guardian, chuckling and rambling on about the weather, the journey, the time we had not seen each other, ushered me into the sitting room, and yet

64

a while longer before I got to see his wife and daughter, who had been watching over the arrival of my belongings from the upper floor.

The appearance of the two ladies at once set me at my ease. Not that they were particularly considerate or able to help me tactfully past my shyness; oh no, on the contrary they seemed very reticent, even surly. What got me going was the shoddy furnishings of the room. It was as if the good cut of my own clothes gave me an advantage. In my heart sounded the words: "These people feel that they are your inferiors, so they dare not judge you so harshly."

I produced my phrases of apology, and did so quite easily, about the inconsiderateness of my coming to stay and the trouble I was causing.

The good-hearted rambling of my nervous guardian got me further into my stride. His stream of words still murmurs in my ears. "Yes, yes, a drink? But...do sit down, eh...a comfortable chair, eh. Yes, yes, a drink...how would you like that?...Such a journey...eh, in our damp climate, eh. You're looking well. What?...Come, just one, eh? Equilibrium inside and out. You'll never do it this young again....You'll say yes, eh?"

Seeing that on the marble top of the sideboard a pair of decanters stood ready, I accepted. A glass of strong drink would perhaps give me the courage to address a few words to the girl, who had already picked up one of the decanters and was looking questioningly at her father.

"Gin or port?"

My answer was "Gin," and silently, with downcast eyes, Anna offered me the full glass on a tray. For a moment it seemed that the downcast eyes said, "You are a low person, something I cannot possibly look at"; but the impression did not last long.

The old gentleman took port and we touched glasses.

Ever as hurried in his faltering speech as he was subdued in his movements, he gave expression to his pleasure at my visit. After his wife had concurred, he began to talk about my father. First came the observation that I strongly resembled the deceased. Then he computed how far the latter would by now have been into his sixties, confessing that he himself was nearly sixty.

65

"A jolly chap, you know...yes, yes...always cheerful, eh...
at least in his heyday. Later on...well—we all have to pay, eh...
but a nice chap...yes, yes...a success with the ladies...at least
with some of them."

"I am sure the pair of you had quite a lot on your conscience,"
his wife observed in a lightly jesting tone not without a touch of
disdainful jealousy.

A crooked smile played over the pale, chubby face between the
wide, thin-lipped mouth and the narrow gray side-whiskers. The
small eyes, from which radiated a spider's web of furrows, flickered
roguishly, and he would surely have volunteered a pretty set of
reminiscences had his daughter not been in the room. For the
child's sake he held himself in check, and, taking another sip,
spoke to excuse himself: "I beg you to believe that my role was
always that of spectator."

A barely noticeable shrug of the shoulders was Mrs. Bloemendael's only response.

It was only too often in later years that Anna, by a similar
wordless jerk of her shoulders, put me in mind of her mother;
and I felt regret every time at not having paid more heed from
the first to my future mother-in-law. Who knows whether our
marriage would even have come to pass if I had detected in time
the Anna of the future in this taciturn, conventionally prim,
pedestrian matron. But being too irresponsible not to restrict
my interest to those few people from whom I personally expected
something pleasant or feared something unpleasant, it did not
occur to me to deign to pay much attention to the aging Mrs.
Bloemendael. I remember finding her always tense, genteelly lined
features, from which blue eyes peered out sharply, neither pretty
nor ugly. If I think back to her I believe I can assert that she
was someone with a talent for understanding people who lacked,
however, the intellectual development and power of thought that
would have got her further than obstinately holding to her
own opinions.

Bloemendael proceeded to expatiate on Father's married life,
which had not been happy.

"He should not have married; but that goes for her too. And
as it is in these cases, the children suffered the worst consequences—

not so? Yes, yes...your education, my boy...well now...eh?...
During the last years I no longer visited your father much at home.
I always say, one doesn't have to go out looking for unhappiness,
eh?...if one couldn't help anyhow—not so?...But that doesn't prevent...after all, I was your guardian—not for long, eh?—that's true
—but long enough to know...eh? It was all over with your studies
at once...then came all that traveling...Amsterdam...I don't
know it all exactly—only from hearsay...I'm not reproaching you
with it...youth must let off steam...your father's nature...it
isn't my business either; but...it's a pity, eh, and if you had had
a better education..."

I would have preferred to see the subject left untouched; however, the fact that the old gentleman termed my wretched life in
Amsterdam "letting off steam" gave me pleasure. Though I did
not thereby become an amusing rake in my own eyes, the possibility
of appearing as such in the eyes of others strengthened my self-
confidence.

"But, Mr. Bloemendael, what must your daughter be thinking
of me?"

The phrase was barely uttered before I found it ridiculous; but
the fact that it made Anna blush raised my spirits further. I went so
far as to look at her, even smiled at her—and she smiled back.

That soundless little laugh, in which her light blue eyes seemed
to join, while two even rows of white teeth gleamed through
the pale red of her lips, exercised a rare charm on me. It was
not the shy, childlike laugh that makes a woman seem naïve, even
stupid. No, her laugh—which I was later to assess differently—
gave her, at the time, the semblance of an intellectual advantage
with which, from a high elevation, she looked down upon mankind
and smiled kindly. Besides...I was not used to being smiled at,
and when, suddenly blushing, she cast her eyes down again,
something gave me the impression that she was implying a kind
of silent declaration of love.

For my part, I did not find her in the least attractive; but a
lover of clear lines would probably have come to a different conclusion. The blue of the eyes was too light for me, the almost
imperceptible lashes and eyebrows did not set the eyes off, the
small, tilted nose gave her a childlike quality, and the cool, marbled

skin aroused not the slightest sensual desire in me. If at that moment I had been permitted to give her a kiss, I would not have done it, or have done it without pleasure. Outdoors in a crowd she would certainly have passed me entirely unnoticed; in these stuffy domestic surroundings we saw each other as two prisoners who could escape only by combining forces.

I remember that at table that first evening I at once took over the conversation. Such was of course part of the role of amusing chatterbox which I immediately began to perform. The character I had hitherto acted—among others, to the Swedish girl—was but a pitiful caricature of the merry Don Juan I played, with all the superior airs of a widely traveled man addressing dull homebodies, in my stories. Yet the more stories I told and the more wine I drank, the more my belief in my own boastful anecdotes mounted, and I would certainly have been deeply disappointed if father, mother, or daughter had in the end decided I was a liar. Fortunately these simple folk had picked up too little knowledge of people and of the world in their monotonous existence to see through my playacting. They listened attentively and swallowed everything. Still, I have not forgotten that the old lady often fixed me with a long hard gaze.

A faint sparkle in Anna's eyes gave me the courage during dessert to address myself more particularly to her. We were talking about music. I did little more than ask, "Do you know this? Do you know that?"—yet the girl, seldom coming into contact with men, was delighted. I noticed that a pretty compliment had had less power to send her into raptures than the naming of a favorite piece of music. She even began to hum the melodies and promised to play them later. The consequence was that she spent an hour at the piano that evening, beginning various pieces whose technical difficulties were too much for her powers, while I, standing beside her to turn the pages, felt an intimacy come into being between us which made me as happy as it surprised me.

Meanwhile her father and mother attentively read the newspaper. When we said goodnight, I imagined that in the pressure of Anna's hand there lay a particular meaning, and a presentiment of a richer, better life coursed through me from the touch of her fingertips like a warm vibration.

68

The Bloemendaels' guest room was and is both stiff and middle-class, both neat and stuffy. The window sashes do not move more than a handsbreadth; plain dark green curtains hang ponderously before the windows and around the double bed; formless mahogany furniture gleams overbearingly at the visitor, and from the coarsely flowered wallpaper shine the glass frames of steel engravings mounted on cardboard mottled with damp.

Only with reluctance would I now sleep there again. At that time, however, nestling down under the cold, starched linen that puffed up around the thick blankets from the old-fashioned bedstead, I felt like a recuperating smallpox sufferer who for the first time has had a bath and cleansed himself well. I seemed a new being, purer, healthier than before: it was as if a better self had now really triumphed over the wretch in my heart. How easy it appeared to become an ordinary person, at home in society, surrounded by a circle of acquaintances and friends. Never had there been more cheerful jubilation in my usually dull soul. I still remember exactly what I dreamed that night after my excitement had finally subsided and sleep had taken pity on me.

I was lying in bed in the guest room of my ex-guardian; it was totally dark and quiet. With a soft creak the door opened and someone stepped inside. I knew for sure it was *she*; but I did not stir, convinced that she would leave if she noticed that I was lying awake. Slowly she came closer and, right in front of the bed, stopped. I was sure that despite the darkness she could see me. For a long while she stood motionless. Finally she bent her head down; I felt the fresh warmth of her mouth approach, and then... then she pressed a long kiss upon my lips.

Oh, why have I tasted this bliss only in my dreams? Why has a real kiss never given me the sensation of this dreamed kiss? Why is it that only in dreams have I been deeply in love, only in dreams have been loved warmly in return? All that I envy in others I have enjoyed in my dreams: even pleasure fully experienced has never been able to equal the aftereffects of these dreams, to equal the paling emotions that lingered with me for a day afterwards.

Is it like that with other people, or does nature grant them the reality of which she concedes me only the reflection?

The next morning I was in as good a mood as I had been in all my life. My longing to be a good person, to begin living a good life, to be among good people in a good way, was entirely sincere. I spurned my past as a hideous, heated sickness, and thought I had all at once become healthy and calm. And from this bodily and spiritual health I expected the highest happiness: contentment and pleasure.

Was I in love with Anna at that moment? Certainly I imagined I was. My weariness of spirit had vanished; my gnawing desires were stilled; my misanthropy paled; a delightful sadness trembled through my whole being like seductive music; within myself I addressed Anna, whispering words of adoration to my Madonna.

But...was this love? I do not believe so. If two men, one thoroughly healthy, truly good, sincerely in love, the other I, had been able to bring our feelings out from our hearts, our heads, our senses, into the light and to compare them, what a pitiful sight my thin-blooded, melancholy little inclination would have made beside his overpowering, exultant urge! Was my so-called love really more than a wish to marry, coupled with this unexpected discovery of a simple obliging girl at hand, or more than the self-satisfaction of for once finally having acted with some gallantry toward a women, joined to a fear of not finding such a favorable opportunity a second time? In fact, it is already a bad sign when someone asks himself, "Am I really in love?" True, I did not ask that question for my own sake. Yet in such questioning lay doubts as to the quality of my feeling which would have made an impartial third party say, "Don't marry." Today this is clear to me; at the time I saw in it precisely the proof of a lofty love full of concern.

The sum of it all was that I was as fond of her as a being like myself can be fond of a woman who does not arouse his sensual desire; but to make her believe that this touch of feeling, this alms-offering by a poor devil, was no dissimulation, I had to lapse into exaggeration and thus necessarily again...play a role.

All this deliberating not only quickly soured my touch of happiness but also for a long time held me back from the decisive step. Not long enough, granted; still, this hesitation was one of

70

my few acts—if I may call it an act—that have not done me discredit.

Just as true and unadorned as is this story of my sorry colloquy with myself, which I see stretching behind me to form a pitifully meaningless and empty life, so is my confession that during those days of incessant inward conflict I never consciously wished for anything but to make Anna a happy person and myself a good one. It was no so-called impure desire or ignoble ulterior motive that brought to my lips the few loving words my tongue has ever uttered. They were sincerely meant, and it gave me satisfaction that I dared to say them.

If there was one prospect that enticed me, it was the opportunity of becoming content with my lot, as I thought the majority of people were, and then, at least in the eyes of one being, of being held a good person, at least better than many others; of associating freely with people in general without feelings of shame, and of being on intimate terms with *her*, admiring, cherishing and cherished.

For me, love had always been deeply melancholy. In it there lay a presentiment of threatening calamity, calamity above all for the woman, which could be conjured away only by total self-sacrifice on my part. But now this sacrifice no longer consisted in my renouncing her and going away forever: now it seemed to me that I could make her happy by no longer seeking, desiring, or hoping for anything for myself. In the future everything would be for *her*: every thought, every wish, every deed, every abstinence.

In the meantime my feelings, however weak, were far too much in control of my suspicious intelligence. It is true that I wanted it so. It gave me pleasure that her laughing mouth, her softly questioning glance, and the countless indescribable, perhaps even undetectable feminine peculiarities of form, color, movement, tone, action that charm one man, leave another cold, that sometimes repel, could now—in an ill hour—smother my suspicion. I *wanted* to be taken in, and for that reason—perhaps only for that reason—I was.

So, unexpectedly I came to the point of proposing to her.

We were sitting in the theater; it was between two acts, while the orchestra was playing a fantasia on themes from *Lohengrin*. As usual, the boulder of clumsy shyness lay before me blocking

71

my way. But for once the music dragged me over it. I did not say, "Will you be my wife?" but, "I love you so much, Anna."

She did not speak at once. I had to repeat my words and add, "Don't you believe me?" When she spoke, however, her reply was to a proposal of marriage, which she had apparently been expecting. Quite calmly, blushing only faintly, with sobering self-possession, in fact in a cheerful, eager tone, she said, "I certainly want to; but I must first talk it over with Mama and Papa."

What a disappointment for someone who had been counting on a warm, tense handclasp, on a long, penetrating look of surrender, on an ecstatic fusion of two emotions, on the soaring on high together of two souls transported from a hostile humanity by waves of erotic music! It was as if a ray of sober white daylight all of a sudden pierced the mystically colorful theatrical splendor of my fantasies.

And things went on in this disturbingly ordinary way.

The next morning the parents gave their consent. When Bloemendael began to cry I found him utterly ridiculous. I was not questioned about my past—the old gentleman, who still managed my inheritance, knew that the capital was untouched. As for the future, they indicated that they would like me to look out for a regular occupation.

So all at once we were engaged!

Before long I felt unsatisfied; my new condition did not correspond at all to my expectations. I had imagined being in love as something if not forbidden then at least hidden. Like a treasure of which only Anna would know but whose name even she would not utter, I wanted to guard and cherish it in the deepest darkness of my soul. Now it seemed to me to have been profaned by rude disclosure, enfeebled by the shared knowledge of third parties.

I realize now that Anna saw the matter in an entirely different light. She wanted to get married because that was the proper thing for a girl to do, while staying unmarried seemed to her a kind of humiliation. She accepted me because I had been the first and as yet the only man to propose to her. There was not much more going on in her mind. I believe, certainly, that she imagined she liked me; but what interested her in me was the Don Juan I played, not the Termeer I was.

So it would seem that it was as much my fault as hers that between us there was so little of the staring into each other's eyes, the long hot kisses, the sitting hand in hand and all the delicious contacts from which a magnetic life-stream vibrates through all the nerves, rising to an overwhelming chord that echoes through the soul like organ music through a Gothic cathedral.

In the rare moments when my inner being shone through the mists of my depression, I had imagined all this to be so beautiful and had expected of it a renewal of my whole spiritual life. Now I felt at best like a man in church among believers: the ceremony moved me, but as for sweeping me along as it swept others, as for wrenching me for a while from earthly concerns—no, that was not in its power.

Day after day I kept hoping for improvement. Convinced that I lacked enthusiasm and sensitivity, I tried repeatedly to compel her and myself to a warmer intimacy; but our fingers, though intertwined, seldom pressed each other involuntarily, and it was unmistakable that neither she nor I enjoyed it when our lips touched. Only in the evening, when I sat down next to her at the piano and the harmonies filled in what we lacked, yes, only then could I recapture the mood of an earlier time, when in my lonely room I stimulated myself with books and liquor. For a while I felt my cold, drab thoughts glow again with color and become a self-sacrificial sentimental lovesickness. The skeptical questions that kept rising within me died down, drowned by the music of the emotions.

The first thing we had to do—after I had moved to a hotel—was to pay visits to relatives and friends of the Bloemendaels. They had almost no close family; their friends were for the most part old and middle-class folk. A few of their friends did have grown-up children; but this younger generation, having seen that there was no chance of fun at the Bloemendaels, had not kept up the acquaintance. So Anna hardly ever came into contact with young men of her own age.

This round of visits seemed to me outrageously like a freshman initiation ritual, but I subjected myself to it, thinking it would be the bridge over which I should return to society.

73

Almost everywhere I picked up nasty impressions. Looking from the street into the half-light of apartments, I have always had the feeling that the people in them are spending their lives in a kind of stupefied half-sleep. And now, entering the stuffiness of these banal sitting rooms, hearing the conventional formulas of friendship run from bored lips like rote lessons and stifle in the dull silence, feeling time and time again the transition from the fresh outside air draw an insuperable drowsiness like a black veil over my mind, hearing now and then from afar the tedious mournful whimpering of children find its way to me as if through a thick cloud—now a cold, dulling fear of the life ahead began to seep through me. At the same time I could not shake off the thought that all these people were inspecting me from head to foot, were reading weakness and perversity in my face, in my figure, in the way I looked at them. Surely they were pitying Anna for her miserable intended. Again I felt I was disdained, laughed at behind my back, and while my timidity increased rather than decreased, hatred for commonplace people content to be commonplace welled up undiminished in my heart.

Yet all the time I still wanted to be one of them, to learn to be happy like them with a calm life that did not damage my health, that did not blunt my mind.

Back at the Bloemendaels I usually volunteered all kinds of sarcastic remarks about people with whom I had spoken barely half an hour. I imagined that Anna with her pleasant ease of manner had been ashamed of me, and behind my sarcasm lurked the instinctive intention of trying to stand higher in her eyes than the people I criticized and ridiculed. And it seemed that this goal was being attained. When her mother, who always accompanied us, one day made the observation that on a certain visit I had been almost impolitely taciturn, Anna took my side and called me an exceptional person, out of place among their acquaintances. Then she too—to the astonishment of her parents—began to make fun of these acquaintances, and, seeing what an influence I was exercising on her thought and judgments, I reached the point of having spells of believing in my superiority myself. Should chance have it that someone came up with such a boring little piece of pulpit moralism as "Everyone can amend his faults" or "Every good

74

deed is rewarded, every evil one punished," then my feeling of superiority expressed itself in hateful remarks that might perhaps on the one hand be difficult to refute, but on the other were again demolishing the bridge to normal humanity piece by piece beneath my feet.

Our most important visit was to Anna's married sister in The Hague.

Suze had made a rich marriage to Baron van Swamelen, a senior civil servant in the Ministry of Justice. They lived in style, knew plenty of people, had two children, and were—according to the old people—extremely happy.

When Van Swamelen heard that we would like to come over, he at once invited us to dine. Of course there was no question of declining the invitation, but I was not looking forward to the evening at all. For all that, I saw that a man of Van Swamelen's name, fortune, and position was just the right person to open the doors of one or two homes to us and supply us with a few acquaintances. So I decided not only to do my best, but even suggested the plan of eventually settling in The Hague.

Van Swamelen received us most cordially, but with such reserve and condescension that I immediately felt there would never be any question of friendship between us. He probably took an intense dislike to me at first sight.

Suze was much like her sister, but prettier. Her figure had something regal in it that impressed me, and it was as if everything in her house, from the manservant who answered the door to the wine on the table, was pervaded with this regal quality. The gleaming silk covering the chairs in the salon looked too beautiful to sit on; the thick carpets on the stairs and in the dining room felt too soft for ordinary leather shoes; the fine porcelain, crystal, and damask shone as if never sullied by greasy sauce or wine dregs. The silence of this stately, spacious house was even denser, even more oppressive than that of the homes of Anna's hometown friends. We saw and heard nothing whatsoever of children, while the subdued tone of both Van Swamelen's and his wife's responses smothered every attempt to become familiar or even simply openhearted. I found myself less at ease here than anywhere else, and when after dinner I was left alone with my future brother-in-law, I felt like a boy who has overestimated himself at the moment when his examination is about to begin.

And it was in fact an examination, this after-dinner conversation of ours over coffee and liqueur. The Ministry official, the man of society with connections, the inhabitant of the capital in a position to see behind the scenes, put the loafer, the outcast, the vapid provincial through his paces, and it was clear that I failed in politics, failed in sociology, failed even in general knowledge of the news of the day. At his wit's end, Van Swamelen steered the conversation toward travel, and in this field too the unsystematic and inartistic adventure-seeker must have made a sad impression on someone who had himself traveled much, using his eyes and studying seriously. With a woeful feeling of inferiority, a feeling which to my annoyance expressed itself in a stream of exaggerated protestations of thanks and flattering phrases, I left Van Swamelen's house. And as Anna and I traveled back, each huddled in a corner of the railway carriage, wakeful and yet as if by agreement silent, it became clear to me that I had not only made an unfavorable impression on Van Swamelen and Suze, but had also in the eyes of my future wife lost quite a lot of my seeming prestige. Struck by the contrast between her brother-in-law and me, she was beginning by degrees to distinguish the true Termeer who would one day fill her with such deep repugnance.

The next morning I stayed in bed and sent word that I was sick. It seemed to me that all kinds of things had come out about me the previous evening which I ought to feel ashamed about toward Anna. At the same time the prospect of our future existence oppressed me like a nightmare. When I had still been sitting alone in my hotel room in Amsterdam, always weary and exhausted, harried yet aimless, with burning cheeks and stinging eyes, haze-shrouded brain and dull pains in the back, the vision of a restful married life had floated before me radiating happiness and exuding health, just as the prospect of a sunny southern mountain floats before the eyes of a feverish consumptive in the chilly gray of a Dutch November day. But now that calm had been returned to my blood by several weeks of a healthier, even life, the future gaped before me like one of those houses with

76

thick carpets and heavy curtains in which the daylight pines away, in which every sound is stifled, and in which boredom hovers like an oppressive gray fog. I saw myself waking up, oppressed with fear at the thought of the long empty day; I saw myself wandering about in the streets, spied on by malevolent eyes, with no desire but to kill undying time; I saw myself going to bed again, embittered against a life that crumbled in my fingers joylessly and aimlessly, like all too thin ice in the grasp of a drowning man.

If I had at least been able to take pleasure simply in having children, in filling some honorary post, or in putting together a collection of some kind! But nothing—to want nothing, to be able to do nothing, and yet to flinch from a life without any interest, not to dare risk the leap into the endless sleep—the martyrdom was so exquisitely cruel that only that gruesome power which marks out our lives—call it fate, circumstance, heredity, God—could invent and execute it!

Aversion to everything and everyone, fear of every word that might pass my lips, kept me bedridden for two days, powerless. I shrank from the marriage like an exhausted traveler from the endless zigzags of a mountain road, while from bachelor life I recoiled like a healthy person before the hot mustiness of disease.

On the third day I had an early-morning visit from my future father-in-law, who came to find out how I was. Without really knowing why, I jumped out of bed, hurriedly put some clothes on, and went to meet Bloemendael with a smiling face. Before he could say a word I asserted that today I felt much better and planned to visit Anna at the usual hour.

I can still see the astonished face of the kindhearted old gentleman, who had expected to find either a very sick man who did not dare to admit the worst, or a healthy man who had been lying because he did not know how best to break off his engagement.

"Well, well," he began to mumble, "that's good.... Look, we didn't understand quite...eh? We were beginning to think...and I intended...unless Anna...but...so much the better...then. ...Yes, that certainly changes...though...go out, eh...it's really bleak outside today...so..."

Pushing a chair up, I gave no more answer than, "Oh, is it bleak."

Bloemendael did not sit down. More by the tone than by the

content of his words he had betrayed to me that he had come
to do more than merely see what was doing. And so, pacing in
circles, he began: "I have actually come to ... yes ... to have a talk
with you. But look ... yes ... that is actually no longer so necessary
... unless ... go to Anna today ... yes, that is best ..."

"That was what I intended."

"Oh ... yes, yes. ... Do you mind if I take off my coat? It is
quite warm in here ... eh. ... Thank you. ... Don't put yourself
out ... all right. ... No, no, I would rather stay on my feet. ... It's
a habit of mine, eh. You know: habit is second nature, eh. ... And
you can also talk more comfortably, eh, don't you think?"

I said nothing. So after a moment of silence the poor fellow
had to stumble on. He did so, still nervously pacing back and forth
between chair and window and gesturing expansively with his pale,
blue-veined hands, whose broad fingers seemed to stick to each other.

How he introduced the subject I no longer remember, but before
long he was again talking about my father, saying that though he
had not exactly become a useful member of society, and though
he lived a life of pleasure somewhat longer than most people, he had
still been a good fellow who had meant well by his wife and child.

At once I felt an urge to contradict him, but as usual controlled
myself fairly well, bottling up my rage, only to lose my self-possession
the more completely later on. So Bloemendael could proceed.

"He died ... quite suddenly; but it was after all a blessing ...
in the circumstances, not so? I only saw you once, when you were
such a tiny toddler ... yes ... you were so tiny and so sweet ... yes,
I had only one sight of you, eh. ... Then all of a sudden I became
your guardian and ... yes, yes, I could soon see it. ... The boy
knows he has money. ... He prefers having fun to studying ... his
father's son, eh. It's in his blood. Well, not everyone has to have a
job, not so? ... My heavens, my own work isn't exactly elevating,
is it? So if he can perhaps find himself a decent occupation later
on ... not so? Some hobby or other ... a job ... in short, whatever
you like. After all, there are superfluous people all over the place ...
so ... and then the death of your mother, eh? I had nothing against
it that you wanted to travel and see the world. After all, it's
educational, too, isn't it? You had had enough unpleasantness ...
and then, youth must blow off steam ... an old libertine is much

78

worse than a young one. . . . You are at a good age . . . not too young, not too old. . . . You have money—not wealthy, but enough to live on decently, not so? So I didn't have anything against it; but . . . look . . . that does not surely mean . . . I have always found you strange, I must admit. . . . Speaking frankly . . . I have never quite known what to think of you, eh? . . . And then you don't have any friends . . . whether that's true or not . . . but . . . you will say, seeing that Anna knew it . . . well, you're right there; only—look . . . it's always better to change your mind than to lose your way. . . . So . . . you see . . . perhaps one day you will come to regret it . . . I don't know anything about it . . . but—well? You are, after all, cold . . . in fact, strikingly cold . . . I'm not the only one who says so . . . I don't often see the two of you together. Anna doesn't complain either; Anna never complains—very reticent—always has been; but your mother-to-be has sharp eyes and it was actually *she* who noticed it . . . at least, she thinks that . . ."

Through all this I had felt a tingle of rising temper spread through all my nerves. I saw what he wanted to say, where he was steering; countless potential objections whirled around in my mind. I knew for sure that I would go much too far as soon as I uttered one word. After the word *cold* I was no longer master of myself at all. The old gentleman—I realized perfectly well—was quite right, but the fact that he reproached me with being what I was annoyed me terribly. Was I not doing my best to transform myself and become a good person in all respects? Ought he not to have recognized that? The reproach I heard in his words intensified my bitterness against normal people more than ever. What made this bitterness foam up into rage was the gathering realization that I was not after all going to become as I wished to be. So in place of refuting him, I burst out into a diatribe against those whom I envied and whose equal I would never, despite all my efforts, be able to call myself.

I think that a thief must have roughly the same feelings toward honest people as I have toward normal people.

What precisely I said has slipped my memory. It came down to the following.

"How do you know I am cold? Can you read my soul? I don't think so. But I don't act like other people, do I. That is really your

79

grievance, or rather your wife's grievance. She seems to be one of those people who know beforehand how a person ought to behave at every stage of his life. Everyone must be the same and act alike. Everyone must be broken in. People who have not a single spark of natural feeling left because for centuries they have been crushed in the straitjacket of social forms demand of each other that they behave as the law prescribes. Oh, I know very well that this law is nowhere written down; but what does that matter when it has been impressed by heredity on every—no, on nearly every brain? If there were still a little nature in us we would enjoy love the moment it welled up in us; but that is branded as immoral! Coldly and formally we must keep our distance from each other. However—once the town hall clerk has issued his license, it is all the other way around. Woe to the man who then does not put on an exhibition of passion! On the other hand, during our engagement we must show some warmth, we must make love-talk, we must kiss, we must hug, mustn't we? Excuse me for saying so, but...I find this way of seeing it disgusting. I loathe every form of coercion under which natural, true, pure feelings are stifled."

Having let loose to approximately this effect, but at greater length and in more detail, with various expressions of hatred directed at society and social man which had nothing at all to do with our topic of discussion, I saw clearly that at best I had given a few truths mixed with sophisms, that I had not answered Bloemendael's question at all. Later on it grew plain to me that I had involuntarily tried to mislead not only my future father-in-law but also myself by putting my undeniable coldness toward Anna on the same level as natural feelings held in bonds by the latest conception of good manners. What was happening inside me was so strange that at that moment I would have been incapable of saying honestly whether I wanted to marry or not. To get back to some extent to my point of departure, perhaps also with unconscious intent to give him an opportunity to break off the engagement, I ended with the words: "I am what I am! If you don't like that, just say so! I don't go in for hypocrisy!"

As if everything I had said had not, from my point of view, been uninterrupted hypocrisy!

80

The result of my outburst was that the old gentleman thought he had deeply wounded and misjudged me. Humbly, stuttering worse than ever, he asked for forgiveness, began to cry, laughed through his tears, and finally assured me with a heartfelt handclasp and a flood of broken phrases that he had nothing in mind but the happiness of his child and his ex-ward, whom he had always thought of as his child too. Certainly I should not make myself out to be what I was not. As long as I meant well by Anna, that was all it came down to.

Had I for once been capable of noble and deep feelings, or even of a good impulse, would I not at that moment have fallen into his arms? However, I felt nothing at all, and even reached the point of feeling inwardly uneasy that I could watch the spectacle so coldly—in fact, frankly speaking, that I could find the old gentleman ridiculous for giving way to his emotions.

I do not know how many generations of forebears had to have lived exclusively for their egotistical pleasure before a being like myself could see the light of day, but I do know that in each and every case they would have done better not to have propagated the species long enough to have a creature eventually spring from it which would recognize its ineradicable misery and thereby pay the price for one and all.

That whole day I was so displeased and discouraged that there could not fail to be a reaction. This came in the evening, when a half hour of music had given me back the belief—no, the illusion of a better self.

While she had asked before dinner about the state of my health, Anna had said nothing about my coldness. Had her parents then kept their observations to themselves? I have never been sure, but I tend now to believe they did, and am convinced that at the time Anna was not bothered about this coldness. But that evening I did not yet realize it. I thought that she was saying nothing in order not to hurt me. This idea mollified me, and during the piano-playing I suddenly gripped her hand and began to stammer through unfeigned tears: "Please don't be angry if I am dull or unpleasant. I can't help it, and it weighs me down more than I can say. Be patient with me, Anna. I would so much, really so very much like to make you happy. Then for at least once

81

in my life I would have done something good, something truly good. Look, if you sometimes find me indifferent, just take me by the hand, look me hard in the eyes, and say, 'Think of me.' That will help. Just try it. Would you like to try it?"

I was sincere, entirely sincere, yet it was perhaps at just this moment that I gave the impression of being a playactor. At least Anna answered with a laugh, "How silly you would find it if I did! I keep noticing that music makes you terribly sentimental. You're a bit dull, I'll admit; but I think all men are like that."

That evening for the first time I found her laugh no longer enchanting.

So our engagement stood, though the unratified union already lacked all luster, all color, all freshness. A change came over my behavior only insofar as I began to give Anna little presents now and again. It was certainly not to satisfy a heart's need—though not stingy I have never known the pleasure of giving—but I understood that this was the proper thing and did my best to appear in a favorable light in Anna's eyes. Whether she appreciated this, whether she even noticed it, I never found out. I believe that during this period, unthinkingly content with fulfilling her little household duties and looking forward to a vaguely attractive future, she neither desired many things nor appreciated them. Only later did she change in both respects, after she had been, as it were, awakened from her somnolence by the disillusionment of our married life and the comparison of herself with other women and of me with another man. For my part I did my fruitless best to understand what Anna thought a man should be, with the intention of then realizing this model as far as possible. Although I had only in rare spells felt the singular enchantment of the soul in which, for me, love had to consist, my abhorrence of the past sustained the desire to be a better person. To put it more precisely: in the expectation of *becoming* better, I wanted to *appear* better.

Unfortunately this did not prevent my moments of fear of the future from becoming more frequent every day. I persevered, but not out of a conviction that grew from any inner impulse. Just as a nocturnal walker uncertain of his way carries on in a straight

82

line because standing still does not help and turning off in a new direction is even more dangerous than keeping going, I found myself pressing on along the road I had chosen though it grew steadily darker.

Finally the day for publishing the banns drew nearer. This formality made an impression on Anna at which I stood staring in astonishment. What solemnity in heaven's name was there in the declaration, made before a bespectacled petty bureaucrat, that we intended to enter upon marriage? If I had been able to discover anything in it, it would have been something shocking. Afterwards we made our wills, and whereas the thought of death turned Anna's cheeks ash-gray, I found it hard not to burst into a fit of laughter at the seriousness with which she, who owned nothing and had little to expect, made over to me whatever she had and whatever she might in the future acquire.

Then there was the question of two practices with which I wanted nothing to do: a reception and a church consecration. Anna and her parents were set on both; *I* was so scared of them that I would perhaps rather have broken off the engagement than do their will on this point. But I did not admit that it was dread of cutting a foolish figure in the (to me) unfamiliar terrain of the church, and fear of the formality of a large gathering of friends and acquaintances, that made me dig in my heels so stubbornly. Again I put forward neat arguments, such as an un-believer's reluctance to be a hypocrite, or the desecration of our happiness by the insincere congratulations of inquisitive people; and so I got my way, though the parents, particularly Mama, found me stranger than ever, and though even Anna plainly found the contrariness of my behavior unpleasant.

We were married in the simplest possible way: now that the church ceremony had been cancelled the Bloemendaels no longer took any pleasure in the event. I certainly had my suspicions that Anna herself would rather have been driven to the church in bridal array than to the town hall in a simple traveling dress, but I did not dare say so openly. It would anyhow have been impossible to satisfy her in this respect and overcome my timidity. The result was that she did not take the ceremony half so seriously as the publication of the banns, for which the official had come by

83

carriage to Bloemendael's home. She did not even think of crying, and when I whispered to her that one of the witnesses had a piece of thread hanging out of his trouser leg, she almost burst out laughing.

Back from the town hall, I saw that the moment had arrived to clasp my wife in my arms and say, "I am inexpressibly happy."

I did not do it; I could not do it! Whether I was gripped by a presentiment of things to come or simply by the somber chill of the autumn day I dare not say for sure. I remember only helping her pack the suitcases in an unheated room and feeling so weighed down, so numbed through and through, so feeble, so deeply unhappy, that despite myself I found myself whispering, "What misery, what misery!" To add to this, I had never found Anna, with her skin mottled a brownish red by the cold, so little seductive as in this first hour of our alliance.

The lunch with the four witnesses—Van Swamelen and an old friend of Bloemendael's for Anna, Van Dregten and a distant cousin of my father's for me—was a veritable martyrdom.

The old people, very much upset, could not keep back their tears. Anna wept too, probably only out of nervousness. It was just as impossible for me to join in with all the crying as to set a jollier tone, and I imagined that the witnesses were scrutinizing me all the time and wondering at my nonchalance. A painfully stretched-out farewell ended the series of formalities. Of Papa's words I remember nothing; of Mama's I have retained, to Anna, "Always submit, child; do your duty without murmuring," and to me, "Don't forget that you now have the happiness of two people in your hands."

Then there ensued a seemingly endless train journey through the dark and cold, and then ... I enjoyed my first wedding night.

I do not know whether there are people who can honestly testify that of all the joys of life termed the highest, the most beautiful, the greatest, such as a first kiss, having a child, attaining a lifetime goal, or a first wedding night, a single one came up to their expectations.

Little has fallen to my share in life, and this little has always been disappointing. Is this the fault of my imagination, still too

84

lively, or of my nervous system, too slack? Perhaps of the latter.

If my first dream in Bloemendael's house, the dream in which I saw Anna near my bed, bend forward, and kiss me, if this dream had only come true, yes, then perhaps I would have enjoyed a bliss so intense that, like an electric lamp over a nocturnal sea, it would have cast its brightness over the whole of my future existence. But ... I have already said it: only in my happy dreams—and how rare these are—have I experienced life as something good and at the same time pleasurable. With Anna I found neither the voluptuousness that had occasionally been given me for a few seconds by a pretty whore, nor the ecstasy for which, sitting beside her at the piano, I had so often hoped. Yet I needed the one as much as the other for my happiness.

Did she notice it?

I suspect she did. In any event, it could not have escaped her that we did not behave like most newlyweds. Between us there was little or no question of the mysterious whispering, of the urge to touch each other or stare into each other's eyes, of being rapt together from the world, and this lack of overpowering mutual interest was not in the least compensated for with the kind of exaggerated interest in the outside world in which, in the case of other young couples, the temporary bubbling over of animal spirits also finds relief. Our behavior was as cool and indifferent as if we had known each other for years and had traveled together all that time.

Much of this can be laid to my account, but not all. In the beginning I certainly sensed that happiness—the mighty happiness exulting through body and spirit, the happiness I had imagined as a foaming music of the soul—that this happiness continued to shun me. But the fact that Anna remained so coldly composed and wordlessly disappointed was only partly due to my incapacity to acquaint her with the glorious intoxication of such happiness. As for myself, I am now certain that while I can feel it at a remove, divine it, behold it from afar, as a cardiac patient feels the stimulating steepness of a high mountain peak, I will never see it from nearby, never grasp it, never enjoy it. But as for Anna, it was largely due to the singular conception of a honeymoon trip she had formed. From my stories she had inferred that being on

85

a trip meant being taken into a wide circle of fun-loving and diverting people. Such a circle was not to be found, at least by me. Perhaps I might have been able to provide Anna with the best approximation to what she wanted in Nice and other such places, if I had only been a little less unsociable and gauche. Insofar as I had dressed my stories up and invented them, I suppose it was all *my* fault; but would a sensitive woman with warm feelings, truly in love, not have formed a different, a more intimate picture of a honeymoon, in spite of these stories?

I hear the objection, "Such a woman would not have taken a Willem Termeer."

Anna did not complain. For years I did not know at all, and only recently have I guessed, how from the child with nothing to say, from the girl with an empty altar in her heart on which she was ready to set as an idol the first man she met, she grew into the woman who scorned to speak her mind and admired and adored only her own perfection.

The clearest indication she gave of her disappointment was when she asked that the scheduled journey be curtailed. I did not venture to ask her for a reason, but agreed to turn back as soon as she wanted. The upshot was that we immediately cut short the visit to churches and museums and asked Anna's parents to put us up for a few days. Back in the parental home Anna showed particular pleasure in seeing again her girlhood room, her piano, her birds, and everything she had occupied herself with in earlier days. She laughed, she clapped her hands and gave everything pet names; I had never yet, and have never since, seen her so nervously excited.

Of course I was puzzled about these tokens of an attachment I had not previously guessed in her, but at the time did not draw any conclusions. I was too preoccupied myself to do so, and anyhow it gave me too much pleasure to see her in high spirits again to go and search out an unpleasant cause.

After we had frittered away a week with her parents, we moved into the house in The Hague that Mama had hired and put in order during our absence.

In this house I killed Anna and in this house I am now sitting and writing.

86

I can barely grasp that the same walls, the same furniture that my eyes beheld when I came in here with Anna still surround me. Everything looks different now, has, above all, a different tinge. It is as if the chairs, the tables, the cupboards, the curtains earlier on spoke, and now must hold their silence... forever hold their silence. It is also as if earlier they kept each other occupied but now only look at *me*—always *me*. They frighten me, these pieces of furniture: there is something ghostly about them; particularly in the evening they frighten me terribly!

Of our first two years of marriage I remember almost nothing. They constitute probably the best period of my life. Not that I felt happy—oh no. What happiness means I do not really know at all. I was quite content with my lot, felt no insatiable desires, was not engrossed in the difference between myself and other people, kept myself busy with the thousand little tasks that belong to the first stages of setting up house. When Anna wanted labels for canisters, jars and bottles, I cut out the pieces of paper, wrote on them, pasted them on. When workmen came to knock in staples, to lay a pipe, to hang pictures, I supervised, made remarks, and give bits of advice.

So the days passed one by one.

Looked at more closely, does contentment perhaps always turn out to be the product of diversion, of an enforced absence of reflection?

Playing the master within narrow precincts behind four walls and not being noticed was something utterly new which disarmed my diffidence, and as long as trivial cares like these filled my days I did not find it difficult to convince myself that for the present I did not have time to get to know more people and to see to a regular occupation in the much-feared public world. These matters would surely take care of themselves later on. First of all I was pleased with my home. Inside there seemed to exist a lighter, warmer atmosphere than outside, and whenever, after a walk through the crowded center of the city, I closed the door behind me in the quiet of Bosch Street, I felt myself revive like a hunted criminal who, having fled to a hiding place, hears his pursuers rush past.

From these very feelings I should undoubtedly have been able to infer with near certainty that nothing would ever come of my transformation into a normal person, a being at home in society, capable of associating with his fellowmen without timorousness and suspicion. But I did not at all realize this at the time, imagining that any difficulties could be overcome with the aid of my brother-in-law, overcome gradually... later... much later.

And Anna too seemed to be content. At least she was so busy all day that in the evening she usually felt too tired to play the piano. Being busy like this kept her in a good humor. Although we lacked the poetry with which other young households seem to be permeated, we had not yet had any unpleasantness. For the most part we talked about our trivial little affairs, and as long as I could comfortably give Anna her way, since fitting out and running a household did not in the least interest me, I lived in the illusion that I had really set aside all my own wishes and desires and was devoting myself exclusively to *her* happiness.

Meanwhile, but for Suze and an aging friend of Anna's mother, no friends or acquaintances crossed our threshold. Begging letters and circulars constituted, together with tax assessments, our only link with society.

The Van Swamelens had invited us over on several occasions, sometimes to a big formal dinner, sometimes to a so-called informal party with at least six strangers. We had made a few return invitations, always to them alone, because no one called on us. These visits neither increased our intimacy nor did they initiate us into a circle. I have never dared to appear on my brother-in-law's doorstep without being invited or else having an answer ready to his stock question, "What can I do for you?" As for the friends of his we had met, we greeted each other in the street, but there it stopped.

In the beginning I did once or twice turn up at his club between four and six. Here Van Swamelen daily gathered a dozen friends about himself. But I always lacked the courage to take a place at his table of my own accord, and I never detected an overture from the other side. After taking a turn around the billiard table or hiding my embarrassment behind the illustrated weeklies, I had

88

each time to leave with nothing accomplished, a swelling rancor in my heart against all those indifferent, arrogant, public people.

So I rather stayed at home, gathered the news from my paper, and sought compensation in taking walks and going to the theater. I foresaw that Anna would eventually complain about this uncommon isolation, but what in heaven's name could I do about it?

True, Van Swamelen had offered me jobs through which I would have come in contact with a variety of people, and I...I had declined them. But could he not have done more than simply say, "There is going to be an opening in A or B; if it appeals to you, I advise you to go and speak to X or Y"? He could surely see that left to myself I would never take such a step! That he did not want a familiar relationship was clear enough; but if he already knew me well enough to consider me too unworthy for that, must I not assume that it was also clear to him that I sincerely wished to change and to like society, or at least learn to view it with interest? And if he knew of this sincere wish, why had he, who to me represented society, always kept me at a distance, not once stretching out a hand to make the leap easier from my lonely little island to his densely populated coast? Is it conceivable that he gave any credence to the pretexts under which I refused his jobs? Was it not clear as daylight that, in shrinking back from formalities unfamiliar to me and from being forced to meet men in their official capacity, I was struggling with the oppressive feeling of never being able to get anywhere? How easily a little help pressed upon me in a friendly way would have put an end to the feeling!

However...we remained isolated in the heart of The Hague. And slowly, very slowly, an embittering boredom slunk into our house.

One day when there was again no break in the cold, wet mist which, dirty and gray, had suffocated the city for twenty-four hours, obliterating all color, smothering all sound, so that I no longer saw anything but wraithlike trees in front of the house yet endlessly far away, no longer heard anything but the dripping of rain in the street and the drone of the maids' voices in the kitchen—on such a day I saw that what I had feared had come about: stagnating in the gray vapors of a dark house with thick carpets and

89

heavy curtains. And it was as if all this grayness issued from my own interior, wrapped me in a cloud, and separated me from mankind, just as the veil thickening over cataracted eyes looks to the sufferer like a mist behind which the world is vanishing.

Rising aimlessly in the morning again became a martyrdom. The long mornings I would spend stretched out on a sofa staring at a book from which, as before, my attention wandered to unattainable dream visions. I would take a walk, and a gleam of longing for something different, something more lively, a longing to run away, to escape from my surroundings, would briefly evoke again impossible fantasies full of tender love or of brutal sadism. Then the stillness of the evening would blur all this back into a gray drowsiness, and exhausted with doing nothing, I would retire to bed before night had even fallen.

No matter how calm, how healthy, how moral my life now was, I again began to loathe myself.

As I said, on odd occasions we went to the theater. Here it was that the extinguished urge to write flickered up in me again. We saw among other pieces Marcellus Emants's *Artist*, a play which Anna found revolting but which made a deep impression on me because of the many features of resemblance between the artist and myself. I too had suffered from an artistic impressionability not directed and made fruitful by a capacity for solid work; but how much happier was someone like Gérard, who could at least write something beautiful, at least meet with love, at least experience passion! Undoubtedly he stood higher than me; yet I still asked myself whether it was not a fault in the play that he was not depicted as a hypocrite. Are people like us not compelled to play a role, since we cannot possibly find the courage to reveal our true self once we have learned how far this self deviates from the normal human essence? I believe this is so, and because I believe so I also believe that among those who condemn us the most harshly there are more degenerates than the superficial observer of humankind might realize.

Seeing this play again made me want to record my own history. But in the sober light of the next morning clouds of apathy welled up in me higher than yesterday's tiny glimmer of energy.

I noticed that Anna too was beginning to find the days long,

90

no longer occupied with seeing to our modest household. Her activity in setting up our home had for a while misled me—perhaps her as well—into believing that she was reconciled to her fate. Now doubt loomed up in me again like the thought of illness in someone who has dreamed he is well.

That she had formulated no high ideal of married life had grown clear to me in the course of time. But what does the quality of our ideals matter? It is after all simply a question of whether we are more or less satisfied. What Anna had desired was a perfectly ordinary course of events, namely, a *good time* on honeymoon, followed by the *novelty* of playing the married woman, both inside and outside the home, and then finally the *cares* of being a mother. She had not even entertained particularly highly colored expectations, yet despite all she found herself disappointed! Poor creature!

She had already faintly felt this on our honeymoon, and she felt it more sharply when she compared our life with that of Van Swamelen and Suze. Suze had many friends and acquaintances, went to dinners and parties, had so to speak a firm place in society. We knew no one, lived in isolation, like people who have something to be ashamed of in their birth or their conduct.

A long time passed before Anna allowed a trace of her daily mounting dissatisfaction to appear in her words. In the meantime the expression on her face slowly changed. The soundless laugh seldom creased her lips any more, her eyes acquired a staring, almost burning quality—it was as if their blue became steely gray—and between her eyebrows a deep vertical groove, caused by their repeated contraction, established itself. It was clear that a peevishness was stirring through her which she was not yet fully prepared to admit to herself.

Finally, at table she brought up the subject. We had been sitting across from each other for at least a quarter of an hour that afternoon without uttering a word. What news could we after all have had to tell each other!

Suddenly she began: "Have you again been to see no one? We live in The Hague, but for all that we might as well still be in the province."

I said nothing, understanding what was weighing on her yet at the same time feeling powerless to change her life. The bitterness

91

that settled in my soul like dregs from the thought that "this existence is all I can give you"—this bitterness seethed up, not only against myself, but against Van Swamelen, against her parents, against all members of society, against her. I had wanted to do something good, something beautiful; I had done something ugly, something bad, and I felt that not only I but the whole world was to blame for it. Could I not even once achieve what I had undertaken? As before, I felt everything and everyone conspiring against me: the old hatred which I had each time imagined smothered, annihilated, was still haunting my heart unabated.

Testily she continued: "And to think that you don't have one friend, that you haven't been able to make a single new contact! I can't understand it! Must we go on sitting opposite each other like this until we are eighty?"

I grew angry. "And do you have a single woman friend here? Is it my fault that your sister's friends don't visit us? I don't want to see people, and even if I did, I can't pull people here on strings!"

"No, that's true. Apparently you can only repel people! Are you really a man of barely thirty? You act as if you are in your sixties!"

I have never been able to forgive Anna this outburst.

Today I admit that all my spurts of interest in doing something or other or at least showing myself in a better light were the stillborn children of an impotent spirit; but at the time I still imagined that at any moment there could be a change for the better as long as everything, including Anna, would assist me instead of opposing me. "Who will lift me up, who will give me confidence?" was the instinctive supplication of my soul, and then Anna trod me down and ridiculed me into the bargain.

She came back to the same subject several times more, and each time reproached me more sharply with the laziness and gaucherie that prevented me from getting to be anything. "Then how do other people do it?" was the question with which she beat down all my objections. I answered less and less, more and more convinced that it lay beyond my powers to modify my attitude toward mankind. When she reached the point of claiming that it was all the fault of my conceit, I felt a burst of joy that this gross injustice gave me the right thenceforth to hold my silence.

The first time I brought this stratagem into play she gazed at me fixedly for a while with wordless astonishment in her eyes. Then a contemptuous little laugh passed over her lips, the wings of her nose trembled, her shoulders jerked slightly and...never again did she broach the subject to me. In one respect old Bloemendael seemed to have known his daughter well: she was truly amazingly reticent. It was perhaps on account of this reticence that then only for the first time did I ask myself, "What kind of person is she actually?" Though married for two years now, I did not know her. Quite often before my marriage I had asked myself, "What kind of person am I? Can I make her happy?" It had never occurred to me to find out about *her*, whether she could make *me* happy.

To the extent that I, as an exception, am in a position to judge a specimen of the rule, I believe that Anna was in the fullest sense of the phrase a person of principles. It was as if instead of milk her mother had fed the child precepts for what a woman of the right sort should and should not do. In Anna's case these precepts were so faithfully absorbed into the blood that she never hesitated with regard to her "duty." I envied this certainty. Yet at the same time I found her narrow-minded. Many mountains of difficulties had been leveled for her by her upbringing, but it had also made her surprisingly inflexible. As long as she did not deviate from this stamped and approved "duty," she felt that she stood on a high pedestal of excellence, and condemned people of a different mold with a mixture of one-sided injustice and haughty pride. She looked down from a great height upon those who, while strict and demanding in their dealings with others, were soft and indulgent toward their own faults. But the other side of the exacting demands she made on herself was the strict demand she made on her fellowmen to recognize her merits and esteem them. She wanted to be found spotless, even if she had to sacrifice the satisfaction of ardent wishes to this ideal; but she also wanted to draw from her spotlessness the right to look down arrogantly on those who did not admire her.

And *my* admiration—which had never been very ardent—grew even fainter the more pitiless she seemed toward my weaknesses, the more blind to my spark of goodness. Duty was her idol, its fulfillment her life; but as for what her duty consisted in, that no one was allowed to decide but she herself. Whether fulfilling her duty thereby degenerated into the worship of an image of her own excellence was a question which never occurred to her.

Between self-esteem like hers and self-disparagement like mine it was obviously impossible for that mutual confidence which should be the natural issue of true love to come into being. She did her duty to me; I did my best for her; she did not deign to complain. I did not presume to ask questions; and so we went on existing side by side without our inner lives touching at any point.

Would she have been able to evolve differently with another man? I am inclined to admit this; I would almost say that she later gave me proof of it; but our relationship could certainly have been a better one if Anna had not let me know so clearly and so often that I was incapable of representing anything good or pleasant in her life.

Perhaps—I go so far as to think—everything would have been quite different if her physical beauty had aroused my sensuality a little more. The contrary surely did not escape her, and who knows what she made of it. In any case, we were married as if we were two people who, in pursuit of marriage for different reasons, met on a long, lonely road. With a slightly wider choice both of us would have mated in a wholly different way.

Anna was going to have a child.

It is said, according to books—and I believe it—that there are men who greet such tidings with a shout of joy. It seems to make them love their wife all the more. For such couples the child becomes a new, strong tie. I find myself envious of such people, but as for understanding them, or rather feeling as they feel—that I cannot do.

The news widened the slowly yawning rift between Anna and me.

She must have sensed this in advance. It was not sitting in my lap with an arm around my neck, nor with downcast eyes and a voice trembling with emotion, nor with a blush that she whispered the tidings in my ear. Oh no: she said it in passing, in an artificially casual tone, as if embarrassed about the subject and prepared for

94

an outburst of anger. I fancied she thought, "You will never be fond of the child, and the time will come when I will be ashamed of it."

Later, when the doctor said, "The little thing is very weak," I did not dare look at her.

The night after she had told me she was positive, I found my bed moved to another room. The first thing to strike me about this act was that it was done without a word of consultation. Had she then no respect left for me at all?

Of course, as usual, I did not dare say anything or ask anything. Perhaps—I still flattered myself—she had only done what is customary in these circumstances. Perhaps I lack the antennae to sense what is appropriate in such a case.

She was succesfully delivered of a daughter. The little thing lived more than eighteen months. During these eighteen months Anna was so anxiously happy that the most obtuse of men would have understood that she had found compensation for a great disappointment.

I never felt one moment of love for the child. I never felt an urge to so much as take it up in my arms. Many will call it a shame, and I understand that it is their duty to talk like that; but whose shame is it? The shame of my egotism, which compelled me to do without something in which others find their greatest happiness? Rabbits are especially unfeeling animals. Is that their fault and therefore also a shame?

However strange it may seem, I felt more affection for my cat than for my daughter. At least I took all kinds of trouble over the cat and was at the selfish animal's beck and call. On the other hand, I was also more indifferent to that beast than to the child. The child scared me, and had it stayed alive I would have felt my fatherhood as an oppressive responsibility. Every little fault in its system, in its character, in its very appearance, I would surely have reckoned up against myself, and who knows whether I would not have concluded by hating it just as I hated Anna! It was also as if the little creature suddenly turned me into an old man. I searched anxiously in the mirror for gray hairs at my temples, for wrinkles under my eyes, and self-reproach for having reached my thirties without having lived quivered up again from the depths of my soul with the ominous gnawing of an incurable illness, like a cloud of smoke from the abysmal crater of a volcano. This did not, however, prevent the old, sadly delicious yearning for self-sacrifice from welling up again on those many evenings when I heard Anna, more cheerful, more healthy, more lively than before, making her plans for the future. It gave me a painfully pleasurable feeling to be able to think, "This happiness of yours is after all due to me."

In the mornings too, when I saw her kissing, hugging, chucking the infant, fondling it in countless ways, I was always more or less jealous of all those soft, tender, truly womanly touches. Anna was never sensually affectionate, as a wife should have been to me. Yet in the early days of our engagement she had once or twice unexpectedly kissed me or stroked my forehead with her hand. Now I recalled how these endearments had grown scarcer and eventually ceased altogether. In the morning and at night she still presented me with her cheek; but that was all.

The child caught a chill, ran a fever, and in a trice the poor little flame of its life was puffed out. Anna was bewildered with pain. She could not cry, could not sleep, and for the first time had recourse to chloral. For days on end she sat staring blankly in front of her and I—I had trouble hiding my singular feelings of joy.

I have tried to analyze these feelings. How complex they were! Relief about having escaped the responsibility, deliverance from having to go on playing the hypocrite, the illusion of rejuvenation, avenged jealousy, yes, even compassion for the baby which I thought destined for much suffering—all these played a part.

Until the funeral I did not speak to Anna. It was anyhow unnecessary; she had her mother with her. The old woman must have found me a strange person, perhaps a bad one too by now; I felt that I would not find it easy to dissemble as long as the child, our child, was in the house. And what could I say that was not dissembling?

Coming back from the cemetery I wanted to give Anna a kiss on the forehead, but with a hurried motion of the hand she warded me off.

"What have I done wrong to you?"

"To me? Nothing!"

"Is it by any chance *my* fault that..."

"I'm not saying that; but you are glad about it. It seems to me that is bad enough."

So she had noticed it after all. In her eyes there was contempt again, the contempt to which perhaps everyone was entitled except...she! Yet once again there was nothing I could respond with: what she had said was true.

This last fact—which would constrain me never to speak about the child again—fed the rancor in my soul so furiously that hatred could not but burst out. From damp compressed hay a flame always shoots up sooner or later, sending up itself and everything around it in smoke and ashes.

My bed was not brought back to the main bedroom. On the other hand, when I finally visited Anna there one night, she did not ward me off. Oh, she knew her duty, and no one should have the right to accuse her of falling short in her devotion to it! That she performed this duty as coldly as a woman who accepts money was a matter about which I was not of course entitled to complain.

Behold then what delight was mine from the only chaste, sanctified, legitimized, decent love, love in marriage, that soul of civilized life!

Was it to be marveled at that, in the abstinence and the barrenness to which Anna condemned me, a blaze built up in my nerves that sought an outlet? From my erotic dreams a mawkishly melancholic mood often lingered with me for days, and on my walks I looked out for lovely eyes I would have liked to stare into, mouths I would have liked to kiss, shoulders I would have liked to snuggle my brow against. The old Adam who, exhausted and overfed with bad food, had only been slumbering awhile, awoke again. Bouts of sentimental lovesickness that brought me almost to the point of hearing the voice I yearned for, the voice that called my name alone, though with deep melancholy, alternated anew with fits of plain filthiness, when I saw naked women before me so clearly that my hands sometimes grabbed at them. At the same time I could not shake off that feeling of getting older. The

97

race of the hours sometimes made me so nervous with fear that I stopped the clocks so as not to hear the incessant ticktock of fleeting time. It was often as if minute by minute I felt my hair graying, my eyes growing weaker, the wrinkles on my face deepening, the strength of my muscles drying up! Oh, those days that shot past, days that I could have enjoyed but that disappeared empty into the abyss of the past! I *had* wanted to clutch them. Many times I started up from my sleep in the middle of the night, wakened by that cry in my innermost that could not be silenced: "Take your pleasure, take it soon, just a few more years and it is all over...over...over...forever over!"

Then I thought about what I would do if Anna died and set me free again, free as before. She impeded me now, as a physical defect or lack of money or having committed a folly impedes a person. The situation in itself can be borne, but if this impediment only did not exist, how much better it could all be. Yet it was precisely during this period that all of a sudden I would happen to desire Anna more powerfully than had even been the case before. I remember particularly a beautiful autumn morning, the light golden, the air calm, fresh, yet still warm. Not for a long time had I felt so firm on my legs, so strong and supple in my muscles, so pleasantly aglow.

Wandering about the dunes, I began to ask myself anew why other men can find in one woman, their wife, a wife often of little charm, whatever they desire, while I had not only found no satisfaction, but had aroused such aversion that I was begrudged what was after all without question mine. Thinking back to the days of our engagement, I felt all of a sudden the first and rare pleasant sensations from this period come to life again: the touch of velvety girl's fingers entwined with mine, looking into a young face that smiled at me, thinking, "This woman has never belonged to another man and never will." Why, at moments like these when I came to life within myself, had I not thrown my arms around her neck, clasped her to my breast, whispered to her, "Give yourself to me, now, at once, here, in the middle of living nature!" Was my shyness and fumbling not the cause of everything? Could *she* give me pleasure before *I* taught her what it meant to have pleasure?

98

All this time, I felt, she had not yet wholly been my wife. I was sure she would have to become wholly my wife when, unexpectedly, in an attack of powerful desire, I possessed her. By keeping me off she had become forbidden fruit to me, but forbidden fruit which no feelings of diffidence prevented me from plucking. The urge came over me to overcome her resistance by force, to virtually rape her at an impossible time and in an impossible place.

There was something in this that excited me; but alas—back at home my desire at once faded. It was as if the rooms—the rooms in which *she* reigned—radiated a chilly primness which turned all sensual desire into an obscenity, and I had only to behold Anna herself, with her downturned mouth, her stuck-up nose, her marbled skin, and her pale cold eyes always looking past me, to again feel hurt by her pride, embittered by her thanklessness, repelled by her color, and turned to stone by her stony face.

She never made any further mention of possible changes in our life. Nevertheless I saw that her suppressed annoyance was not only at my lack of friends and acquaintances, my isolation in society. She despised me in *all* respects; she despised me so deeply that she even thought it beneath herself to let her contempt be seen. In quiet resignation she awaited the moment when some remedy or other, preferably the most conclusive, would free her of my presence. Then she would have done her duty and played a fine role to the very end, while I would never have understood anything about her, never given her what is due to a woman. "And,"—she would add—"I never complained, because only a fool speaks when he is sure he will not be understood." And besides, had I not taught her myself that keeping quiet is the most sensible thing when one has anyhow to resign oneself to the inevitable?

Meanwhile Anna had had a visit from the Reverend De Kantere.

For a short while now this ex-clergyman had been our neighbor. With him, as with the other neighbors, we had exchanged visiting cards. There, at first, it had stopped on both sides.

I remember it as if it had happened yesterday. Coming downstairs to take my daily walk, I heard coming from the hallway a man's voice that made me stop on the stairs. The maid went inside, came back, and showed someone into the back room. Descending the stairs cautiously, I heard how this person had himself announced.

Any other man would now surely have gone in too. *I* quickly slipped out the front door, and a few hours later told Anna that I had already been out when De Kantere came. She believed me and said that the minister had come to condole with us on the death of the child.

Whether from her tone or from her eyes I no longer know, but I was immediately sure that De Kantere had made an impression on Anna, and I could not take it calmly that she should speak so very highly of his great friendliness, his pleasant voice, his sincere concern.

"In fact a minister through and through!" I burst out.

At once she caught fire.

"I suppose you mean something spiteful, but I don't see what. First of all he is not a minister any more, and second it is no disgrace to have been at least *something*!"

I pretended that the allusion escaped me.

"I mean that the fellow probably makes himself up as carefully inside as he does outside. Haven't you noticed that he shaves all around his mouth and leaves only a stiff little fringe? Why must a minister look different from a common mortal, after all? It is simply affectation, playacting!"

"I find it worse than childish to blame a person for conforming to a general custom. If it were a matter of something important ...but the shape of a beard—something so utterly insignificant! *I* would prefer to see people follow the general example in small, everyday matters and stand out in great ones, rather than... the reverse."

This conversation too I remember as if we had had it only yesterday. It would have held little of interest to someone not directly concerned; *my* ears heard in Anna's voice as much glorification of the other man as humiliation of myself.

The outcome was that I declared I would not return the visit. To no one did I give the right to force his company on me, as De Kantere seemed to want to do. To my surprise Anna let the matter rest here, though she called my attitude rude. "I've known for a long time," she said with her most self-satisfied laugh, "that you aren't ever going to change."

About a month later De Kantere's little daughter threw a hoop she was playing with over the wall. De Kantere himself came to fetch it, and seeing the garden door open he entered without ringing.

Anna, who from a back window had happened to see the hoop glide over and had gone out to throw it back, was looking for it under some rhododendrons when suddenly the minister was standing beside her.

I heard this story only at lunch. Though Anna knew I was upstairs lying on my sofa playing with the cat, she had not had me called. When I remarked about this, her answer was, "After all, you don't want to see the man."

The next morning De Kantere came back, now with his daughter, therefore presumably invited to bring her by Anna, and when lunchtime came she told me she had met her. The little girl was twelve and was a sweet, pretty darling. Her mother had died of tuberculosis, and since De Kantere himself had coughed up blood in his youth, there were only too many reasons for him to fear for the preservation of his Sofie. So he was thinking of spending a few years in the bracing air of Davos. Naturally Anna had dwelt at length on her own deceased darling, and the upshot had been that De Kantere had gratefully accepted her offer to be something of a mother to his daughter.

"All the love of a father"—he had said—"can never wholly take the place of a wife's care."

In these circumstances any other man would probably by now have eagerly sought De Kantere's acquaintance. This became daily more impossible to me. I became more obstinate toward Anna and more diffident toward De Kantere as I grew more certain—in her case—and more suspicious—in his—that these attitudes had been noticed. From my room I saw the minister saunter around my garden with Anna and little Sofie almost every day for hours on end. I studied his affected gestures, caught echoes of his rich voice, yet not once did we exchange even a wordless greeting when by chance we met in the street.

In the end the silliness of this attitude began to disturb me, and over tea one evening, after the two of us had again brushed past each other in the city, I brought up the subject. Not one angry word escaped me this time. I simply said, "Mr. De Kantere seems to believe that I am a lodger in this house."

But at once Anna flared up, snapping: "If you like I will tell him tomorrow that Sofie may no longer enter the house because everything here is yours and nothing mine! The poor child has no mother any more and likes to play with me in the garden; but if that is cause for you to treat her father impolitely then the two of us can just as well go and walk in the woods."

I did not say another word; yet it struck me that she had once more replied by referring to Sofie when I had spoken to her about De Kantere.

What she thought about *him* she never told me. If she mentioned his name, then it was exclusively in connection with his great fatherly love, for which she often expressed her admiration, not without offensive intent toward me. So I had actually not one sound reason to pass unfavorable judgment on him, and yet I did so as often as was in any way possible.

There was undoubtedly jealousy beneath this churlishness. I envied him his strong build, his regular features crowned with his heavy black head of hair, and not least the clerical polish of his appearance and manners, which I felt probably bewitched women and could perform the function of a social grace for him. I also remember that one day, on a walk, I so to speak found these words on my lips: "The woman who has secrets from her husband invariably sets someone else, even if it is herself, higher than him." On the other hand, I had to admit that in the recesses of my soul there lurked the wish that this cool, dutiful woman for once make a false step, seduced by this of all men. So I was certain that she was mistaken in him, and this certainty could have no foundation but my groundless conviction that De Kantere was really a hypocrite. Whether he was a petit bourgeois afraid of betraying his extraction, or whether as a minister he knew that his conduct was at odds with his tenets, I was not yet in a

102

position to say; but it seemed to me impossible that his downcast, furtive eyes and his affected tone of voice could belong to a person who simply presented himself to the world as he was. And hypocrites are the more unendurable to me as I see that they play their role better than I do. In only two cases can I bear people who are like me: when they are inferior to me, and when they know themselves as well as I know myself and therefore think as little of themselves as I do of myself. As far as De Kantere was concerned, I suspected that he not only fancied that he was my superior in all respects, but was also blind enough to see his own playacting as nature ennobled. And since Anna did not see through him as I did, in consequence looking more and more down on me as she looked more and more up to him, this worship of hers irritated me just as strongly as I longed for the moment when she would be revealed as deceived and I as clear-sighted. With what joy would I take my chance to look down in disdain for a change and think myself justified in acts which I already felt I would go through with anyhow!

Yet on the other hand I felt like simply ordering Anna not to receive this man any more.

Unexpectedly one morning De Kantere was announced. The maid had said I was at home; it was so sudden that I could not find reasons for excusing myself; there was little else to do but receive him.

As usual, the unexpected flustered me completely. The feeling of not yet being properly dressed made me doubly embarrassed, and the dullness of my brain, which on warm, rainy days in particular felt to me like a mist in which my thoughts grew pale, oppressed me, as I imagine premonitions of madness oppress someone descending into insanity. The questions, "What does this man want?" "Did Anna put him up to it?" "Is he only coming for her sake?" "What does he know about me?" "How should I behave?" whirled about quite bewilderingly in my head; but not a single answer materialized, and De Kantere was already standing in the room before the role I wanted to play floated into clarity before my mind's eye.

He was as usual all in black, the long shiny coat carefully buttoned, a gleaming top hat in the dark-gloved left hand. There was no trace of diffidence to be discovered in him. It seemed to me that the smile on his ivory-pale cheeks and the gaze from his jet-black eyes, which, despite his height, seemed always to dart upwards from the depths, were as studiedly friendly as the sound of his deep voice was studiedly sonorous, the sweep of his pale hands studiedly beautiful, the stringing together of his words studiedly graceful. What a pitiful figure my awkwardness of speech and gesture must have made in contrast!

He began by excusing himself for his impoliteness. A combination of circumstances had led him to make the acquaintance of Mrs. Termeer; he would long ago have called upon me had he not been prevented, morning after morning, he being aware that I spent the afternoons in long walks and in the evenings often went to a concert or play.

I gave a little laugh, thinking myself as silly as his politeness was exaggerated, but responded with nothing in particular. I have always disliked the clergy. In these expositors of the unknowable, these official envoys of the truth and distributors of consolation, I have never been able to see anything but power-hungry fools or like-minded swindlers. This view could undoubtedly have given me a sense of superiority, but such was not the case. Was this the result of my involuntary deference to the hold they had exercised over the mass of men, or was it a disguise for the same unpleasant suspicion of being seen through which left me so childishly weak when faced by a doctor?

I remember offering De Kantere a cigar and blushing when he said that he never smoked. "Of course you haven't a single failing," said a voice inside me, and instinctively I cast my eyes down, afraid that he would read the thought in them.

This first time we discussed only subjects of little importance. De Kantere expatiated on the sunny situation of our houses, on Anna's exceptional friendliness toward his child, on Sofie's sudden fondness for Mrs. Termeer. I answered no more than was strictly necessary. What lingered in my memory from this visit was that while most people express their introductory remarks with a smile, perhaps even a broad smile, De Kantere remained entirely serious. Even later on I do not remember ever seeing him laugh.

Two days later he came again, though I had not in the mean-

104

time returned his visit. This time our discussion took quite a different turn. As soon as I asked in passing after his daughter, he began to speak on the subject of children, and it was not long before he was saying: "Ah, yes, to deal with a child one must like children, and to like children one must have children oneself, or... have had them."

It was obvious that these words referred to my circumstances, but they had a quite different effect from the one De Kantere must have expected. They gave me the impression that I was being drawn out. I felt something shut inside me, as if my soul were closing itself up so as not to be seen, and was incapable of saying one word in reply.

Gesturing meaningfully, he continued. "Of course you know that as well as I do....I have inwardly shared in your loss, Mr. Termeer....But for the grace of God there go I, not so? I don't mean to say that my own little daughter is not healthy; but so delicate, so delicate....If I were to lose that child..."

There followed a long, painful silence. De Kantere looked out at the window while his ever-roaming eyes began to glisten damply. I still said nothing, not knowing what to say. Eventually his eyes returned to me and he went on: "You may still hope for a little substitute. I...would lose all, and forever."

For a while he now discussed parental love, which according to him was the most beautiful and unselfish disposition of the human heart. I agreed, not wanting an argument; but it was on the tip of my tongue to say: "Why? A person already loves his children before they are born. So there is no question of his appreciating them individually. He begets them and keeps them to satisfy an instinct. He does not hesitate to bring children into the world even if he can be more or less sure they will be degenerate or predisposed to miserable sicknesses or destined to suffer lifelong poverty. What is beautiful and unselfish in that?"

Had De Kantere read the objection in my eyes? Without transition he suddenly said, "Yes, only love can sanctify our deeds. Still, I once asked myself: people who are afflicted with some so-called hereditary ailment—can love be an adequate justification for them to marry?"

With my usual suspiciousness I could not accept that what

105

De Kantere had said referred only to his own past. I imagined again that he wanted to sound me out, and found his words, seen in this light, so remarkably callous that, like something hot forcing its way up my throat, I felt the urge tingling in me to hurl my peculiarities at the fellow with equal callousness. And I wanted to add: "Looking at me from a distance you have decided that I do not amount to much. You have heard from Anna that I am nothing exceptional. You have come here out of inquisitiveness. Well, now you know all there is to know of me! Behold the handiwork of the God whom you worship, the God whose justice visits the guilt of the parents not on them but on their children, who are guilty of nothing!"

But I did not find my tongue quickly enough, and so began simply by replying, "I think not."

This answer surprised him very much: he was visibly disconcerted, and with two deep furrows in the middle of his forehead drawing his eyebrows together, he cast repeated glances toward me. However, the furrows disappeared, a strange fanatical glow began to shine from his dark pupils, and shaking his head softly he spoke.

"I just cannot accept it. If we were entirely sure of the theory of heredity—yes. But we are even less sure of this theory than of others. Do you not think that for the present we should do better to follow the mighty voice of the heart rather than the weak utterance of a disputed and most disputable doctrine?"

I began to suspect I had mistaken his meaning, but did not immediately grasp that he had been referring to himself. The ceremoniously clerical tone of his last words aroused me to a rebelliousness which was reinforced by the feelings of brutal callousness that had been brought to the surface but no longer had any cause to burst out as I had initially planned. With a sarcastic laugh I struck out at him: "Your heart . . . yes, perhaps; but what we take to be the voice of our heart is usually something quite different."

"You mean calculation."

"Sometimes calculation, sometimes also impulses of all kinds having little to do with the heart."

It was some while before De Kantere continued. He glanced at

106

me repeatedly, sometimes with a most suspicious look in his eye. Under this inspection my embarrassment returned; yet the urge to sling my cynical view of life in the face of this apparently excellent man persisted. I was prepared to believe that he would prove to be my superior in debate. Nevertheless, I wanted to shove this under his nose: "Look, not only do there exist people as insignificant, as perverse, as barren, as wicked as myself, but the fact that these people are so miserable is as little their fault as your so-called goodness is your reward. And while you are distilling beautiful theories out of all the beauties of your soul, out of all the hideousness of their souls there waft up hideous theories. Yet as people they are just as good as you; in their words too there is truth, just as much and just as little as in yours."

After a long pause De Kantere said, "You seem to be a cerebral."

"What do you mean, a cerebral?"

"Well...a man of intellect rather than a man of feeling."

"Oh yes—if you put the question like that, I am a cerebral. Feeling is a blind guide; I believe more in a guide with sight. Otherwise I do not think that the word cerebral means a great deal; for the brain is after all as much the seat of the feelings as of the intelligence."

De Kantere showed none of the irritation I had expected. "I see, Mr. Termeer, that you have read and thought about the difficult problems of our spiritual life. But...may I speak frankly—or rather ask something? Will you permit me? We have known each other only briefly, and I should be most sorry if as a result of careless-ness on my part..."

As he did not complete the phrase, I shook my head, smiling faintly, but at the same time felt my courage ebb away like foam from a glass of sparkling drink. What frightful thing was this man going to say?

"Haven't you argued somewhat too exclusively with yourself?"

The question relieved me, and went so far as to revitalize my urge to pursue the theme. I guessed that my answer would reach Anna's ears, and, at the same time, that she could not yet have disparaged me very badly to him.

"Perhaps," I said, "but what difference does that make? After all, what one thinks the truth, is wholly true for oneself only."

At this juncture De Kantere surprised me with measured words uttered in a tone of fatherly authority: "You are not happy, Mr. Termeer."

I considered taking offense at these words, but dared not. I was at a loss for a fitting reply, and the minister continued.

"Von Feuchtersleben says in his *Spiritual Hygiene*: 'When man reflects on his physical and moral condition, then he feels that he is sick through and through. He is suffering from life.' That is true, if instead you say: *reflects too much*."

The opportunity to announce without a long preamble one of my favorite and to a minister's ears (it seemed to me) most unpleasant propositions was too inviting to pass. So my reply followed hastily, as if I were afraid that something might prevent me from getting it out.

"Only a fool can be happy. For happiness consists of two contradictory elements: contentment and pleasure. Enjoy pleasure and you have no contentment; be content and you have no pleasure. For this reason happiness is conceivable only for those who enjoy themselves without thinking that they will always want more and thus be discontented, or for those who are content without thinking that they have no pleasure. Whoever reflects can never be happy, unless..."

I arrested myself, for I did not dare utter what was all of a sudden on the tip of my tongue.

"Unless..." repeated De Kantere; and growing all at once more reckless again, taking malevolent pleasure in wounding this plainly not unhappy man, I stuttered out, "Unless he is a fanatic and thus blinded...thus exercising control over his intelligence with his feelings, instead of the other way round."

De Kantere remained perfectly calm. "Then I would have to class myself among the fanatics; for, however much I have lost, I can and may not call myself unhappy. Yet I do not believe I am one. Certainly I am an idealist, but that is not the same thing. You call pleasure and contentment contradictory elements; but why? If by pleasure you mean simply misguided pleasure, pleasure at the cost of other people, or to your own detriment—yes; but, after all, there is another kind of pleasure too, isn't there?"

I was silent. Having come so far, I had either to lay bare my

108

innermost soul or hold my peace. Like someone who, stubbornly standing by an assertion without being prepared to name his source, prefers in the end to confess to sly eavesdropping rather than have it said, "That is only talk," or, "You lie," so I felt tempted to confess to the spiritual life on which my opinion depended. But it was again as if, in my heart, I had to clear away a mighty boulder to open a passage for the rush of words.

Meanwhile De Kantere resumed. "I define happiness as follows: happiness is the fulfilling of our desires. Note well that I say the fulfilling and not the fulfillment. Happiness is a state of activity, not of rest. Perhaps you know the just observation that if you were to offer the hunter the hare he has spent all day pursuing, he would surely refuse your offer. By the word *desires* I understand spiritual desires as well as physical desires, the wishes of the heart as well as the demands of the stomach. Now it is beyond question that a human being is acquainted with a greater number of desires than an animal, and that a highly developed person has more of them than one who is rough and unfeeling. (You will perhaps say not more, but more difficult to satisfy; for my part, I view the refined desire as a complex of many simple ones.) So the higher we stand, the more happiness we *can* participate in, and we *shall* also participate in this happiness as long as we know how to adapt ourselves to the circumstances on which the fulfilling of our desires depends."

I was already in a position to find fault. "And if we don't know how to do so?"

De Kantere again had a quotation handy. "Von Feuchtersleben says, 'Create conditions in which you have to.'"

"And what do you do with those desires whose fulfillment makes you resentful and sad rather than happy? There are even some that we cannot satisfy without danger to our liberty."

"You must mean the depraved need for sensual pleasure, the impulses of a thief, and so forth. But I was not speaking about *all* our desires. Is it not the task of our reason to winnow the chaff from the wheat? Just as we can cultivate, refine, purify our desires, so we are capable of suppressing them, even of killing them. That is the purpose of our will, which must be directed by the intelligence!"

At these words I remember standing up and walking around.

I could no longer remain seated, my nerves were trembling so much. The blood rushed to my head, images danced through my brain as if I had a fever, and the more I exerted myself to stay calm the less I succeeded. I fancied that I saw quite clearly through the apparent truth of De Kantere's argument, yet I was unable to refute it neatly. It felt as if I were hunting for a forgotten melody: my ears heard it, but my mouth could not reproduce it. As I walked about, however, I inveighed against the dualism which postulates an independent intelligence, the better to exercise police surveillance over our desires; I referred to how a disturbance in the circulation of the blood, an overstimulation of the nervous system, even an impairment of the air supply through the nose could have the most fateful effects on both our thinking and our willing; but in saying all this I still did not say what I actually meant. Meanwhile De Kantere interposed various new arguments: spirit is dependent on matter, but matter is equally dependent on spirit; do not doubt the strength of your will and your will will be strong. I heard them as if through a mist, until at last there burst from me what I had unconsciously intended from the beginning of our conversation to hurl in this minister's face, sooner or later.

"Ah, what is the point of all this verbal skirmishing! I have a proof which topples all your subtlest arguments, a proof which is irrefutable, for my proof is myself. His own feelings are the only thing which a person knows with certainty. Your prescription, 'You must do thus-and-thus,' is fine; but if a person cannot, that is the end of all musts. Tell a drunkard as often as you like, 'You must stop drinking—see how wrong it is and you will want to find a situation in which you cannot possibly drink.' He will see how wrong it is, he will want to find such a situation, but he will not do so and he will go on drinking. The insuperable urge is in his blood, just as in someone else's blood there is a tendency to deposit calcium in the joints or stones in the gallbladder. Despite all his willpower, all his intelligence, he will achieve nothing. As a rule such a propensity is inherited. It is too late to change or destroy the inheritance. It is not the heir but the testator who should have been reformed. Teach a dog to guard sheep and its young *must* guard sheep. Control of your mind? Do you think I would be such a good-for-nothing, such a mis-
110

anthrope, such an abortion if my mind had turned out to be less powerless against my propensities and weaknesses? It is true, I am no lawyer, no minister, no engineer, not even an artist! Not one title to show that I lay claim to a mind. Nevertheless, I dare assert that I possess one, which has spells of being clearer than the minds of a lot of so-called useful people. Nevertheless, I am conscious of having used and developed this mind at every moment of my life when the mists of my nervous weakness were not hiding my brain in gloom. And what has this mind done for me? I have found out that I am a wretched exception to a miserable rule. Almost all my desires are warped, perverted. For things that make an ordinary person happy without doing harm to him or anyone else, I don't give a damn. In the course of my life I have, with one exception, always done things for which, according to conventional morality, I should have felt remorse. Well, I admit it openly that while I may perhaps have felt really sorry about the one exception, I certainly never felt sorry about the rest of my acts. Actually not even that is true: I have been thoroughly sorry to have been too spineless to give full rein to these warped inclinations of mine. If I had only been one of those utterly degenerate natures whose entire mental capacity is at the service of their warped impulses... but again that is not the case. I despise myself; I feel that other people despise me; therefore I hate other people, and yet want to be like them. Not happy... no, certainly; but..."

A slight faltering in my words was all at once enough to fill me with alarm at everything I had so unexpectedly blurted out. I was sure I had cut a clownish figure before a man I had not met till a few days ago, and a reaction against my openheartedness came over me in the form of a longing to run away and never again lay eyes on the minister.

Meanwhile, not in the least surprised, he had calmly replied, "You are not the first person I have heard speak like that. To ministers like myself much is revealed of what goes on at the bottom of the human soul. Do you know what has always struck me most about it? It is that the unhappiness—or shall I rather say the feeling of being unhappy, which is not the same thing—felt by these people is as a rule chiefly their own fault. Take yourself as an example... that is to say, if you will allow me..."

111

Of course I again grew frightened, and so simply nodded assent.
"You paint yourself far too black, and you brood too much.
Thought is a good and beautiful thing, but it must remain a means
and not become an end. One must think to be able to act, not
think just for the sake of thinking. If you thought a little more
highly of yourself, you would regard yourself as fitter for life's
task, and that task would in turn make you happier, for you have
a glorious task, Mr. Termeer, but... above all... in your home...
among your family. I am sure it was a great disaster to both of
you to have to lose your first child; but is it not a great joy to
be able to comfort each other?"

In spite of my self-knowledge, a word of flattery from no matter
whom has always made me rise in my own estimation. De Kantere's
declaration buoyed me up, and the strange thing was that it made
my love of truth suddenly disappear, while the old urge to present
an attractive figure arose again. Perfectly aware of the false the-
atricality of my answer, I said in almost a whisper, "He who
wishes to give must find someone prepared to receive, and that
is less easy than it seems at first sight."

At these words De Kantere stood up so suddenly that I thought
he had not understood me. But now I believe that the opposite
was the case. He acted as if he had lost track of the time, stuck
out his hand, and said in parting, "If you will give me the pleasure,
we shall on another occasion continue with this discussion, which
I have found remarkably interesting. I flatter myself—it is perhaps
somewhat presumptuous—but I flatter myself that I may be able
to bring you to a new way of seeing things. But for that I should
need more time than I have left."

I declared myself honored, showed him out, and then for the
first time realized with astonishment how excited I was. My cheeks
were congested to a dull red, my eyes burned, and my whole
body was trembling. It would have been impossible to go on
reading, even to sit still. After snatching a hasty bite, and evading
Anna's curious questions—which I had so easily answered the
previous time in a dry word—I went for a walk in the woods to
go over the conversation in my mind.

I rehearsed it not once but a hundred times. Incessantly I heard
De Kantere begin again at the beginning, heard my responses

recur. There were moments when I was sorry I had told him so much, and, all by myself, I would blush. But at other moments I thought I had expressed myself too briefly and unclearly. Then my heart would begin beating faster and I would feel an urgent longing for the next interview. In the end a wonderful sense of completeness radiated through me, as if I had enjoyed a deep and beautiful emotional experience.

Back in my room I wrote down the conversation, and at dinner I was uncommonly voluble, like someone who has made a small mistake and wants to forestall discussion of it. However, over tea Anna returned to the subject of De Kantere. She said that she was glad I had at last found someone to talk to.

"How do you know I can talk to him?"

"Well, that is what he told me this afternoon while you were out on your walk."

"So—he was here. Anyhow, he can only speak for himself, can't he?"

"I suppose so. All he said was that he had had an interesting discussion with you; but I concluded that you, for your part—"

"Oh, certainly, for a minister he is far from being a fool."

The words rolled, so to speak, from my lips. Yet I felt nothing of the presumptuousness from which they seemed to spring.

Anna remained calm: apparently she was quite satisfied with the course of events. I can still see her quietly going on with her tapestry-work, and, with her eyes on her wool, talking as if in a dream: "He understands you so quickly and so well. And what a melodious voice! When he speaks I feel as if I am listening to music. Everything seems to become prettier...lighter...more colorful."

It suddenly occurred to me that since her confinement Anna had not touched the piano. Without any spiteful intention, in fact in order to be pleasant, in a spirit of good-heartedness I asked, "Talking of music—why don't you play any more?"

She stared at me for a moment, smiled (it seemed to me contemptuously), returned to her work, and said, "Why should I play?"

Her answer made me feel very bitter, for she knew that I liked music. Did she then want to stress our silent enmity with the

113

utmost force at her disposal? Is it strange that all the cordiality vanished without trace from my response?

"Well ... so as to see everything become prettier and lighter and more colorful. After all, it is easier to provide such harmless pleasure yourself than to have to wait for someone else to give it to you!"

She looked up, then went on with her work in silence. The maid brought the newspaper in, and that evening no further word passed between us.

Not long after, I happened to meet De Kantere near the house, and took a stroll with him. Later on we went for a long walk together, which was succeeded by many others. On these walks I gradually poured out the whole story of my life until the time of my marriage, and while De Kantere heard me out patiently, I felt myself grow interesting in my own eyes.

In contrast the minister told me almost nothing of the vicissitudes of his life. It was as if he were as willing to engross himself in my existence as he was reluctant to do so in his. Only now and again, when he felt the need to illustrate one of his many hints or pieces of advice, did he allow me a fleeting glance into his past. Thus on the occasion of a conversation about my lack of perseverance he set himself forward as an example of a self-made man. His father had been a small shopkeeper, and he had had to earn the money for his studies cent by cent, first as a servant, later by giving lessons.

"And if I had not broken off my career, first to go south with my wife, then to devote myself wholly to Sofie, I would have become whatever I wanted to be. It is all a matter of resolution and perseverance. I am quite sure I could take a seat in the Chamber within two years and be a Minister within five. I do not want it, you understand; but if I *did* want it, I would achieve it. And, who knows, perhaps one day I *will* want it."

As he made this declaration, there was something challenging in his voice, something that testified to his relish for struggle and his belief in his own powers. But at the same time I heard in his words, or rather in his need to utter them, the disappointment of an ambitious man who has not reached his goal. Had he simply been boasting, or was there something besides all that seemed attainable to him which experience had taught him was un-

114

attainable; and did he feel this unattainability as a defeat in his life's struggle, a defeat whose significance he was trying to minimize for his own sake?

In order to find out more about him, I once asked whether he had felt the call to the ministry from the very beginning of his studies.

"Oh no! In fact I began by studying law; but I soon saw that I would get much further—and get there much more easily—as a minister."

I ventured the remark, "What I do not at all understand is that someone with your ambitions should have got married."

The words had barely escaped me when I felt that, as he walked beside me he had his eyes fixed on my profile. Was it because he wanted to find out with what motive I had spoken, or had there been something mysterious about his marriage, and was he asking himself, "What does this man know about me?"

After hesitating briefly he answered. "It is true that the tie of marriage will often hinder the movements of an ambitious man; but on the other hand, too much freedom is not good for anyone."

And after further hesitation, he added in almost solemn tones, "He who bears about with him a profound need to love may speak of happiness if he has a wife and children to whom he can devote his affection. Do you not agree with me, Mr. Termeer?"

The last sentence sounded so threatening that I did not dare ask for a clarification of the one before. Only much later did I find out that his ambition had been not in the first place for social position, but rather for the idolizing affection of beautiful, cultivated women of high rank. He too had wanted pleasure, as I had, and he too had not succeeded. Succumbing to both the adoration and the fortune of the first woman on the scene, he had found his efforts as much handicapped by his marriage as he was protected by it from much that was unpleasant. While he tried to pretend to himself that he was thankful for the latter he was in fact dissatisfied about the former. Had he not had Sofie or had he loved her less, who knows what he might not have done. But his fatherly fondness for the child kept a rein on his need for passion, just as in a miser greed for money restrains all other cravings.

Anna's name passed between us. In fact, De Kantere made

115

oblique provoking references to her. Thus, for example, he said, "You know what a great joy it is to have a wife who desires nothing for herself but is absorbed in the husband she loves," or, "It is not always in the worst marriages that man and wife appear little concerned with each other." Once he let slip, "It must be one of the most glorious things a man can imagine—to so fascinate a woman of character that, conquered and so to speak tamed, she abandons herself in adoration."

Perhaps he said this on purpose. Most of the time, at any rate, he was clearly expecting rejoinders. But remembering our second interview, I would not let myself be seduced into further careless utterances. I did not know whether or not Anna had yet complained to him about me, but in either event I saw I could not do better than maintain a haughty silence.

Accompanied by Sofie, he continued his regular morning visits to Anna. However, I was seldom present. I have never known how to treat children; girls in particular make me even shyer than grown-up women. But whenever I made an appearance, it struck me that I seemed to be disturbing them. As soon as they saw me they broke off their conversation, and after I had greeted De Kantere they never continued the interrupted discussion. It was difficult to believe that at the point of my arrival they had each time wholly disposed of a subject.

Meanwhile there was no improvement in my relationship with Anna. I often made up my mind to bring up the subject of the removal of my bed, but as often postponed discussion of the question. Despite my conviction that I had honestly and sincerely done my best to make Anna happy, at heart I felt that she had every right to treat me with contempt. The reception I had had last time in our erstwhile bedroom—now *her* room—had left nothing to be desired in clarity. So I had decided no longer to force the performance of this duty upon her, and, leaving aside the isolated rushes of sentiment of which I have spoken, I found it easy in the beginning to hold to a resolution which gave me the right to look out for another avenue for my desire. I had even felt daily more indifferent to what she said, until De Kantere had appeared between us. Thereafter, the more certainty I distilled

116

from thousands of small details, certainty that with every meeting she fell further under his influence, the greater became my desire to reassert my marital rights. No doubt there was an element of harassment in this, and it certainly showed how stone-dead my affection was by now; but was *I* not being harassed? Was I not being harassed by desires of mine that I could not satisfy, by efforts that had been thwarted, by people who despised me, by Anna who misunderstood me?

During this period I went to the opera frequently, and almost always alone, though without fail I invited Anna to accompany me. In part I went to have my fantasies stimulated and given color by the music, for the rest on the off-chance of an adventure. Usually I came home unsatisfied, and it was this feeling of being unsatisfied, coupled with a flickering up of sensual desire, that made me decide one evening to assert my rights after all.

This time I found the door of her room locked. I knocked, but she did not open, in fact at first did not even answer me. I knocked harder and finally heard her voice: "Let me sleep, please. I have a headache and I am sleeping badly nowadays."

Annoyed I slunk off, and next morning asked the meaning of this way of carrying on.

Cold and surprised, she stared at me. "What way?"

"Well, locking the door of your room."

"I have told you already, I sleep badly nowadays."

"Sleep badly...sleep badly.... A person doesn't suddenly begin sleeping badly without reason."

Without another glance she shrugged her shoulders and left the room, saying only, "Then it is probably *with* a reason—let us say nerves."

And De Kantere, said a voice inside me.

I remember a pleasant morning when, after a long, blustery north-wind period, mild spring weather returned. The still, milky-blue air vibrated with melancholy; it was as if the sunlight had to break its way through tears, as if it trembled damply down to earth. And melancholy seeped back up out of the black, soggy ground, oozed through the plants, whose tender green life fearfully unfolded itself from the indifferent gray stem.

117

I got up feeling torpid, and immediately after breakfast sank back on my sofa. I was lying in a doze when in the distance the church bells began to ring.

Few things have the same power to transport me back to the past as the far-off sound of a church bell. All the sensations of my youth reawoke so clearly that I might have imagined I was reliving them. I saw again those long-vanished faces and rooms and furniture; I heard again those long-stilled voices and sounds; I felt again the caress of hand and glance, and the stirring of thousands of painful impressions, half expired, suppressed in silence. How little I had enjoyed of all there was to enjoy, what horrible voids there were in my existence! Mightily and swiftly had the dense stream of humanity rolled on, and I had stood to one side watching, barely suspecting what was going on in that thunderous maelstrom.

And it was still like that. Even this lovely day, this day full of life, this day which would afford feeling and pleasure to thousands of people—for me it would pass by empty again, leaving not a single trace behind on the even, gray surface of my existence, which wound on in silence. So it would go today, so it would go tomorrow, so it would go in a month, in a year, and meanwhile my hair would be turning gray, my arteries calcifying, my brains hardening or softening. Already I had stopped hankering so incessantly after sensations; already they were less intense than in earlier times. Already the life of my nerves was drying up. Already what little soul I had was withering away completely. At the age of forty I would be like a normal person of seventy!

No, no, this could not go on! I wanted to get out—I must break through the invisible walls of my prison. For once at least I must know genuine emotions, for once feel that I was not only living in my imagination, for once desire, love, enjoy, and suffer to the full! And this must happen soon, very soon, very soon, or it would be forever too late! What use was it to anyone, who would thank me, if with the idiotic courage of an ascetic I sat and grew dull in this monotony? Did so much as a pretense of love still exist between Anna and me? Had love ever truly existed between us?

Oh, to stare into a woman's beautiful eyes, to kiss tender young lips with genuine desire, to feel the pressure of a soft, warm
118

hand, to clasp my arms about a gloriously white form that yielded itself ardently to me! And then once, even if only once, in the midst of this bliss, to whisper, "I love you!" Oh, soon, let it be soon, before it is too late!

The echoes of the bells died away, the memories faded, but desire went on thrilling in my nerves.

I tried to read, but my attention wandered. De Kantere had given me a book, a book he had written, a book that had gone through three editions and was entitled *The Army of Man*. In this work he compared mankind to an army that is going into battle. "Why?" ask the soldiers, officers, generals, and to each the answer is different. The highest leader alone, with an overview of everything, sees the final goal, while those serving under him can only give account of the limited task entrusted to them. Thus the simple soldier—and the simple soldiers are by far in the majority— sees nothing but his immediate duty and remains entirely unaware of how, in fulfilling his duty, he cooperates toward the attainment of the great victory. Yet he does his duty just as well as a general, and once he is fully alive to this truth he will cheerfully fulfill his duty and in turn draw new cheer from fulfilling it.

From this comparison the author went on to derive the formula, "Our life consists in dedication," and to make the reader feel what he meant by dedication he said, "Look at a plant, which brings forth beautiful flowers and exhales glorious scents: it gives itself and gives itself, as it is, without knowing why."

At that time I still enjoyed talking to De Kantere, but I did not like his book much. I found it nothing but fine words. What in heaven's name might *my* duty be, and how could working for mankind, which I hated, cheer me up? And then this comparison with a plant—thereby he surely proved precisely what he did not want to prove! Or is it not true that there exist plants which stink, in fact which give off such poisonous exhalations that the traveler who falls asleep under their foliage never again awakes?

I asked myself who was being misled by De Kantere: only his readers, or he himself too? However, I still wanted to read the book properly so as to be able to discuss it. What a pity that I was so seldom able to read properly. Women floated before my

119

eyes, gradually losing their poetic charm. I saw them more and more clearly in color and line, until eventually I felt at heart as I had in the morning hours of my youth, when I found myself vile and bad.

At two o'clock I left my home for the park.

During my walks, as a rule, I stayed as far from the throngs of people as my whole life was remote from the great stream of mankind. I still know too many people—even if for the most part only by sight—not to feel lonely and ill at ease in a crowd. But this time I made my way into the middle of the crush and looked about surreptitiously for a woman who might whisper her address to me in passing.

I felt that I had again become the same person as in earlier days: the awkward starveling who had to satisfy himself with crumbs that fell from the great pleasure-dish. More embarrassed than ever by faces completely unknown to me, I slunk around the bandstand in a state of nervous tension for two hours, only to end up, as in earlier times, in a bawdy house.

Back in my own street I felt revolted by myself. To shake off this revulsion I had three glasses of cognac. The result was a growing sense of bitterness against Anna, who had rejected me with cool haughtiness, with wounding contempt, and whom I blamed for all my miseries.

What did she observe in me that evening at bedtime? For the first time she did not stick out her cheek to receive the obligatory goodnight kiss. It struck and hurt me; but less than ever before did I dare ask questions.

Some nights later *Carmen* was being produced at the opera house. For both music and libretto, *Carmen* is my favorite opera. At least once a season I have to see it.

As I was taking off my coat in the passage behind the boxes, I heard the Sevillans singing: "*Et nous vous suivrons, brunes cigarières, En vous murmurant des propos d'amour!*" and at the moment when the parterre door opened, the refrain resounded from the chorus with voluptuous allure: "*Des propos d'amour, des propos d'amour!*" The ravishing harmonies coursed through my nerves like warm Burgundy. "Love, love," it echoed in my soul,

120

and only nervous weakness seemed to prevent me from feeling love, only cowardice from finding it. At this moment I would have dared much, would have been able to feel deeply. Why could there not always be such colorful, exciting music breathing about me? Did other people carry it around in their souls, and thus have only to listen to themselves to be lifted out of the gray tedium of the everyday?

Then Carmen appeared. There was nothing of the gypsy in her, but with the fiery camellia in her jet-black hair, with her eyes glowing against the white greasepaint, she looked quite seductive. To feel those arms about my neck, to kiss those eyes—what unattainable bliss! I felt as if I were tasting her lips, so completely did the music isolate me from everyone else, so much was my imagination spurred by it.

"If you do not love me, I love you; if I love you, beware!"

Yes, that was it, that was it! She would cling to me, almost suffocate me in her embrace, and I should find it bliss to die like that, to feel my life being scorched away in a mighty flare of passion!

But where would I find such a woman? Where would I pick up the courage to seek her out, to address her? And even if I succeeded in all this, and she were still not a Carmen, to me—?

The curtain closed, and it was as if in a flash I had been returned to the bright light of the emptily babbling crowd from the depths of a tête-à-tête in a twilit boudoir.

The longing for a Carmen filled my whole being! I could no longer think of anything else; I still saw her so clearly before me that the whole hall intermittently grew dim and disappeared from my sight.

Should I wait for her at the exit...write to her...call on her? All the possibilities passed in review; yet at the same time I knew very well that, timorous and awkward as ever, I would do nothing but wait...wait...wait...forever wait for something that of its own accord would simply never come.

Casually I began surveying the audience through my glasses. In the dress circle I saw numbers of white shoulders bending back toward men in evening dress, numbers of bare arms which, as they toyed with their furs, shone like ivory beneath the light of the chandelier.

121

So this was the highest, the must unashamed revelation of the world I had earlier dreamed of, the world in which I had imagined fresh passion unfolding before the faded one has even withered away completely. I did not even know the people by name, yet saw clearly that these circles had never been open to me. But lower—not much lower, but somewhat—my pleasure-world also branched out. Was it true that even there I would never penetrate, never discover by what sign the members of this freemasonry recognized one another?

My glasses ascended, and all at once there came into view a blond head which laughed enchantingly as it leaned back in lively conversation with a somewhat older, heavily made-up woman. It was a blond Carmencita, nothing more or less: the same animal eyes, the same provocative mouth, the same bright complexion.

That this was not the she whom I sought I understood at once; but... perhaps it lay within my reach to possess her. This thought drove the blood to my head. I grew dizzy. I was sure that everyone was watching me grow dizzy, that they must have guessed what was going on inside me, and I no longer dared look up, particularly not through my glasses.

The second act commenced, but I saw everything through a mist and heard everything through a veil. It was impossible to keep my attention on the stage. The music no longer gripped me, and slowly I felt the certainty arise that in a minute I would go upstairs and speak to this woman. It was not a decision that I took, that my reason took: it was decided for me somewhere deep inside, and my will merely obeyed.

Since then it has always happened like that. Perhaps it was no different earlier on, perhaps this was simply the first time I realized it clearly.

As soon as the curtain had fallen, I left my place and made my way with big, hasty strides, without looking at anyone, to the second tier. I felt myself growing pale, and my heart was in my throat by the time I arrived in the cramped little passage behind the boxes. Some of the usherettes and an idly sauntering servant stared at me, but said nothing. Boxes opened and loudly talking men appeared from them. I did not yet look at anyone, imagining that only if I did—and then for sure—would they look at *me*. I saw quite clearly how crazy the idea was. Nevertheless, this sense-less notion overmastered me.

Where exactly she was sitting I did not know. Therefore I too sauntered up and down for several minutes, struggling with the timid wish to have one of the doors opened for me. As if to conceal my intention, I first walked to the opposite side and looked out through an opening.

The pretty girl had left her place.

Slowly, with poorly feigned nonchalance, I returned along the curving passage to the original side. Again my heart began to thump heavily, while my lips grew as dry as if there were fever glowing in my blood. There she stood, leaning against the wall, a shining patch of blue silk, white skin, and blond hair against a dull red background. Opposite her I vaguely made out a thin young man in evening dress.

I stood waiting sheepishly a short distance away. To create an appearance I again stared through an open box door toward the third tier.

The conversation with the young man seemed to be getting on famously—at least, I heard her burst out repeatedly in darling little peals of laughter. I was getting anxious that the third act might begin before I could get a word in to her; but finally the fellow in evening dress gave her a parting handshake, strode past me humming, and disappeared. At once I stepped up and stammered out a few words, not looking straight at her. I no longer know what I said: it was as if she radiated something that blinded and confused me. There was no more laughter from her, but at least she did not turn her back on me. With affected politeness she asked me stiffly what I was trying to say.

At this moment several gentlemen approached, returning to their places. A foolish fear that someone would recognize me whipped me on. Harried, I asked simply, "Your address, quick, your address!"

I turned half to one side, as if by so doing to create the appearance of not speaking to her, heard her response, called out, "Good—I'll see you afterwards then!" and ran downstairs.

Back in my seat I saw her scanning the hall through her glasses. After a while she found me. Then she let the glasses masking her

123

face sink, and smiled at me. It was as if a wide-open shining heaven of blessedness unfolded before me. "Soon, soon," my soul rejoiced, and compared with this chorus within me the music of Bizet sounded so feeble and thin that I barely recognized its melodies.

As soon as the last chord of the orchestra was drowned in the noise of clapping hands, shuffling feet, slamming seats, and babbling voices, I left the hall, quickly put on my coat, and jostled impatiently through the exit with the stream of upper-circle spectators. For a moment the fresh night air cooled my warm brow, but within a dozen steps the muggy atmosphere had eradicated this sensation of coolness, and I felt the sultriness of the spring day hovering unabated under the thin leafage at the pondside. With a drab aluminum sheen the moonlight trembled through the damp of space. The brown-gray government buildings were sharply outlined against the blue-gray sky, and their dark reflection slept restfully on the unruffled surface of the water.

Oh, how beautiful it all looked!

A mystic stillness, a stillness full of warmly germinating life, lay spread out over nature. It was as if I heard the lament of tones in the mild air, and these tones were also scents, and these scents wafted about me, snuggled against me sensuously, forced their way into me like a deliciously enervating poison. A voluptuous languor slid through my muscles, blurring the keenness of my thoughts until they became pearl-gray visions of love and pleasure. I walked in a waking dream, and in this dream-illusion I became another creature, full of deep feeling which coursed through me like music of noble melancholy.

On a bench sat a pair of lovers whispering, their heads inclined, their fingers interlaced, their shoulders pressed together. I bent my gaze on them feeling less hostile than before toward the humanity I had shunned. Now I would share their feelings: at last I was getting my portion. True, I had hoped for a different, a less soiled pleasure; but is the scent of a rose less caressing because it is nurtured with manure? What difference could her past make as long as today, for a mere five minutes, she desired me as much as I desired her? I had far to walk, but the walk did not disturb my mood.

When I rang at the door, my heart was throbbing in my throat

124

from anxiety that one of those small disillusioning details which I had so frequently had to contend with would again spoil everything. But no!—Caroline was tastefully set up, she was no less attractive at close quarters, there was nothing about her that irritated me, she behaved neither coarsely nor as if bored, she acted as if money were not involved, and for the duration of an hour I enjoyed something approaching what I had fruitlessly pursued so often, in so many places.

Oh, the caresses of a lissom white woman's body, itself longing to be caressed, the intoxication radiating from clear, pale-blue eyes that do not despise, do not reject, but entice, ask, even beg! And then those kisses from fresh, warm lips to which kissing is a joy, that indescribable luxury of being able to give pleasure in attaining the highest ecstasy! It was probably all playacting on her part— but she acted so deceptively well, and I let myself be deceived so willingly.

Is everything not illusion, and is illusion not everything?

In fact, even the word "illusion" here is too pretty. Illusions too pine and shrivel in a tainted atmosphere, like plants in a hothouse that is overheated. But alas, a person like myself then sets up imitations in their place: imitation flowers in his hothouse, imitation illusions in his soul.

What had never happened to me before happened that night: when I left Caroline, it was not with revulsion—my whole soul exulted with yearning love.

A pleasurably contented, drowsy languor stayed with me into the next morning. I was still living in the previous night. After so long a period in which bouts of impotent exasperation recurred more and more oppressively and finally deposited a persistent embitterment in my heart as heavy as lead, it was a veritable relief at last to have tasted pleasure, and to be able to think, "As soon as I want to, I will taste it again." Caroline was certainly not— if only by the fact that I paid her—the ideal woman who could satisfy both the cold-eyed morning sensualist and the highly strung, overimpressionable evening self in me; but besides possessing a whiteness of skin, an ampleness of bosom, a curve of neck, arm, and shoulder, in a single word a luxuriousness that gratified my eye and aroused my lust, she made love deliciously. Oh, what a glorious moment when she had taken my head between her hands, pressing her lips slowly tighter and tighter to mine, and I had seen her close her eyes as if in a swoon of pleasure! The mere memory of it glowed through me like a warm wine that leaves one feeling generous and happy. More and more I felt my longing for her as something novel in me, a desire in which the morning man and the evening man really both had a share, an integral need for this woman, a need, too, that she should be entirely mine.

Was this all self-deception?

I became much better disposed toward Anna as well. I was dominated by the thought that our cohabitation could become at least bearable if I simply found elsewhere what I had to go without at home. True, I would not confess it to Anna; but had I no right to give someone else what she scorned? And, since she never came to ask me anything, not once revealed surprise at my uncommonly late homecomings, since, like myself, she looked remarkably cheerful and even walked about the house singing softly, was it not clear that she too had found a compensation for the disappointment of her marriage? Presumably her happiness, like mine, was a compromise with her ideal; but, good heavens, what happiness, in the series of illusions followed by disillusionments that one calls one's life's course, is anything more? In fact, it seemed to me piquant that each of us should have his secret, which the other, by tacit agreement, should respect.

Yet by lunchtime a cloud had fallen over the radiance of my inner life.

Getting up late, I had heard Anna from afar but not yet spoken to her. After her singing I was not surprised to notice an unusually happy expression on her face. While the maid was telling her about a beggar with all kinds of fantastic stories, I saw clearly how her soundless laugh from the old days came back, that laugh without contempt in which her light-blue eyes seemed to laugh too. Her movements, which since the death of our child had become somewhat listless, had gained a new liveliness, and—though I was perhaps imagining this—the furrow between her eyebrows was not so deep.

The question, "Was De Kantere here last night?" had barely

occurred to me when she told me that he had come at eight o'clock and stayed until half-past ten.

"Because he knew I was out?" (the words slipped out).

Anna shrugged her shoulders faintly, but with a rather indifferent expression on her face. "How should he have known that? If you had let me finish you would have heard that he came to see you."

"I see. And to what do I owe this honor?"

"Well...I think to...to a feeling of friendliness."

"Yes, of course: out of friendliness to me he stays until ten-thirty—with you."

So my tone had become spiteful again after all. What had done it? A last spark of jealousy? Perhaps; but in that case it was certainly not jealousy of an affection which I no longer in the least desired for myself. If I understand it properly, I was jealous of the nature of the affection that I suspected between Anna and De Kantere. That these two people cherished feelings for each other in which neither money nor fantasizing played a part, that they had found something so fine and beautiful without looking for it, that they enjoyed it without having to hide—this was what vexed me. In the same way, I suppose, a diamond on the breast of an actress vexes a fellow-actress who has to wear imitation jewelry. Their relationship, or at least the relationship I supposed between them, spoiled mine with Caroline, as at an exhibition a picture painted from the heart in vigorous colors spoils the dull, contrived piece hanging next to it.

Would it remain so beautiful?

If I was not deceived in De Kantere, I would venture to say, only very briefly. Yet how long such a "very briefly" was compared with my "never attained and never to be attained!"

"What did he actually want from me?" I asked a moment later.

Anna, who had left my spiteful words unanswered, now said quite calmly: "To ask you why you had not taken a walk with him in the last few days, and whether you would like to go for a walk today, or otherwise tomorrow."

Although I saw it was a pretext, the explanation satisfied me. Unfortunately, without a smile yet in a faintly mocking tone, she

127

added: "He seems to want to reform you. He even believes he is well on the way to doing so!"

I knew that De Kantere, despite his capacities and his experience, belonged among those zealots eager to lay everyone on the Procrustean bed of their opinions, but it annoyed me that he had discussed his plans for reform with Anna. What could those two have told each other about me, I asked myself again. To Anna I replied, "Quite possibly! At any rate, he seems to have a lot of influence over certain people."

These words annoyed her in turn. "Oh, anyone can exercise influence who takes the trouble and...who means well by the other person...unless...unless the other person is...how shall I say...as surly, as unapproachable as someone I am acquainted with."

"What do you know about it? I do not claim to know what is going on inside you. You have always done your best to keep that hidden from me, and I am quite willing to acknowledge that you have succeeded. But trust breeds trust—and the reverse is also true."

I can still see the insufferable little smile with which she looked me for an instant straight in the eye, and then, with her nose in the air, replied: "As if it were so difficult to know what is going on inside you."

It was not possible that she could already know anything definite about my relationship with Caroline, yet I lacked the courage to ask her, "Go on, tell me!" But seeing that silence on this point would be a more or less clear acknowledgment of guilt, I said, "You can imagine, if you like, that you know me. Knowledge of other people is anyhow usually three-quarters imagination!"

"For those who think they can only understand other people with the intellect, I suppose that is true."

Anna, cold Anna, recommending feeling as an instrument for penetrating the inner life of others!...There was no doubt about it, in this she was simply mimicking someone, which meant De Kantere. Which brought me back to the thought that they had been putting their heads together about me. What could they—in particular, what could he—have said about me? I very much wanted to find out, but again dared not ask directly. So I tried to discover it in a roundabout way.

"So...De Kantere stayed such a long time....It must have been an interesting evening.... What did the two of you talk about?"

"Oh, about all kinds of things. I don't remember exactly. He told me about his book—the book you are reading. He knows it almost by heart. What wonderful things there are in it, and so true! Of course you find them untrue. That is what you were going to say, but you needn't. Then...then we talked about Sofie, and also about his wife."

She was right: a discussion of philosophical topics with Anna seemed quite superfluous. So I let De Kantere's book pass and asked only, "Has she been dead long?"

"Oh, no, only eighteen months. He sacrificed his whole career to go south with her, and now here he is full of worries about his child."

I said nothing, expecting that a comparison would follow between De Kantere and me. But I was wrong. Without pause she continued, "He has told me a lot about his life, and...though he will neither speak nor hear ill of his wife...I do not believe that those two were happy together."

"Who is?"

She pretended not to hear my gibe. "But it seems that he looked after her in an exemplary way. Yes, he is a superior man, and that must have been the reason for his unhappiness. He must have been too far above his wife."

Not a word about me, yet I had no further doubt that Anna had given De Kantere a clear insight into how inferior I was to *my* wife.

Oh, that cursed feeling of forever—and never quite without reason—knowing or fancying yourself humiliated!

Simply to say something I remarked that De Kantere did not like to hear himself called unhappy. This statement had no effect that I could see, nor did it receive a reply; but suddenly she said, "He has been most friendly toward you. I think that before he leaves we should at least invite him to dinner."

With my head full of my adventure, and little inclined to have my time taken up by this excellent minister, I would surely have turned down the request point-blank if I had been less curious to observe Anna and De Kantere together. Besides, since he would soon be leaving, and for a long time, this one dinner surely committed me to nothing. So I consented at once, noting with satisfaction that my promptness greatly surprised Anna.

Alone in my room I conjured up as usual visions of what our conversation at table would be, and determined for once to bring to light how oddly Anna's hysterically grateful adoration of De Kantere, who had done nothing for her, compared with her cold contempt for me, to whom she at least owed her independent situation.

De Kantere accepted the invitation.

To his suggestion that we again go for a walk together I had made no reply. I felt that he was far too much on Anna's side for me to go on being able to speak to him frankly, and in addition I preferred to keep my available time free so that I could visit Caroline at any hour of the day.

As early as our second meeting Caroline had told me that an elderly gentleman who had died four weeks ago had kept her. While he was alive she would not have received me, for she was neither unfaithful nor thankless. But now she needed a new protector, and since it was not in her nature to become involved with a different man each time—for she was not common—she asked whether I would like to be her protector.

It would have been nicest of all to know that she was the property of another man, and then to deceive him. This would have given me a kind of certainty that she really loved me with all her heart. But since this was as much an impossibility as the alternatives of giving her up fairly soon or sharing her with someone else on an equal footing, there was little for it but to consider whether I could not accept her proposal. So I named a sum. Her only reply, however, was to ask with a laugh whether I took her for one of those lieutenants who puts a painted side of beef on the table and bacon on his plate. For a moment this revolting valuation she put on her caresses made my illusions fade almost quite away. If these words had occurred in a letter to me, I would never have returned to her. But as long as my eyes were enjoying her, my mind was powerless to detach itself. I swallowed the painful impression like a fish swallowing the hook hidden in the bait.

130

Anyhow, I had offered the highest figure I could afford, and I saw no chance of laying my hands on more money even temporarily. Anna's father still retained the administration of my fortune, and there was not a single reason why I should deprive him of control. Indeed, since he possessed a safe in a strong room and I neither the one nor the other, the very reverse was the case. So what was there to do? To gain time I promised to think the matter over, and in return extracted from her a promise that in the meantime she would be satisfied with whatever I gave. I believed this promise because I did not *want* to doubt it. However, the very next evening she sent me away as quickly as she could, claiming that she was going out to tea with a lady-friend. I asked whether this lady-friend was perhaps the young man in evening dress from the opera, and with a provoking little laugh she answered, "That's right."

Was she lying, I thought, or was she only teasing me?

It had not escaped me that Anna took far more trouble over receiving the minister than she had taken over her sister and brother-in-law. All sorts of little refinements, picked up from other people or from when we were abroad, like hors d'oeuvres before the soup, rose water in the fingerbowls, and so on, were now deployed, and she saw to a particularly elaborate dessert, supposing—or rather fearing—that after the meal De Kantere would leave in a hurry. In the morning she herself tidied up all the magazines and books lying about, arranged the ornaments above the fireplace, and kept an eye on the preparations. Then with unusual care she wrote out the long menu, made one or two suggestions to me about the wine, and finally made an appearance in a new black velvet gown which suited her and was in good taste.

Her gaiety of mood had not yet given way. I kept hearing her singing, and besides the soundless laugh of earlier times, which I rediscovered at moments on her lips, I detected in her eyes a dreamy tenderness which she had never shown to me. As if to escape my gaze, which must have expressed amazement as much as ridicule, she suddenly sat down at the piano and played from memory several bars of the Moonlight Sonata.

It was as she played that I could best see the change in her

131

being. The unreflective child who had married only because that was what one did and someone asked her, who had formed no more exalted idea of marriage than of living as other women *appeared* to live, who might have been perfectly satisfied with an expansion of her limited powers in the day-to-day loving of a husband, looking after a household, caring for a child, keeping up an interest in a small circle of friends—this child, through an overwhelming pressure of circumstances, had become a woman who lived a strange life, whose energies, everywhere repulsed, had quietly entrenched themselves in the depths of her soul, where they were now devoted to the service of a self so beautiful in its self-denial that only he who was prepared to kneel with her before that ideal and ascetically adore it had any chance of being touched by a reflection of her worshiping love. And I guessed that De Kantere understood perfectly what kind of role he should play in this spectacle.

But could he and would he persist with the role?

Apprehensive—without reason, of course—that De Kantere might know something about my relationship with Caroline, I had downed several drinks before his arrival so as to be able to comport myself well—in this case with insouciance. So I was fairly irritable, ready to go too far in whatever direction I took.

When I saw the minister, with his friendly, almost condescending smile, with a slow nod full of ill-concealed pride and his downcast eyes full of feigned humility—when I saw him, lisping an over-cordial "How are you?," stick out his pale hand to Anna, I felt like crying out, "If you two are playing these pretty roles for your own pleasure, well and good—but don't think that you fool me!"

In her nervous excitement Anna did not at once offer her guest a chair. So for a few minutes we went on standing and talking in the middle of the room, and as usual I cast a glance at the mirror. Oh, how thin and sallow I was beside this big man with his foursquare shoulders and his aristocratically pale face framed in jet black. And he used his hands well; *my* hands looked fettered, so tightly did they remain clasped together behind my back. He stood calmly talking; about *me* there was always something jerking nervously.

I saw that Anna's eyes did not stray from his face for one

132

second, and knew that I was a negligible quantity, superfluous. Like hunchbacks who, mocked for deformities for which they are not responsible and unappreciated for all they have won at the cost of much bitter experience, end by adopting a sarcastic tone, as if thereby to set themselves above those who look down on them, so I too felt mastered by an urge to be sarcastic, an urge usually foreign to my diffidence and my slowness of thought.

At first, however, I said almost nothing.

When De Kantere asked whether we would not be going walking together again, I answered with the excuse that I had had errands, and Anna quickly changed the subject. At table the minister was for a long time the only one to speak, while Anna, smiling dreamily, stared into his eyes, now and then giving the maid a hasty word of instruction, or swiftly and softly, as if to remain unobserved, serving the minister herself. I could almost feel the influence that went out from him like a magnetic stream and intoxicated her like heady champagne. He soon arrived at the subject of his child, telling us that he had been advised to leave for Davos at once rather than wait and find that the treacherous sickness had lodged in her chest. Prevention was always to be preferred to cure; in the high mountain air her youthful lungs would perhaps grow so strong that they would soon be unassailable. There was nothing to tie him down, so there was no reason to hesitate.

When—more to say something than out of any conviction—I remarked that it would be difficult to give the child a good education in Davos, Anna, with flashing eyes and a shrug of the shoulders, called out, "As if the Reverend could not do that himself!"

Then she asked when he planned to leave, and I saw her eyebrows rise and fall, the line of her mouth grow rigid, her pale cheeks pale still further, when he answered, "Quite possibly before the summer begins."

And looking past him, she said, "I am sure you are right. There is nothing to tie you down here, and ... to have to lose someone your whole heart depends on—that is terrible! How fortunate that you can still strive to save her!"

Never had Anna said a sentence of such significance to me. It spurred me to interject quickly, "But surely that is a striving against

133

Providence, and Providence demands resignation and gives to each what is good for him!"

Anna blushed and cast me an indignant look. She was probably ashamed at such language toward an ex-minister, who was besides at this moment my guest. I saw perfectly well the loutishness of using an argument I did not at all believe in to fence with; still, it pleased me to see that I vexed her and drew the minister into difficulties.

De Kantere seemed not to mistake my intention; at any rate, he replied in an almost jocular tone, "Do you want to drive a theologian into a corner with his own weapons? Be careful, Mr. Termeer: it is dangerous to handle a weapon whose sharpness one underestimates."

And going off at a tangent, he continued: "I believe that it surprises you to hear an ex-minister talk so little about God. You are not the first to find it strange. Yet I flatter myself that I can give a good explanation. Suppose that you wanted to sell me this house. Would you, to recommend it, tell me how clever the architect was, or would you praise its solidity, its construction, its workmanship, and leave it to me to deduce how good the builder was? As Schiller once said, 'The handiwork should praise the master.'"

"And do you really find that the handiwork praises the master?"

"As long as we are prepared to look at it attentively and without prejudice—yes. I am well aware that in your eyes there is much in life that is unjust, since wrongdoing does indeed yield a brief satisfaction and since all good deeds are not at once followed by their reward. Not so? However, you cannot give me a single example of evil bringing happiness, and though good often causes us pain at first, it thereby makes us receptive to the highest happiness. Is it not so, Mrs. Termeer? Suffering is simply the price at which such happiness is to be bought. Whose fault is it if we are too greedy to pay the price?"

As he spoke, I had seen Anna's eyes regain their clear, fanatical glow, and now she called out in a transport, "Oh, Reverend, how true that is, how true!"

This hysterical assent left me feeling particularly peevish, and with an unpleasant little laugh I said something like, "An excellent

134

truth! I would have expected better from an Almighty than to offer at so high a price what he could have given free. And I know what you are going to say to that: that we cannot understand his ways, not so? Fine; but then I want to ask, can the handiwork ever praise the master when the handiwork consists of the impulse to strive toward a goal plus a ban on ever understanding that goal?"

"You feel the goal," Anna blared out triumphantly. "You feel it at every moment, if you do your duty, and you also feel that that is where your only true happiness lies!"

I was growing more and more sour, and after De Kantere, with all the emphasis of a teacher who sees that at last he is understood, had said, "Precisely, Mrs. Termeer!" I broke in: "Yes—if you are naïve enough to think that giving in to your impulses is doing your duty."

Anna again had a refutation ready. "If you're not a child any more, you have put aside all other impulses. Doesn't Feuchtersleben say that as well?"

For the first time I heard this name from Anna's lips. Since she had previously hardly ever read a book, even a light novel, she must surely have owed her acquaintance with this superficial philosopher to De Kantere. So for his sake she was now immersing herself in more or less profound speculations! Using other people's wisdom to spar with was something that irritated me; in Anna I found it unendurable.

While De Kantere answered her question, I calmly poured wine; as soon as he had finished I spoke with a teasing smile, "Since when have you been reading philosophical books, or rather, since when have you been reading at all?"

A dull red overspread Anna's cheeks and I saw the glass in her hand tremble as in calm but biting tones she replied, "Since I have known someone who is capable of explaining to me what I do not understand."

De Kantere at once intervened. "Ah, Mrs. Termeer, with you the explainer has an easy job. Your husband saw that long ago."

Neither of us spoke, I laughed nervously, afraid of losing my self-control completely, she controlled herself more easily, but deep down still was excited and indignant.

For a while De Kantere went on about Von Feuchtersleben and

135

other thinkers, but I was no longer listening. What difference could this chitchat ultimately make to me?

I now poured a finer wine, drinking a lot of it myself, and lost the thread of the conversation. Willy-nilly my thoughts wandered to Caroline. There was my reward. I saw myself sitting beside her, my head leaning on her shoulder, her shapely arm about my neck. Her soft hand stroked my brow, her head bent over me. I saw her mouth, her eyes coming nearer, and I whispered, "Love me, give me pleasure, so that I can forget all the vexations, all the humiliations, all the barrenness of my day-to-day life." I felt that no one else could give me what she gave. I could never again do without her; a future without her seemed like a living death. I *had* to—and no vileness would be too vile for me, no treachery too base, to get the money for the annuity she asked. Such happiness as she gave me I had never known, would never know again. There was no question of hesitating: the very next day I would go to Utrecht to take my assets away from Bloemendael. What nonsense—I did not have to account to him in any way as to why I chose to control my own resources and what I chose to do with them!

Only when we reached the brandy did I return to reality and hear what was being said around me. And I remember getting the impression that they had not so much as noticed my absence of mind. Anna was wholly immersed in gazing at her minister, whom her ecstatic stare did not leave for one second, and he— probably used to such adoration—strung his fine sentences as tastefully together as if he were standing in a pulpit speaking to the multitude.

Suddenly Anna called out enthusiastically, "Exactly, exactly! I have often thought so myself, but how wonderful it must be to be able to express so well what is going on in you!"

De Kantere smiled with feigned modesty, and I made use of the pause to say, "If I had to live my life over, I would be a minister! It must be nice to have so much prestige in the eyes of the ladies that they take every word that falls from your lips for the very truth!"

"As if that would make any difference to you!" said Anna with a cutting smile.

136

De Kantere changed his tactics. "I do not deny that prestige is involved. But what is concealed therein is the danger rather than the satisfaction peculiar to our profession. What constitutes its attraction in the long run is having people's trust and thus being able to comfort and support them."

"Do you find that without danger?"

A long excursus from De Kantere about the duties of a minister and all the tact he requires ended our gathering. I made only one further observation: "Sorrows for which comfort, or rather a comforter, can be found do not amount to much."

It vexed me that in spite of a challenging stare from me, Anna remained perfectly calm at this point. She pretended she had not even understood me.

Rising, De Kantere now declared that he could not stay for tea. He wanted to see Sofie before the child went to bed, as was his regular habit. Anna gave him some candy to take along, and made an appointment to go for a walk with the child the next day.

No one mentioned a walk with me.

Is it a peculiarity of mine only, or have other people also had the queer realization that the presence of a third person—say A—can give one both the desire and the courage to direct sarcastic and nasty remarks at B, remarks which with only the two of them present he could not and would not utter? Once De Kantere had left, I had no further inclination to exchange words with Anna, let alone say unpleasant things to her. So each of us took a page of the newspaper, and for more than half an hour no sound passed our lips. However, there was no further trace to be found of the subdued cheerfulness with which we had begun the evening. We chafed worse than ever before, each feeling the other's presence as the insurmountable obstacle between him and the satisfaction of his desires. In addition, it kept troubling me to see that her attachment was so much more beautiful—or let me rather say, so much less ugly—than mine. But what pained me most was the thought that she could torment me so much more than I could her. Public opinion and my lack of courage to defy it boldly, the circumstance that her father still had my money in his possession, and then, yes, finally, if she wanted it, the police and the powers of the courts—everything would aid *her* work against *me*. And I could do nothing as long as she did not cross the prescribed boundary line that conventional morality had drawn between forbidden and permissible pleasure. As if the offense called adultery, which is nothing but a consequence, and sometimes only a piece of carelessness, were not always preceded by a split between two souls or two sensuous dispositions, a split in which the entire rupture already lies in embryo! The difference between us, in a nutshell, was that for me satisfaction began only with the act, while she reveled in wanting it, and was soothed too by being conscious of a temporary self-control. But mankind wants facts, sees only facts, judges only on facts.

Which meant that it was again not only Anna who was hostile toward me: behind her stood the entire human-social community with its rigidly arbitrary distinction between good and evil and the irrational rules according to which it acquitted or condemned.

It was Anna who, stammering somewhat and still flushed with excitement and anger, began the conversation. "Since De Kantere is leaving so soon, I suppose he will not come to dinner here again. That would not anyhow be much pleasure for him after today's experience. But we may still meet him together. I ask you in a friendly way to address me—in his presence—a little more politely than you did this evening."

I can still see her sitting there. Gone were the moments of pleasure she had looked forward to, turned to gall by my sharp outbursts. Now she was once more the Anna of a few weeks ago, the cold, inscrutable image with the steely gaze, the nose in the air, the downward-arching mouth.

Heated by the wine and liqueur, I had little wish to be reprimanded with such icy control. "And I ask you in a friendly way henceforth to moderate your tone of contempt a little in the presence of third parties. Not that I care one way or the other; but if you find it necessary to communicate your opinion of me to other parties, at least do so in my absence. What De Kantere thinks of me is a matter of complete indifference to me; but you should have understood that it is not exactly pleasant for me to have to put on a ridiculous act."

"I don't know what you are getting at."

"Oh. Then ask De Kantere. He will understand it all the better."

Uttering not another syllable, she got up and left. From that moment onward she did not even offer me her hand any more.

Left to myself, I brought out the brandy, poured myself a drink, took the cat upon my lap, and immersed myself in a whirl of incoherent thoughts.

If at an earlier time I had felt safe when I closed my front door, cut off from the hostility of people, now the house had shrunk to a room and the hostile force had penetrated all the surrounding passages and rooms. I felt it everywhere, invisible, oppressive, condemning all my desires and trying to smother them in the stuffy atmosphere of this tiny space. I wanted to get out, out, and I did not know how!

I felt deeply wronged and offended, yet I had to admit that in fact it was not Anna but I who had misbehaved.

But whose was the fault, the original fault? Had I been asking too much in expecting from my wife the tenderness that even an affectionate cat gave me? True, even if she had given it to me, I should in the end not have been satisfied. Nevertheless, I had a need for it and a right to it!

Then it was as if a voice called in my innermost: "Right or no right, no woman in all the world will give such tenderness to a man like you except for the sake of appearance, out of necessity!"

The thought was certainly no novelty to me, yet at once it paralyzed my will to go to Caroline that evening.

Was it the flush of the wine, or what was it that suddenly prevented me from being content with an illusion in which I had a moment ago been seeing my highest happiness?

I drank more and more, and gradually all kinds of visions from my youth returned, and I experienced feelings such as I had experienced then.

What did my most intense pleasure of today signify compared with the imagined pleasure of earlier days, and why had those imaginings not been enough for me when they had given me so much?

The next morning I awoke as I had so often awakened in Amsterdam before my marriage: frightened of the new day, of the long sequence of miserable hours that had again to be struggled through. And as before I asked myself, Why had I opened my eyes? Was the nastiest dream not better than the reality of embitterment and envy alternating with disappointment and indifference that was mine?

My cheeks glowed as if at fever heat. Clouds of smoke seemed to draw endlessly past my eyes. My brain, heavy as lead, was incapable of reflection. I felt too tired to stir a foot, too agitated to go on sitting or lying down another quarter of an hour. Shrinking from the first words I might have to exchange, I shut the door of my room and yet yearned for diversion, for something new, something unexpected.

An evening alone with Anna seemed unendurable, being with Caroline not in the least tempting. There was nothing I wanted, yet I wanted to want something. As soon as lunch was over—a meal during which we said not a word to each other—I went outdoors to pull myself together; but the north wind that cooled my brow could not drive the rancor against everything and everyone from my spirit. How unusually dour and chilly and unpleasant I found the world that afternoon! The sunlight seemed painfully bright, all colors repellently hard. It was as if the pulses of warmth were being driven away before me by a cold stream of air, and the heavy shadows overhead looked like tatters of a winter blown apart.

I had set out with the firm intention of walking among the lonely dunes. However, at three o'clock I was at Caroline's front door.

What an empty and shabby and deathly aspect her street had! Yet I pressed myself fearfully against her door, peering around to see whether anyone had spied me! My fear was annoyingly foolish and cowardly, but it was by this very fear that my rage was reawakened and swept up against the injustice of life that denied me everything and thus forced me to steal my pleasure as it forced the unemployed to steal their bread.

Caroline offered me port, plenty of port, and, with her white neck enticing me anew, with her hot kisses arousing me, I felt myself gradually grow in heart and strength and clarity. She lavished endearments on me, and though I tasted something false in them, they soothed my soul as warm water soothes one's hands in winter. Suddenly a separation from Anna seemed unavoidable.

140

I wanted an unambiguous situation, and Anna could not refuse it to me—at least not if she truthfully wanted to be called a gentlewoman.

As soon as I was free again, my acts, if not justifiable, would at least be excusable, and no one would have the right to call me to account for them. I declined to serve as a foil for Anna's show of excellence or to let myself be encumbered by a millstone around my neck.

As she sat on my lap, kissing me and giving me pet names, Caroline reintroduced the question of money.

Oh, I can feel it still—how I could not keep my eyes from her delicious lips, which with a continuous undulation, as if kissing each other, kept a misty sheen over their soft carmine, and how, at her question, I suddenly felt as if a gush of gall had risen from my stomach to my throat.

"Be quiet," I shouted, "nothing more about money—or I will walk out and never come back!"

She started at my vehemence, kissed me again, and whispered, "Now, now, now—only don't get angry, be a darling." But after she had been silent for a while, smiling and stroking me and kissing me all the time, she began again from the beginning, and now it seemed that harmony gradually crept in between her demands and my desires. I fancied I had been unjust. If I demanded that Caroline be entirely mine, then I should be entirely hers. As long as she had no certainty that I would provide for her longer than a woman's first charm usually lasted, she had every right to leave no means untried to gain as much money as she could from our relationship, thereby safeguarding herself against poverty in her old age.

If she had not liked me a little, or at least had pleasure from me, as I from her, she would long ago have found a replacement for me or shared her favors with other men. A pretty girl like her surely had to turn down more admirers than she could accept; therefore she, despite the money, surely favored me above the others.

Ridiculous reasoning and adolescent self-deception, I will not deny it—but also the only way to make life bearable. If I lost Caroline, then—I knew from experience—I would not be capable of finding a woman whose attentions could replace hers.

With the image of her beautiful mouth in my eyes, with the

141

taste of her kisses on my lips, I went home, determined to part from Anna at any price. I could no longer understand that only yesterday evening I had scorned Caroline and about Anna had thought, "If ever she wants to leave me so as to marry De Kantere, she will feel who it is she has treated so contemptuously!"

During this period my personality sometimes changed completely three or four times a day.

At table I raised the question. We had, as usual, exchanged not a word for the first fifteen minutes. However, the changed expression on Anna's face showed that my silence did not disturb her at all. It was as if not only her eyes but her whole face glowed with a still, inward, secretive happiness. She had undoubtedly been talking with De Kantere, and in her thoughts still lingered with her minister. She was staring not past me but over me.

It took me some effort to break the unpleasant silence, but I succeeded. "Listen, Anna, I know that you care less for me every passing day. You have even had occasion to reveal some of your complaints against me. May I now finally hear all of them?"

The mere uttering of these premeditated words was enough to convert my resentment into an ill-controlled fit of irascible temper. My voice quivered as I went on: "Of course you think, or you have thought, 'I'll just keep quiet—after all, it doesn't help.' But don't...don't be so sure!"

She threw me a swift, quizzical glance, but did not even stop eating, and answered with a near smile and with the amused air of someone who thinks he can escape a pointless squabble by being calm: "What do you mean—my complaints?"

"Well...your comments...the reasons you give for being offended...your...surely you are not going to claim that...that you still have the same opinion of me as when we were engaged!"

"Oh no. I think I now know you better, and after all...we both have changed. People keep changing. One gets ahead, another falls back, we all grow older. But I am not complaining."

"That's just it!"

She did not forget the usual contemptuous shrug. "I don't understand you."

She was lying. I was convinced that she believed she understood me very well. However, she found it better to act as if the opposite

142

were the case. I was infuriated by it—by this trick of hers of attributing to herself powers of discrimination which enabled her to decide what I should or should not be allowed to know. But as usual, in my nervous state, I could not find words for all the thoughts that whirled around in my brain. I apprehended them no more clearly than as a persistent tremor, much like the impression one has walking past the bars of two gates which are perpendicular to each other. I saw no chance of coming properly to grips with the subject of De Kantere. I could not yet in all justice reprove her with more than overfamiliarity, and this reproach would make me look ridiculously stupid if there were more between them, or ridiculously jealous if their relationship were limited to familiarity. In incoherent fragments of sentences, however, I went on about the grand enthusiasms in which she seemed to be looking for comfort and diversion, and about the absurd pedestal on which, in her imagination, she seemed to be placing herself. But with up-drawn eyebrows she simply went on shaking her head and throughout my jumble of words repeating, "I truly don't understand you!"

So I did not succeed in striking one painful blow, while she went on imperturbably looking down on me—in other words, persisted in her estimate that she stood high and I low, that she might, could, and must mislead me.

This calm presumption enraged me. Interrupted by the entry of the maid, I had for a while to hold my peace, and during this interval managed to calm down somewhat. I found a few phrases that would enable me to approach my goal gradually, and so resumed as soon as we were alone again: "You do not complain, that is true. But we exchange unpleasant words, don't we? Is that evidence of a good relationship?"

No reply.

"And then—also without complaining—by one's attitude, even by keeping silent, one can indicate quite clearly that one is not happy. Isn't that so?"

"Being happy depends on yourself. Happiness resides inside you."

In true feminine fashion, her answer was beside the point. On the other hand, it was also an expression of her self-sufficiency.

"Good," I cried, already much less under control; "but if your

143

happiness no longer depends on *me*, then mine no longer depends on you, and if that is so then our marriage becomes a senseless exhibition, in which I am once more putting on a ridiculous act, and of that I have now had enough—I refuse!"

"I do not see that you are in any respect putting on a ridiculous act, nor have I any idea who or what compels you to do so."

I felt like boxing her ears, with such icy coldness, such haughty defiance did she stare at me all the while she was making this declaration. A curse hissed through my teeth. "Damnation...!— Why do you think I married?"

For a moment there was no answer, and I had to repeat my question with a snarl before she said, "I think with the best intentions. It appears that you have not found what you have been looking for. I am sorry; but... it is not my fault. I can do no more than my duty."

At these words my rage foamed up in such a paroxysm that my grasping fingers involuntarily curled around a silver fork and twisted it into a corkscrew. My voice could barely pass through my pinched throat, and the words trembled on my lips as I shrieked out, "Your duty... aha! So—you think it is your duty to *seem* to be my wife, but not to *be* my wife in one single respect!"

Anna did not lose her calm. It would seem that she had been prepared for this interview for a long time. "I understand what you mean; but you are wrong. You know yourself, from experience, that you are wrong. I will say no more about that. I find it unpleasant to talk about such things—almost more unpleasant than... and it does not matter, after all."

This enigmatic statement affected my anger as oil does the waves. It was as if a lock were clamped on my lips, and a dry cold seeped through my whole body. Does she know it—I thought— or does she mean that as a man I am so repulsive? I was so amazed that I could not immediately choose between these alternatives. The one possibility looked as bad as the other, and it was quite some time before I could force my brain to occupy itself with the question, "What now?"

At last, with well-feigned indifference, I continued: "We seem to have most divergent ideas about marriage."

"Yes, it certainly seems so."

144

"Oh, I thought you did not want to talk about it."

No reply.

"Consider one thing carefully. I certainly have no intention of being a millstone around your neck; but nor do I want a millstone around mine! Tormenting each other can never, in my eyes, even in marriage, be a duty. In my opinion, people who are as totally at odds over the main issue in marriage as we seem to be should not... remain tied to each other any longer." And standing up so as to make an end, for the time being, to this distasteful conversation, I added, "You don't have to give me your answer at once, but I recommend that you think the matter over carefully. When the time arrives we can discuss it further."

I was not yet out of the room when her answer sounded after me: "Do what you like. I am aware that I have never failed in the performance of my duty, and I will not fail in the future either!"

The door slammed shut behind me.

Oh, I knew it all already: where I longed for marks of love, she would serve me dutifully. She would deprive me of all grounds for complaint except to myself, and despite my threats she would go on being a millstone around my neck, ostensibly for my welfare, in fact for her satisfaction. I slammed a second door shut, so loudly that the whole house boomed. Then with convulsively balled fists I fell down on my sofa and in throes asked myself what would be better—to nag her, if necessary abuse her, so much that she would simply have to bend, or to turn a blind eye to her so-called exercise of duty, go my own way as if she no longer existed, and... if necessary move in with Caroline? Surely the latter... but... would I ever dare take such a drastic step?

Meanwhile nothing became of my trip to Utrecht to get my stocks and bonds back. From day to day I postponed it while I sought an argument effective against both my father-in-law and Anna. During my solitary walks I found it enough to think up a meeting at which I simply declared, "My money belongs to me; from now on I should like to administer it myself; be so good as to hand it over." But I recoiled from the unexpected turns the conversation might take. Strictly speaking I did not have to say a word more. Bloemendael could offer any objections he liked—the right to

145

refuse was ultimately not his. But all these considerations did not prevent a chasm from opening before me between the resolve and the act. When I sat across the table from Anna I saw the chasm yawn, and it seemed to me insuperable. Even supposing that her father took my plan for personal control seriously, it was anyhow obvious that for safety's sake he would advise me to take the dividend coupons and leave the certificates themselves behind in his strong room and safe. To buy a safe would still be a defensible act, but to have a strong room built in a rented house was more absurd, and anyhow it would be safest to keep coupons and certificates separate. So what could I say that would not ultimately drive me to respond point-blank, "It is none of your business, I will do what I want"?

From my income alone it was impossible to give Caroline what she wanted: I would need one or two thousand guilders a year of my capital. How would I get the money if I were not in a position to sell some stocks? Then besides, my conduct would unavoidably make Anna more suspicious than she already was (it was obvious that my mistrust assumed mistrust on her part too). So she would probably go to her brother-in-law for advice and help. He would have me followed, would find out everything, and...

Here we come to the strangest feature of the case. By rights Anna would then *have* to ask for a divorce, and I would thus achieve what I desired. But I did not want the divorce to take place in that way, in fact I did not quite dare face divorce. A quiet separation—forcing it on her, if need be, in one way or another, within the four walls of our home—that would be the best; but I lacked the courage to provoke a petty scandal and thereby, if only by my silence, show the world that I paid no regard to anyone's opinion and did as I pleased because it pleased me. Despite—or perhaps because of—my misanthropy, I was and am afraid of people. So I felt like a fly in a spider's web: gossamer thin, almost invisible were the threads that held me captive, yet I was incapable of tearing myself loose with a brutal, powerful jerk.

Meanwhile Caroline grew daily more pressing. At the same time her caresses became daily more precious to me. A future without her lips to kiss, without her neck to stroke, without her whiteness to snuggle against, no longer bore contemplation. Every instant I

146

did not spend with her I experienced as a drab barrenness in my existence, as an insane sacrifice of happiness, as the loss of a part of life. Why had I not met her earlier, I thought continually: why had I not set out with her into the world to roam from place to place, forever following the summer, forever renewing my pleasure in ever-changing surroundings? And in the light of this enticing vision Anna, with her cold prudishness, her bourgeois devotion to appearances, her nagging self-sufficiency, seemed like a prison wardress appointed by society as a brake on my freedom.

I soon saw that she was determined to behave as if I had said nothing at all. She continued to see to everything connected with the household so carefully that it would have been impossible to find grounds for complaint, and in her spare time she went for walks with Sofie and De Kantere, paid the odd visit, or sat in her room reading. Whenever I met her, whatever she was occupied with, she turned on me the same silent expression of contempt and haughty resignation. Every gesture, every glance, every movement of her head said, "You will never have anything to reproach me with; I would rather smother every human feeling in my soul than give anyone the right to doubt my purity." And since in her proud knowledge of this purity she did not deny herself walks up and down the garden arm in arm with De Kantere in full view of the neighbors, the concealed self-righteousness of her attitude and the powerlessness to which she condemned me sometimes drove me half mad with jealousy and rage.

Alone in my room I broke several vases and paper-knives before my passion cooled. When I beheld her I felt that my eyes radiated hatred, and my teeth clenched as if they wished to crush something in their grip. What was there to do against someone who had no desire but to go on clinging to me like a dead body, bound by an article of the law that demands an active will to divorce before it loses its binding force?

One day I again saw her from my room walking with De Kantere, this time—to my astonishment—without Sofie. All at once I heard an inner voice ask, "How far have they actually gone in their mutual idolatry?" Looking for some means of finding an answer, it occurred to me that perhaps a torn-up or discarded note might afford me certainty. I had never meddled with Anna's correspondence. I was aware that De Kantere often wrote her letters to accompany a book or to change an appointment. Who knew, perhaps she was careless with them!

I went downstairs at once, searched through all the open cupboards and drawers in Anna's room and through the wastepaper basket, but of course found nothing. I was just about to leave when I heard voices coming nearer on the stairs. I started, noticed all at once that it was raining, leapt to a side door, and almost fell into the drawing room. The door clicked shut behind me and I stood motionless, confused by the sudden events of the last few seconds.

They had not heard me. Still talking about the unexpected shower, they entered.

The sounds penetrated the thin wood of the door, muffled but quite clear.

"Please sit down," said Anna, "the rain will not go on for long. What I still wanted to say..."

The rattling of passing carriages prevented me from hearing what she said next. When I could again make out the words, De Kantere was speaking: "So I will not claim that I understand him in all respects. Oh no—very often he is a complete enigma to me. For example, I don't at all understand why he has been avoiding me recently. We were getting on so well; he had gained some trust in me; I flattered myself that I could exert some influence for the good on him; and at once... he slipped away again."

"Influence on him? That is an illusion, believe me. There is no one, nothing that has any influence on him. How could it be otherwise? Do you know of anything that Willem gets enthusiastic about, a single person he cares for in the slightest? I don't believe there is a more unfeeling being in the world!"

And now came De Kantere's voice again: "No, no, I cannot accept that. There is no such thing as a person who does not care about anything or anyone. Such a lack of feeling is always only a show. Every living creature has a tender string: it is only a matter of finding that tender string and making it vibrate. Your husband—"

Anna did not let him finish. "In other words, I have been unable to find his tender string, so it is my fault—?"

148

There had been irritation in her tone, surely more irritation than De Kantere liked, for he quickly interrupted her: "No, no, no—I don't mean it in that way! I know very well that a tender string of that kind is not always pretty, so...I am not talking about Willem but...in general....In short...I am quite prepared to accept that you know this string thoroughly and that, deliberately and with good reason, you do not choose to make it vibrate. What I meant to say is that—again in general—the cause of an unhappy marriage quite often lies in a misunderstanding. The people do not know each other well enough. If they were to learn to know each other better, then—"

I had never yet heard him stumble so.

Anna interrupted him: "No, I know Willem only too well! When we got married...ah yes...if someone had only told me then that he was actually quite different from what he pretended to be! But...Papa and Mama did not see through him at all. Mama mistrusted him, that is true; but Papa just kept saying, 'He is so strange!' and this strange side of him—I don't know why, but it was just this that I found pleasant and interesting. Our engagement was boring...oh, very boring, and at the time I even wondered whether everyone found it like that. But what did I know about other people, particularly about men? I believed I did not understand him properly, I believed that everything would get better once we had settled down...once he had an occupation like Papa....Life at home wasn't much fun either....I thought that eventually I would understand him better, and...well...that is in fact what happened. Even on our honeymoon trip my eyes were opened, and now I know for sure that there is nothing—no, nothing at all that he feels interest or pleasure or ambition about. Nothing makes any difference to him! His response is always 'I don't want to' or 'I can't' or...something like that! What you have just said is certainly true—he is a saddened man, and deeply to be pitied. For...I am sure he never enjoys anything; but..."

What followed eluded me. A heavily laden furniture cart rumbled slowly past, and it was some while before my ear, now pressed against the door, could again make out a syllable among all the grinding and droning. And this just when Anna was busy putting her dislike of me into words! The strain of listening without being

149

able to understand drove me half mad. I felt my heart thumping, and with every beat the blood seemed to rise only to my head, while the rest of my body lost sensation and stiffened convulsively. I dared not take my ear from the door, yet was afraid that my panting would betray my presence.

Eventually I could again understand De Kantere. "...then I suppose it is a hopeless task; but...I am still sorry...I feel such deep compassion for you. It would have given me pleasure to think, over there, 'At least there is something she owes me...I have been able to do something for her, however small.'"

Now for what I wanted above all to find out. I yawned with nervous tension and little red flames danced before my eyes.

After a pause she replied very softly: "Thank you for your good intentions....It is kind of you, very kind; but...all that another person can do for me—that...that you have already done....More ...more no one can do....I must bear what has been laid upon me and find my consolation...within myself."

The words echoed in my head. I found them as ungrateful as they were affected, and felt an urge to reveal myself, simply so that I could shout, "Find it then, your consolation, but let me look for my own!" Yet she was right. No matter how fine my intentions had been for a while, had I actually done anything for her? Had I even been capable of anything? Could my self-sacrificing plans have seemed anything more to her than words, empty words?

Noises in the kitchen prevented me from making out the beginning of De Kantere's rejoinder. I distinguished only the following: "I find such a conception of duty beautiful, even noble; but does it really give you the consolation you expect from it?"

Her answer came hesitatingly: "More and more. There are moments...it is true; but...I believe...yes, I am convinced that I would be unhappiest of all if I became dissatisfied with myself."

A long, deep silence ensued. "What are they doing?" I asked myself. "How are they sitting now? Are they staring at the floor or looking at each other?" It was as if through the door I felt some of the emotion that was thrilling through their souls, and also as if they were stealing this emotion—stealing it from me.

150

Eventually De Kantere resumed: "I admire you... and yet... yet your words cause me grief. They tell me that I... that I... mean nothing to you."

What joy this utterance gave me! Certainly I sometimes wished that Anna would misconduct herself. On the other hand, such misconduct would have aroused my jealousy. Since coldness and pride now protected her from this error, I could find pleasure in the fact that De Kantere too was not obtaining what I had always vainly desired. Instead of being the flame in which she should singe her wings, he was only the new shadow against which her own light stood in relief. She was like a woman who dresses well neither for her husband nor for her lover because she has no desire other than to indulge herself before a mirror in the contemplation of her own image.

However, there was still unmistakable emotion vibrating in her voice as she answered, almost in a whisper, "You know better than that."

Now his voice too became uncertain and he too began speaking softly. (Was this a matter of affectation or of natural feeling?) "I—know? Know is... too strong.... Hope?... Have I reason to hope?"

Again there was a long silence. Terrified that some noise or other would prevent me from catching the next words, I pressed myself as tightly against the door as I could, even though my knees gave way beneath me, all my neck muscles hurt, and my forehead burned as if my brains were festering.

De Kantere was the first to speak again. "Anna... you are strict with yourself and strict with others.... Are you not sometimes *too* strict?... Do you not sometimes make too heavy demands on yourself—and on others? In the long run it is impossible for such a complete sacrifice of everything human to satisfy a human being. The life of the heart has rights, sacred rights... and if these are neglected... then... yes, then they end up by avenging themselves. ... I know very well that I am now putting forward dangerous arguments—arguments which I should certainly not dare discuss with every woman. But *you* can understand them... you know how to distinguish between where the rule must be applied and where the exception... and you must know them, these arguments; for

151

otherwise... otherwise what happened to me will happen to you... otherwise you will one day regret what... what has been your noblest self-denial."

For a while he was silent. She too did not speak, and I heard a faint rustling, a sound like the crackling of silk being crumpled by a hand. Then he went on. "Let me give you an example... let me make an admission. I was very happy in my marriage. It would be scandalous to say otherwise. Emma was a noble woman whose memory I shall always honor. And yet... yet I still lacked something. As soon as we were married I felt something missing... felt it as an oppressive incompleteness; and all the affection of my wife, of my little daughter could not fill this emptiness.... Look... Emma was certainly dear... and soft... and full of devotion. But... she revered me too much—she looked on me as a father, and to me she was... a child.... Many a hard battle did I have to fight. Believe me, I know what temptation is, and I know too what it means not to succumb. For a long time this knowledge filled me with pride; but now that a riper stage of life is opening before me, now that old age is visible in the distance, now... I admit it to you honestly... now I curse my victory."

Almost inaudible, yet quite firm, came Anna's voice: "You don't mean that.... You cannot mean it."

Louder, and with a menacing touch to his tone, De Kantere continued: "Ah, don't doubt my sincerity when I open the depths of my soul to you like this!" Then, more softly, he went on: "But ... perhaps you misunderstand me. I do not at all want to say that marriage *cannot* be satisfactory. Oh no: I maintain only that for myself—as well as for others—it *has* not been satisfactory. And I will also maintain that everyone has the right in this life to a certain amount of happiness, and... think carefully for a moment: would he not be depriving another person of it—the person who should share it with him—by not granting it to himself?"

There was no reply.

"What I am saying—do you find it untrue or... or bad?" asked De Kantere.

Again there was silence. Anna must have shaken her head in silent denial, for the minister resumed: "I knew that... and then... look... not only does my heart suffer thereby but also my spirit.

152

The spirit has a need to strive, to be opposed. It wants to struggle and to conquer; repose saps it and eventually extinguishes it. I encountered submission, obedience; you encounter spitefulness, neglect; but neither of us has encountered the struggle that tempers and exalts."

"No, that is true."

"So, you see!...And now...now that...You know that I have earnestly and sincerely done my best to bring about a better understanding between you and your husband....That is true, isn't it? You are convinced of that?"

"Yes, I know it."

"But what if it now seems to be an impossibility?" He stopped as if expecting an answer, but Anna did not give any.

Again the urge flared up in me to make a sudden appearance and show them *my* contempt for a change, throw *my* judgment in their faces. But strangely enough—or perhaps not so strangely in a cerebral and heartless being like myself—my simple curiosity to see how this would all turn out won over my embitterment, my indignation, and my growing hatred. How well I recognized that Anna was enjoying a triumph such as never before, while De Kantere was being swept along by his powerful desire to impose his will and conquer every obstacle. But I wanted to know as well which of them would finally be able to say, "Victory lies with *me*."

Only when De Kantere had repeated, "After all, that is what you yourself said: it is an impossibility," did Anna hesitatingly begin.

"It is true that I cannot do much for Willem's happiness."

"Nothing!"

"Very well, nothing...nothing for his happiness; but...I can still look after him, can't I? My presence at least keeps him...to some extent...in check. I now know what I did not know when we married. My sister Suze has told me...her husband found out...how he lived before his marriage...terribly sad. Now I understand...oh, it's none of my business....I'll never reproach him with anything....I don't even want to hear about it; yet... I can see that his perverted tendencies might drive him in the same direction..."

"Well, then..."

153

"No, no...a bond exists between us, and to me it is sacred. *He* can break that bond, certainly. *I* will not profane it. Willem has a right to my care, to my devotion to duty; I may not abandon him to his fate. No, certainly not! If I did everyone would condemn me, and rightly so. I want to do what I can for him. I will heap glowing coals on his head, and I will have nothing...nothing... nothing to reproach myself with."

So my secret was still mine. She had no wish to hear anything and would never reproach me with anything. There were peals of joy within my head at the discovery, but I had no time to reflect on it. At once De Kantere replied, now in a remarkably pressing tone of voice in which there remained nothing of his usual unctuous friendliness.

"You are right, very right; but...because you have a duty toward him which you must and *will* fulfill, are you going to allow your emotional life, which he does not appreciate, in which he does not even have any part, to wither away? After all, people do not have to find out what concerns only the two of us! You do not want to reproach him with anything—very well. But does he then have any right to reproach you? Can you not give *me* what *he*, who could claim it by right but sets no store by that right, holds to be worthless? Anna...Anna...in heart and spirit you already belong to me. That you cannot deny, that you may not deny. That is something your husband cannot alter in the slightest. Now be mine also..."

I did not make out the conclusion. It sounded hushed, as if he were whispering it in her ear.

That someone could speak like this to a woman like my wife was a mystery to me, though I must admit that—whether through jealousy or through a change of taste—my verdict on Anna's attractiveness had changed erratically of recent times. But...how I envied a man who dared utter such words and who at least once in his life *had* uttered them with unqualified desire!

"And what will happen now?" was the question that beat in my head. The longer it went on the more interesting a performance it was becoming to me.

There was a pause before Anna replied. First I heard her name echo like a cry through the room. Then they both seemed to speak
154

together; but all kinds of noises in the house prevented me from making out what they were saying. When the noises at last died down, her words sounded so muffled, despite their force, that I thought, "He must be pressing her in his arms, and now...now he has kissed her as well."

"...Never again...do you hear me! No, no...never again! I could begin to hate you! I would....Oh God, no, that would be terrible!...Do you want to risk *that*?...No, no—don't ever try it again!...Promise me that!...Swear it to me!...I thought so highly of you. Don't force me...to start thinking less of you. And don't forget...what I am sure you know; the error for which a woman reproaches herself very soon becomes a thorn in the eye of the man for whom she erred."

The surmise that this sentence had been borrowed from a book De Kantere himself had given her almost made me burst out laughing. Meanwhile she went on in a much softer and calmer voice: "I would like you always to be able to think of something beautiful when you think of me. Pure, blamelessly pure—that is how I want to live on in your memory....And I want that not only for myself but also...for you. Come—let me be one of your dearest souvenirs, not one of your most painful." And then, in an even more intimate tone: "Will you often think of me? I shall certainly think often of you. I shall do so every day, when I reread the lines which I found with the page folded down in one of the books you lent me: *Woman, he who is your honor's guard / Loves you best at the bottom of his heart.*"

Such words from Anna's mouth—I could barely believe my ears, and I asked myself whether De Kantere were not now harvesting what he had sowed—phrases. Or...was *I* mistaken? Was I wrong about both of them: did they think and feel just as they said? Had Anna hardly ever spoken to *me* so lovingly because, like a Medusa-head, I made her feelings turn to stone? Was *he* perhaps after all in good faith and really being carried away by the warmth of his feelings? Who knows (the thought flashed through my brain), perhaps people as feelingless as myself always have the impression that every manifestation of feeling in other people is affectation or exaggeration. Yes, perhaps everyone thinks of his

155

fellowman, whom he does not understand and therefore cannot find natural, as more or less an actor.

Now I heard De Kantere blow his nose, like someone who has been crying despite himself. Anna did not say anything to comfort him, but from a faint rustling I thought I could infer that she changed her position. Had she gone to sit even closer to him; had she perhaps taken his hand, bent her head toward him; or had she on the contrary moved further from him because he had already sunk in her estimation, fallen off his pedestal?

After an interval he spoke again in almost a whisper. "Let it be as you will. I bow before the nobility of your heart, before the loftiness of your sense of duty. You are perhaps right...but... ah no...nothing...it is better so!—So...it is all over....For-ever...? No, no, that thought I cannot bear. I must hope...I will not say for what, I do not want to put it into words, but...a person...Please forgive me if I have hurt you without meaning to....I thought...I did not in any event want to...and...oh ...if it has to happen...what shall I...? Oh, you do not know what a horrible feeling it is for me to have to leave you behind so... how shall I say...so lonely, so unprotected! But...we may surely still write to each other, may we not?"

A sob was her reply.

"Promise me then that in your letters you will tell me everything about your life...everything...everything without exception... the good and the bad. Do you promise me?"

There was nothing to indicate to me what she said to that. For a while it was as still as if the room were empty. Then he went on, unctuously again. "In a few days Mr. De Kantere will come and say goodbye to Mrs. Termeer. But now—now our souls must bid farewell to each other. Will it be farewell forever?"

I fancied I heard a kiss smothering the words on his lips. Then he stumbled to his feet and swiftly left the room.

Trembling and glowing with nervousness, I continued for a while to stand in silence behind the door, so as to gradually recover my self-possession. But even before I was able to go over the scene calmly in my mind, the question was resounding inside me: "And are those then normal people, in whose feelings there is nothing

156

contrived, nothing self-deceitful, in whose words there is no hypocrisy, no untruth?"

As soon as I had a chance to escape unnoticed I hurried from the room, from the house, and into the park. As I walked I began to reflect. At first, of course, it was the usual kind of recapitulation —a confused revival of all the feelings and thoughts awakened by what I had heard. Then came the question, "What shall I do with this?" For the first time in my life I found myself with a weapon in my hand, a weapon with which I could strike her who stood in my way and liberate myself. At least...so I believed for a moment, which was why I asked myself, "What shall I do with it?"

What I should like to know is whether among people better than myself, among that great multitude by whom I am spurned, among all those respected, honored, decent, high-minded, well-known, and so forth, men of the community there can be found a single one who, in my circumstances, with my knowledge, with no feelings left toward Anna but hatred and jealousy, would have forgiven her from the bottom of his heart, kept himself in ignorance of what had happened, and resigned himself to the cold, ascetic, utterly empty life, the life of a touchstone for her perfection, to which she wanted to constrain me?

This question will never be answered, for everyone will say, "You get what you deserve. The men of whom you speak will never land in your situation."

Granted. But if such a miserable fate has befallen me solely because I am what I am, and if I see no possibility of getting outside myself so that I can be renovated, as a house-owner can renovate a dwelling unfit for habitation, then do not turn it into a reproach that my situation was what it had to be—my handiwork, my fault. And make it even less of a reproach that, once I was involved, my conduct was as it had to be. For I am simply what I am.

Respected, honored, decent, high-minded reader, if you think you have become so excellent by free will, why then are you not even better? Is it because you have not wanted to be, or because you could not?

Perhaps someone or other may have said or have written of you

157

that you have always shown yourself to be exceptionally good-hearted, a lover of mankind, generous, helpful, and I don't know what else besides; and then, as the plum on top, he will surely have added, "He could not have acted otherwise even if he wanted to."

Well, such is the case with me too. But now I ask, why does the phrase that holds praise for you become slanderous when applied to me?

I no longer thought of trying to do something nice for a change. Once in my life I had tried it. My most serious resolve had not availed. Now I simply wanted to have my way, and how I got it made no difference to me.

"Ah," I shouted in the lonely silence of the park, "all those fine things are nothing but humbug."

Is there a single person who is chaste for any other reason than that he lacks the courage or the temptation to be unchaste? Does altruism exist except to satisfy an instinct, an ambition, or a spirit of censoriousness?

People nowadays are priests of idols in which they no longer believe, prophets of doctrines by which no one any longer acts. They still kneel and pray, that being called for by their office, yet not one of them wholly believes in his neighbor's devotion. Satisfaction of your desires—*that* is happiness, said De Kantere, and he was right. But he was wrong to separate out desires into bad and good, for to the person who feels them there exist only... imperative desires. And unless we are all aware of this we are swindling each other with fine words whose most absurd feature is that we ourselves believe in them, just as revelers who have drunk a lot believe in the vows they make in their toasts.

Thus I gradually grew accustomed to the idea that not only was I going to do things which would necessarily be condemned by those who found out about them, but also that I had just as much right to do them as a cat which assumes the right to overturn and dirty a garden into which its master has allowed it. *What* I was going to do, however, I could not imagine. As usual I found it impossible to define the line of conduct I wanted to follow for any distance ahead.

I saw only one thing: I would keep Caroline even if she were

158

to ruin me; better a year of pleasure and nothing thereafter than another thirty years of unsatisfied vegetating. For the present I was going to give Caroline everything that Bloemendael sent me. Once De Kantere had gone, if it became necessary to settle outstanding accounts, unpaid tax installments, I would go to Utrecht, demand my stocks, and...if need be cause a scandal.

Toward Anna I no longer had any scruples whatsoever. As soon as possible I would reintroduce the subject of divorce, and then at least I would be in a position to repay her humiliations in equal coin.

In the meantime I found it much less easy than I had thought to apply this policy of having no more scruples. If I meant to keep Caroline's attention and protect myself in any measure against rivals then I had to call on her daily and at all hours. I did so. Nevertheless, I was still looking all the time for excuses for Anna's ears, and I limited myself to very short visits to Caroline. I was and am a coward, afraid of prying eyes, afraid of Anna. It did not help me one whit to think that after all she herself had said, "I do not want to know anything, I will not reproach him with anything." On the contrary, I persuaded myself that my situation would be much freer if I could simply assume that she had long ago found out everything and thus demonstrated that she was prepared to let the matter take its course.

De Kantere's departure yielded nothing noteworthy. If I had not overheard his conversation with Anna I would certainly have detected little in either of them. He played his role outstandingly well. Who knows—I thought—how often he has already played it!

As if it had been so arranged, Anna and I actually said goodbye only to Sofie. She was overjoyed to be going on a trip and so was hardly aware that she would have to leave her newest and dearest friend. Toward her father too we comported ourselves very well. We shook his hand and said quite affably, "Have a good journey, goodbye"; to which Anna added, "And write and tell us how you find things there."

On the evening of his departure I went out for the first time without saying where I was going and without being questioned by Anna. The next day we had our last talk. Of course it took place at dinnertime—at other times we exchanged barely a word.

159

My first question was, "Well—have you thought it over?"

She grasped perfectly well what I meant, yet asked with apparent surprise, "Thought what over?"

"What I suggested last time—a divorce."

"I have already given you my answer to that question."

I felt rage boiling up in me again like bubbles in water that is beginning to boil, and reminded myself that this rage—despite my weapon—would go on being impotent as long as Anna would not cooperate toward a divorce.

"Yes; but for that reason—because you were so quick with your answer—I asked you to think it over first, and...now I ask: have you thought it over?"

"There was no need for that."

With superhuman concentration I controlled myself enough to ask simply, "And so?"

"So I stick to what I said then: I know what my duty is, and I will fulfill it."

That was the end of my self-control. The commonest Dutch curse, the irrational expression of exasperation as stupid as it is powerless, rattled from between my teeth, and with a blow of my fist on the table which made the plates and glasses tinkle, I shouted at her, "What is the point of this harassment? Have you made up your mind to drive me mad? Duty, duty! Is it your duty to go on clinging to me like a burr though you care for me less than this cat does?"

Though she paled slightly at this outburst of temper, Anna's tone remained imperturbably calm. "Although we were not married in church, we did vow solemnly to each other that as man and wife we would" (here she faltered for an instant) "we would care for each other. I for one intended that vow seriously, and nothing gives me the right to withdraw from it of my own accord."

"Which you would otherwise do—if you were forced—gladly enough, wouldn't you?"

"Please be so good as not to ascribe your own wishes to me. I know—"

With a bellow I interrupted her. "You know...you know! Come on, confess what you know! But please don't talk about things you know nothing about! You know nothing about me, nothing

160

at all! What you do know...what you know very well, though you do not want to say it, and...what I know too, even if you think otherwise, that is..."

The entry of the maid prevented me from going on with my shouting. I seemed to feel a brake being tightened and my brain being suddenly and violently compressed. Everything spun before my eyes. I wanted to pick up my glass, but my trembling fingers knocked it over, and when the maid tried to wipe up the spilled wine I was barely capable of bending my head calmly to one side to make room for her arm.

Meanwhile Anna said not a word. When we were finally alone together again I could continue somewhat more temperately: "Do you find it nice to stay with a man who wants to leave you...who wants that because he wants a clear state of affairs...because our relationship is false...because you no longer feel anything for me but distaste? Or...is that not so?"

For a few seconds she did not reply. I looked her keenly in the eye and read there that she wished to tell the truth as little as she wished to lie. I was on the point of letting loose another broadside, when in a tone of voice that sounded unbearably theatrical she said, "I pity you, Willem."

What seldom came over me now occurred—I burst out laughing. "So, you pity me! Well, I don't pity you. But if you take your liberty and do as you please, then I will take mine and do what *I* like! You can keep your pity. What I want is a clear state of affairs. I decline to be made to look ridiculous, even if only in my own eyes, and I am made to look ridiculous—ridiculous at every moment you are in the garden or...in the house with De Kantere, walking about or...sitting and talking love! Don't get upset about that word. It is perfectly accurate! Your sense of duty may dictate that for a woman infidelity only begins at the moment when she runs off with another man or...you know what I mean. There are people who think otherwise, and I am among them. I find it sufficient that in your soul you are fond of this other man, and to me it is...too much when on top of that you let yourself be...kissed!"

An ashen hue spread over her features, but no sound left her lips. Motionless as a statue she sat across from me, her trembling

161

eyelids cast down, her hands, clasping and unclasping, hidden away under the table in her lap. I was sure that she was playing the role of martyr to herself, and the thought that even at this moment she could be finding self-glorification in her behavior whipped up my temper anew.

"Would you please tell me whether I am lying when I state that De Kantere and you have kissed each other?"

I had roared these words out. They dissipated in a deathly hush.

"I demand an answer—do you understand me?"

Not a sound.

Now my rage foamed over. With a new "Damnation!" I leapt up, hurling down my napkin, and sprang upon her, fists clenched, hissing between clenched teeth, "Answer me!"

But she too had jumped up at once and regained herself wholly. With her tall, graceful form, her cold, fixedly shining eyes, her contemptuously raised nose, her proudly closed mouth, she impressed me so much that despite myself I retreated a step. I did not dare touch her—so much was clear. Yet precisely this loss of nerve at a moment when I fancied I had all the right on my side made me angrier than ever, half crazed with rage. I grabbed a flask and had the maid not reentered, who knows what would have ensued. The unexpected intervention brought us both to our senses, and as if by agreement we sank down again opposite each other.

All this while my brain was in such wild turmoil that I felt quite incapable of working out what to say next. And yet more than ever before I wanted to get away from Anna, to drive her to divorce. "To her, to her," sounded the words in my head, and the *her* whom I saw was Caroline.

As soon as we were alone I began anew: "Will you now finally give me an answer?"

"I have nothing more to say to you."

"Am I meant to understand that I am lying. Is what I say about you and De Kantere untrue?"

"I am not going to defend myself."

Once more the words burst unchecked from my mouth. "No, you will not defend yourself, but you will do what you like, eh?... You will enjoy the love-talk and love-play of a sneaky minister—

162

and for the world's eyes you will go on putting on that act of yours into the bargain, eh? And I—I will allow myself to be fettered—I will be permitted to look on while you enjoy yourself—I will allow myself to be humiliated, and in spite of that I will be known as the wretch who ruins your happiness, eh? In God's name, do you think I am an idiot? Have your fun, d'you hear me! You are welcome to it! Have as much fun as you want, have whatever kind you want! *I* won't stop you. But I also want to have fun, and that—that you will not stop me from doing."

My rage had no further consequence than an icy answer from her. "Do as you please, and if you can compel me by law—go ahead. I will certainly not offer any opposition."

"The law, the law! What can I achieve through the law if you are not prepared to cooperate? Oh, you know quite well that I am in your power, and that is precisely the reason why you are tormenting me!"

"Oh," was all she said.

My rage knew no further bounds. Pouring forth a flood of words, sheer gibberish and abuse, I sprang up again, grasped my chair, and lifted it above my head. What exactly I planned to do with it I did not even at that instant know. I certainly had no intention of striking Anna with it. I wanted only to grasp and destroy; but when Anna, springing up likewise, and alarmed though fully in possession of herself, ran out of the room as swiftly as she could, I threw it after her, doing no more, however, than damaging the door slightly.

Thereupon I again sank down at the table, boiling yet paralyzed, emptied the wine flask to the bottom, fetched the brandy from the cupboard, and lost myself at once in the strangest projects for rescuing myself from this horrible, nagging tyranny. If I had earlier felt surrounded by a rampart, as invisible as it was impenetrable, separating me from mankind, it was now as if I were sitting in a deep pit, while high above me on the brim of the pit stood Anna and De Kantere mocking and taunting me.

All kinds of plans for freeing myself flitted through my over-excited brain, but there was not one I could retain for a moment to consider it a little more calmly. What any drunk man sees

163

around him—everything moving continually without advancing—I was seeing inside my head.

First I wanted to go and talk to her father and mother or to her sister and brother-in-law, then I wanted to mistreat her so badly that she would have to lay a charge against me. I thought of poisoning her, of letting her play with a revolver, of causing her to have an accident. But while I seemed to be determined to get rid of her at any price, I felt that it was equally certain that, once I was sober and calm, I would not dare undertake anything.

Thus I spent a full hour drinking and working myself up and chafing. Then I suddenly noticed that all this time the maid had not dared come in to clear the table. This brought me somewhat to my senses. I went to my room, had more brandy brought to me there, and eventually—how late I no longer know—fell into bed almost blind drunk.

The next morning I noticed with surprise that in the place where instructions for the maid usually lay, next to a much-thumbed notebook and a pair of worn-out shoes, lay a sheet of paper on which were the words "A phial of chloral as on..." followed by a date I no longer remember. I read it but thought no more about it.

Then one evening it happened that Caroline, who was now receiving the monthly allowance she demanded, to which I had gone so far as to add the previous installments, told me that even with this sum she would not be able to make ends meet in the long run. She told me this almost as if it were a joke, as I lay on the sofa with my head in her lap, her right hand in mine, and stared up at the white chin she bent over me. And with feigned naïveté—which enchanted me nevertheless—prattling all the while like a child, she continued: "No, my doll, really it won't do. If there were no Scheveningen and no opera and if there were no little carriages to be had and no pretty little clothes, yes, then maybe it would still do; but if your Caroline wants to get the benefit of all these things..."

"And if you tried not getting the benefit of *all* these things?"

"Why not, my treasure? Do you think these things are only for other people? Your Caroline is also a person and she also wants to have fun..."

"It seems to me you can get enough fun—"

164

"Oh no, my treasure, no! Don't say that! Never enough! In ten years no one will look twice at your little Caroline. Then I may even have to go out begging. So before that time arrives I want to indulge myself. I must have fifty little guilders a month more, or—"

"Or . . . what?"

Evidently she had put her foot in it, or at least unveiled somewhat much of her most intimate thinking. For now she tried to confuse me by continuing with a smile, "Or . . . you will get fifty kisses a month less."

However, I guessed that a rival, possibly the fellow from the opera, had announced himself, ready to supplant me or take up position beside me. I saw too that there was no question of haggling over the extra fifty guilders. Yet for a moment the business filled me with such repugnance that the formula of agreement would not pass my lips. I promised to think it over and soon left the house, both cross and sad that even this scrap of happiness was constantly being poisoned for me.

When I returned unexpectedly the following day to capitulate as usual and cheer her up with this news, the door was opened by a new maid who told me that her mistress could not receive me.

"Why not?"

"There is a gentleman upstairs."

It was as if the creature had given me a slap in the face. Everything swayed before my eyes, and I must have stared at her in bewilderment for a full minute before I could ask, "Who?"

"I don't know."

There was nothing for it, I found, but to go off in silence.

At first I did not go far—around the corner and back again. Then I stood for at least a quarter of an hour staring at the locked house distractedly, as if hoping that the curtains would part and my eyes see what was going on behind them. But the rigid stripes of light on the ash-gray wall did not widen, the brightly lit steps remained empty, and I ended by wandering off in despair from one street to another without noticing where my legs were taking me.

As I walked I began to see him, this unknown, this man by whom I had been supplanted. No, it was not the youth from the opera. I saw him as a big, broad-shouldered fellow with strong

165

wrists, muscular arms, a tanned neck, a ruddy face, and thick, dark hair.

Emotions, illusions—to such a male animal that was all nonsense. He only wanted a girl to satisfy his animal needs, and she...she did not mind being used and well paid. And as I pictured how that coarse body took her in its arms, kissed her,...handled her, he seemed to be laughing at me, insulting me, staining, befouling my last flicker of affection, devotion, decent feeling.

What hurt me most was that she put up calmly with all of this, that she had casually pushed me aside for a moment. And I could hear her excuse herself: "What difference can it make to you? After all, he hasn't given you any trouble!"

Had she not understood that I longed for more than simply... pleasure? How often had I not said to her, "I love you."

Then suddenly I saw that a woman like her *cannot* believe in the love of a "gentleman." There existed only one means of convincing her, which was to descend to her level, become her equal, cast off all superiority, go and live with her as man and wife.

I awoke exhausted the next morning and at once heard in my brain the question, "Who is that fellow?" I remembered lying awake until five o'clock and then dreaming of a narrow, dark, filthy tunnel through which I had to creep. The further I crept the longer the tunnel became. I could not go back, and the circle of white light I was trying to reach became smaller and smaller in the distance.

A few hours later I was at Caroline's door.

She was most disconcerted to see me arrive so early. "This is no way to carry on! I haven't done my hair yet, I haven't eaten anything. Do you think I can sit down calmly in a chair like a lady and show myself off before three in the afternoon?"

"No; but...who was that man?"

"Ah, that stupid maid! It's no business of yours!...I'm mentioning no names—I'm not a slut. So don't ask—you'll be wasting your breath. Are you going now?"

"While you live on my money I surely have the right to know whom you receive."

"So it's come to that. Well...listen then. That man was a friend of my previous...old friend, you know. Yesterday evening

166

he came for a chat—nothing more. There is something I want you to understand: I have got to know you, and I don't like changing, but if you refuse to give me what I ask then I have only one word to say—"

"Say it then!" I thundered at her, and for an instant I felt like hurling her from me like a filthy alley cat that had clutched itself to me with its claws. But when she calmly replied, "As you choose," I found it incomprehensible that I had let myself be betrayed with such insane carelessness into an outburst which I would anyhow take back.

I did not doubt for a moment that she had lied to me; but if I gave her up, what was there left for me...what could I ever replace her with?

However, I felt it necessary to preserve my dignity as far as I could. So I explained to her that there was nothing I wanted more than to remain her friend forever, and might even agree to her new demand; but...she must never deceive me, nor did I want to hear any more threats, and she must at least try to love me. All of which she at once promised solemnly.

"That other one, that gentleman—you will never receive him again?"

"I swear it to you."

It seemed to me a sign of firmness not to visit her the next day, but to take a few days to think things over. So we arranged on what day, at what hour I should come with my final answer, and I made up my mind not to come on that particular day, but to catch her off her guard by coming at least twenty-four hours earlier.

In the meantime we had to go to a big dinner at my in-laws, the Van Swamelens. Such dinners had always been a martyrdom to me, and I told myself I endured them only for Anna's sake. This time I saw the evening before me as an impenetrable, stifling blackness rearing up menacingly in the middle of the week. Suze had talked to Anna about my past, so I knew roughly what the Van Swamelens thought of me. And who knows—I thought—what they had told their friends and acquaintances!

My urge to decline the invitation this one time was strong, but what reason could I offer? My brother- and sister-in-law knew

167

that I had nothing to do, and Anna, who was glad to see people, would certainly not lie for my sake. The result would inevitably be that I would be suspected; it was quite within Van Swamelen's powers to track down the grounds for this suspicion, and then... yes, heaven only knows what obstacles these people, in concert with Anna, might then put in my way! So I went after all, but with as much rage as fear in my heart.

The beginning of the evening was simply unbearable. In every pair of eyes I read an accusation; every turn of a head looked to me like a mark of contempt; every word sounded like an obscure gibe. I did not dare speak to anyone. At first I stood like one deaf staring shyly in front of me. Then I stuffed myself with food that almost stuck in my throat. And all the while Caroline whirled so madly through my brain that it was impossible to keep my attention on the chitchat at table.

Afraid that someone would see that I was wandering, I again had recourse to the wine. I emptied my own carafe, which was refilled. I did not omit a single choice wine, and drank down my champagne at once every time. The remedy worked. Gradually I became more voluble, even deluding myself that the conversation was beginning to interest me. But when I had also had a few after-dinner brandies, the effect was too much for me. My excitement increased; I adopted an overbearing tone, soon lost track of what I wanted to say, understood less and less clearly what the others were saying, and noticed suddenly that I could no longer focus my eyes properly on them. For the rest I remember nothing of what passed that evening. Only a vague inkling of having become senselessly boisterous, of having shouted and raged, lingered in my brain like an unsightly, lurid wound on the still white skin of a rotten body. No one told me afterwards what actually happened, nor did I have the courage to inquire. So perhaps the worst was only a dream. In any event, I do not nowadays dare show myself to the few people I know.

With Anna I exchanged no word—indeed, at home we hardly spoke at all any more. Only at lunch, at dinner, and at tea did we see each other, and then both of us acted as silent as if there were no one else in the room. When I think of those last days, I hear again the dull clatter of forks, spoons, and knives, the rattle of the blinds, the grumble of tea water, the echoing blows of the pendulum, and about these sounds, encasing them thickly, deathly silence.

One evening there came a letter from Davos addressed to Anna. She glanced through it swiftly, said that De Kantere and Sofie had arrived safely, and put the letter away in her bag.

"Indeed ... I will give you an opportunity to enjoy the rest, which I may not hear, at your leisure, and in your reply to retail all the evil you know about me or are going to think up."

With these words I left the room and the house and went to Caroline.

"My mistress is not at home."

"You lie! There is a light on in her bedroom. I can see it through the chinks of the curtains!"

"Yes, but ..."

"But what?"

"The master is upstairs."

More than once in my life I have experienced the horrible sensation of being both enraged and powerless, but never has it brought my whole being into such tumult as at that moment. It was as if all the thoughts in my head suddenly caught fire and burned away. And it was not only my thoughts that were consumed: all my feelings, my whole inner self swelled up to a surging, chaotic mass whose envelope became too tight, a sea of fire trying to burst and erupt in waves, like an annihilating flood of lava boiling up in the black depths of a mountain. I felt myself going raving mad, and for a few minutes I must have been demented. I had to smash something, the first thing I laid eyes on. All at once I saw my stick waving around, breaking a pane of the front door, though I did not yet realize it was *my* hand that had driven the stick through it. I knew that I was standing on the threshold of a house at the foot of a well-lit flight of stairs, yet I had the feeling that I was again lying on my belly in the dark tunnel and having to creep through it toward the receding daylight. And as if to smash this tunnel, to make space for my exploding frenzy, I began to strike about me like one possessed. Tinkling shards of glass fell on the sidewalk; a blow on the chest

169

smote me backwards into the darkness; the door with the jagged hole slammed shut with a rattle, and there I stood alone again in the gray, desolate street before the dreary housefront, looking up at the unmoving strips of light between the immovable curtains.

My whole body was trembling, and just as in my boyhood, when, taunted to desperation, I finally fell blindly upon my enemies, to be smashed to pieces, if need be, against their heads and fists, so for a second the urge welled up in me to run at the door with bent head, ram it through, and fall down in the hallway with a shattered skull. But just as in the sea a trough suddenly gapes where a moment ago a wave towered, so a groundless fear suddenly replaced my insane frenzy.

That man, that fellow would come downstairs!

I ran up the street, and walked...walked until I had reached the far end of the city. There I entered a filthy little bar.

What was I looking for? Women to shout at and abuse, common sluts who for money, much money if necessary, I might pinch, scratch, thrash, kick.

If only I had found them! But I was mistaken about the character of the house.

I gulped down several glasses of bad gin, went on to the streets again, and for a while roamed around, no longer aware of why I was there or where I was going. I thought only fitfully. Between these fits lay black abysses of utter vacancy. During one of the patches of clarity I decided not to return to Anna at all. The next day I would go to Utrecht, fetch my stocks, and leave the country with Caroline. For money, for *all* my money, she would surely be prepared to do anything, and once I had her among people she did not understand, once I could watch over her every moment like a Cerberus, then she would simply have to obey me and smile at me and kiss me and love me!

More acutely than ever before I felt that voluptuousness alone could no longer satisfy me. My soul throbbed for love, for tenderness; my body ached for affectionate cherishing, and because Caroline could give me all that, if she only would and if I only had her to myself, I had to get away, away with her, away as far as possible! The world would cry shame about me, certainly it would, but what did the world matter to me any more? Was I not doomed

170

forever to remain the unsightly little fellow, the runt whom everyone might look down on with contempt and distaste?

Oh, if I could only revenge myself one day on happy, decent people!

Might I not be capable of a bold deed, one single sensational scandal?

All at once I found myself in front of my house.

I had made up my mind to go to Utrecht—but why wait in the street for sunrise?

Just behind the front door I found a candlestick. There were matches by the low-burning hallway light.

So I had been made provision for; and there would be more of the same.

The solid, gleaming, old-Dutch candlestick—a present from Anna's mother—stood like a spy on duty to see how late I came home and in what condition.

It was neat in my house, tastefully neat, but all these clear windowpanes and marble tiles, all these gleaming doors and stairs, all these shining glass knobs and copper rods glowed balefully at me as material expressions of Anna's self-sufficient prudishness and sterile love of housekeeping. Her surroundings had to frame her worthily and provide a fitting background to her faultlessness.

I felt strange and ill at ease in my own home; it was as if *she* ruled there and *I* were merely tolerated. On the staircase Zola's words came to mind: "No scoundrel like a respectable person!"

At the top of the stairs I hesitated a moment, then went—without knowing why—left instead of right, grasped, as if obeying another's will, the handle of her bedroom door, turned it, and...found to my astonishment that it was not locked. Inside the gas was burning dimly.

I stood listening as the door slowly swung open. Nothing stirred. She was sleeping soundly.

What did I actually want to do? I did not know.

Evidently she had forgotten to turn the key this one night. It would not happen again. And—I thought—she must also keep the light burning every night so as not to be surprised by me in the dark.

Two steps brought me to the hanging lamp, whose flame I

turned up high. Nothing stirred behind the green curtains of her bed.

Again I listened, and now heard the strange silence. The gas hissed; in my ears roared my inflamed blood; further there was nothing but silence—silence in the room, silence in the house, silence outside as far as the ear could hear.

How strange that she did not wake up. After all, I had made noise and light.

A shudder ran through my body. "What if she is dead?" I thought.

Still I did not know what to do.

A curious feeling came over me. It was as if the silence were a black, cold shudder, enfolding the things around me, muffling their sound, covering their eyes, deafening their ears, slowly rocking, smothering, stifling everything, everything in sleep.

Meanwhile on the night table beside the bed I had seen an apothecary's phial one-quarter filled with an almost colorless liquid. Next to it lay a porcelain spoon.

Then, on the table under the gaslight, I noticed a phial of a different shape, as yet unopened but likewise containing a colorless liquid. Despite the dissimilarity of the phials I guessed that they both contained chloral. Now I saw what made her sleep so soundly.

The thought flashed across my mind that she could have taken a little more, that she would then have slept even more soundly, perhaps so soundly that she would...never again awake!

Never again awake!

The idea made me shudder, yet I could not shake it off. On the contrary, it seemed to spread over my brain, and everything grew cold, sober, clear.

A voice in my head began to repeat, "A little more and never again awake!"

All this time nothing stirred behind the still, green curtain. The gas hissed. In my ears the blood roared.

And suddenly, like someone who, walking hurriedly in the dark, comes to a puddle and has to jump to avoid stepping in it— suddenly I was sure of what I was going to do.

A little more and never again awake! Then it would be over; then she would be gone, completely gone, gone forever! Then I would be free; then I could do what I wanted!

172

To be free, completely free again!

First I took the unopened phial and read the printed label: "Insomnia, Pain, Neuralgia—Syrup of Chloral."

Then with a tug I threw open the curtain and looked.

There she lay, pale, motionless, with purplish eyelids, half-open blanched lips—just like...a corpse. She did not awake, but after a moment turned half over.

For a while I continued to stare at her. I was terrified that she might wake up. In the tension of the moment (I remember with hideous clarity) I repeatedly asked myself, "Is it possible that I feel nothing—no pity?" Yes, I tried to work up some pity. I told myself, "She is still the old Anna, the Anna for whom you have felt a touch of sentimental love, the Anna you wanted to make happy!"

It had no effect. It was as if even in her sleep she still taunted me, laughed at me, insulted me. I felt only that she stood in my way, that I hated her, that she had to go, and in my ears the inflamed blood roared.

A little more and never again awake!

Yet I was trembling all over my body when my fingers closed on the half-empty chloral phial.

For a moment I stood with it in my hand like a thief who hears a suspicious noise and thinks he has been caught in the act. But finally I picked up the porcelain spoon too, filled it, and with an unsteady hand brought it between Anna's half-opened lips. At the same instant I pinched her nose shut to make her swallow.

The eyelids parted slightly and she looked at me; but at the same time she swallowed. Then she gave a cough, mumbled with difficulty, like a person who has drunk too much, a few incomprehensible sounds, and slipped back into sleep.

I said nothing, not stirring from my place. For a while I stood trembling with nervousness. Then I poured the rest of the phial down her throat in the same way.

Was she...dead, or was she still going to die, or...what was going to happen?

An appalling fear overwhelmed me. My hands trembled more and more violently, my knees began to knock, I broke out in a cold sweat, clouds passed before my eyes. In the clouds I saw stars, like someone about to lose consciousness. I sank down into a chair, keeping an eye on her.

I must have sat like this for an hour without thinking a thought, simply staring and staring all the time to see whether there was any movement in the waxy paleness of the head on the yellowish white of the pillow.

The gas hissed and in my ears the blood roared.

When at last I could again recognize that she had remained motionless all this time, I felt myself growing more restful, felt firmness return to my arms and legs.

"No half measures," I muttered to myself, and stood up, went to the table, opened the phial of chloral, filled the spoon, and brought it to her mouth.

Thrice more I repeated the dose at long intervals. The third time the liquid ran back out. Did this mean that she was...dead, or would she still die, or...what would happen?

To find an answer I bent over her, and finally...finally she gave up the ghost.

Slowly, dreadfully slowly, her eyelids opened. From that darkly gaping fissure, as if from fathomless depths, a look of icy fixedness shot straight up at me. It was a ghastly sight! Appalled, I started back, finding just enough control over my limbs to turn the gas flame down, shut the door behind me, cross the landing, and lock myself up in my own room. There I stood leaning against the wall and trembling, fully conscious yet incapable of stirring or of thinking. It was as if my brain were paralyzed. I do not even know whether I remained in this posture for a short or a long time.

She was dead. There was no doubt about that, and yet, when life returned to my thinking, I heard again the question, "Is she actually...dead, or is she still going to die, or what is going to happen?"

And if she was dead, had I in fact taken all my precautions? Would no one find anything suspicious?

I wanted to go back and look, but no longer had the courage.

My God, my God, what was going to happen?

Sitting on the edge of the bed I listened and listened, not knowing what I was listening for.

174

For the time being nothing happened. It remained as still as if with one movement of my hand I had destroyed forever not only Anna but all life in the city and beyond.

Once more the urge crept over me to have a look. I told myself I had to, but I found it impossible to stand up. Like a paralytic I sat confined. I could no longer stir a hand, a foot, even my head. And all the time I listened, listened without knowing for what.

I entered a strange state between waking and sleeping. Downstairs I heard two o'clock strike on at least three clocks, and as these sounds echoed through the deathly silence it was as if the emptiness around me began to fill with phantoms. I had horrible visions. At one moment I would see Anna come in, at another moment one of the maids, once even De Kantere. At each apparition I broke into a cold sweat and shivers crept up from my stomach as far as the inside of my eyes. Then the specters vanished into space like pale glimmers of light. Unrelieved blackness closed in around me, and I heard the question anew: "Is she...dead, or is she still going to die, or...what is going to happen?"

More than once I thought, "I have only dreamed it, it is all in my imagination." But then fear reawoke, leaden, oppressive, to fetter me and testify to the reality of what had been done, what eternally and immutably had been accomplished.

At long last, however, I found enough strength to rise and undress, though I kept feeling that someone was standing behind me. Like a madman I whirled about the room, and returned somewhat to my senses only when I lay shivering beneath the blankets.

At first there was no question of sleeping, my heart thumped too frightfully. Downstairs three o'clock struck. I was wider awake than ever. And all the time I kept listening, listening, without hearing any sound but the roar of the blood in my ears, the beating of my heart in my chest.

Again I thought of going to look; again my courage failed me. I saw that I would never be capable of it.

What if she were not dead...perhaps lay dying...or woke up and began to understand? It was impossible, but the sweat of fear would not leave my forehead.

At about four o'clock I must have dozed off from exhaustion.

175

But this sleep could not have lasted very long. A hideous nightmare, a dream of slowly being crushed between two gigantic stones, made me start bolt upright with a heart beating so unbearably fast that I thought I was about to choke with anxiety.

And then, through the dirty, reddish gaslight in the gloomy room, the new day finally began to dawn, cold, blue-gray.

What would it bring, this new day?

Dull sounds rumbled in the distance. A train whistled across the fields. People were waking up. Would they read tonight that a terrible crime had been committed?

If only I had not done it! Oh God, if only I had not done it!

I still had fits when fear rose glowing hot to my head, but the realization that very soon everything might be spoiled by a single unconsidered word, a single careless gesture, a single shifty look, forced me to concentrate all my thoughts on a single point—on the question, "What must I do now?"

It was clear that I should set to work most carefully. Now as never before it was a matter of not only playing a role but of playing it particularly well, of learning it by heart down to its smallest details. To begin with, I must behave just as I did on other days: get up at the usual hour, dress as slowly as usual, go downstairs as calmly as usual...

But then? Anna was always the first downstairs; now she would not... be there.

Yes. Then it would be advisable to ring for the maid, ask after Madame, express surprise at her late rising. Not immediately, but a little later, I should send the maid upstairs, and then...

Yes, and then what?

I felt so light-headed that I could barely think what next.

A doctor... yes, of course, I should at once send for a doctor, refuse to believe she was already dead, pretend to hope she had only had a fainting spell about which something could still be done.

But then?—Then he would ask me all kinds of questions. I could prepare myself fairly well for these questions, but doctors are generally good judges of people. What if he suspected something from my way of speaking, from my eyes, from the gestures of my hands? For *that* I could not prepare myself. The best thing would be to have a story ready and to impress it on myself so well that even I believed in the truth of it—a trick at which I was an old hand.

While I worked it out, my heart gradually grew a little calmer. I was not able to stay in bed, however, until my usual hour of eight. By half-past seven I had risen and begun to dress.

I felt that I could never get through the day.

How marvelous it would be three days from now—or...?

No, no, that could not be, that would not be! After all, there was not a single shred of evidence.

Meanwhile I was exceptionally tired, yet feverishly excited. Hot and cold shivers ran ceaselessly up and down my back.

I looked in the mirror: my eyes were veined with red, my cheeks ashen and sallow, with hectic spots. That face alone would betray me! I washed myself repeatedly, and finally I fancied that the cold water had freshened my appearance a little. Yet—I felt—I would not be able to look anyone straight in the eye.

When, still far too early, I arrived on the landing, I stood staring at the door of Anna's room for a long while. Behind it she now lay with her appalling, half-opened eyes—dead.

But what if she were only apparently dead, and heard everything, knew everything, perhaps...would tell everything. Should I go and look?

Impossible!

As I descended the stairs I wheeled around at almost every step, thinking I heard her door open.

On the first-floor landing I encountered the housemaid, who said "Good morning." I growled something back and stood as if turned to stone, listening. I knew for certain that she was going to the attic, yet I thought, "What if she goes into Anna's room?" Only when I heard her steps fade away behind the attic door was I capable of proceeding to the breakfast parlor on the ground floor.

Eating was out of the question. I drank a little tea and scraped a few breadcrumbs over my plate to create the impression that I had breakfasted as usual. Then I wanted to ring for the maid and ask whether she had not seen Madame yet; but it was still too early.

I was unable to wait longer, however. Suddenly my hand pressed the button. The bell rang in the kitchen and the maid appeared. I did not dare look at her.

177

"Has Madame not yet come down?"

"No, sir, but you are much earlier than usual."

Did this remark indicate that she felt suspicious? All at once I could not understand that she did not know what I knew, that she did not see the corpse lying upstairs as I saw it from where I sat.

With an astonishing effort I tried to maintain my air of indifference, though far from sure that I was succeeding.

"Yes, I too have noticed that. I seem to have mistaken seven o'clock for eight."

A quarter of an hour later I rang again: "I don't understand what is keeping Madame. Go and take a look."

She went. Now the discovery had to come. I heard her steps ascend and cross the landing. Then followed a knock at the door... once... once more.... She opened the door... she stepped inside... a long silence... now she saw it... she was coming back... hurried, rumbling steps... she ran down the stairs... rushed into the room...

"Sir... Madame... oh God, what a fright I had, what a fright!"

Pale as death and gasping for breath she stood there, one hand clutching a chair, the other rubbing her eyes as if trying to drive the horrible sight from them.

"What is it?—Come on, what is it?"

At first the creature was unable to answer. Louder and louder I shouted: "What is it?—Come on, what is it?" Then she began screaming hysterically. I rang for the other maid, but left the room before she arrived, calling out, "There is something wrong with Madame, come along." I raced upstairs and into the bedroom, and... there it was... the scene from last night... now (one shutter stood half open) bathed in the white light of day. The gas flame was still burning but cast no light. There stood the phials. The green curtain was still wrapped around the bedpost. There she lay on the pale pillow: wan, waxy yellow, with purplish eyelids, faintly parted lips... and hideously staring half-opened eyes.

So it had worked, and she would not betray me—never, never! For the duration of a second my soul rejoiced, but at once fear stifled this jubilation. Action was called for.

"Go at once to the doctor. You know where he lives. Say that he must come this instant—this instant, you understand!"

178

One maid went. But now the other reappeared. I saw that it could be dangerous to remain idle.

"Fetch me some milk."

I stayed behind with the body, but could not bear it. One shudder after another went through my body. I tried to defy that fixed stare, but then it suddenly seemed that she moved. I left the room, waited for the maid on the landing, and returned with her to the bedside.

Of course it was impossible to make the numb throat swallow. The milk ran out at once, just as the last of the chloral had during the night. As if to justify myself I spoke of my suspicion that Anna had taken too much medicine and poisoned herself.

The maid was wailing awfully. What she said I no longer know. Weeping and muttering we continued to stand about until the doctor appeared in the doorway. As harriedly as I could I called out, "There—there," pointed to the bed, and went to the window to stand and wait. I dared not look. To conceal my agitation I pressed my face into my handkerchief and the handkerchief against the window.

In deadly fear I listened.

At first I heard only faint, incomprehensible sounds, then the creaking of boots, sighing and throat-clearing coughs, then the picking up and putting down of the phials, and finally, after endless suspense, the approach of muffled steps.

Now he tapped me on the shoulder.

"Mr. Termeer, what has happened here? How has this come about?" His heavy voice sounded more inquisitorial than upset.

Turning, I found myself looking into two penetrating brown eyes which sized me up sharply. I pretended to only half understand him.

"What has happened? Is she then ... dead .. .really dead?"

"Certainly she is dead, and has been for quite a while too."

Frightened of appearing either too agitated or too calm, I fell back on pressing my handkerchief to my face.

"My God, my God! Is it possible? I can't believe it ... I ... yes ... What has happened? Who can say, doctor?"

"You do understand, do you not, what your wife died of."

"Understand ... no ... that is ... I do understand that ... those two phials ... I saw that it was chloral. But chloral is surely a well-known

179

sleeping draft. So how does it come about that...?"

"Did you know that your wife took chloral?"

"Did I know that...? Well...I knew that of late she has often slept badly...but that she was taking something for it—how should I know that? Do you think she consulted me? You know her well enough from earlier to—"

"Was this morning the first time you found such a phial here?"

"Of course...I understand that that surprises you; but I never... came...here."

After this explanation the doctor again looked long and sharply into my eyes, more inquiringly than sympathetically, without saying anything. Then he pushed a chair toward me and sat down. Involuntarily I sank down on the chair; but the fear of being more closely questioned in this room, beside Anna's corpse, suddenly oppressed me so intensely that I stood up and asked him to go to my own room, where we could speak better. Without a word he followed me.

On my own terrain I did in fact feel more at ease. I waved him to a place on the sofa, moved up an easy chair for myself, and began to relate.

"Doctor...I want to...I cannot, in circumstances like these, keep back anything from you; but...on the other hand you need not ask me any unnecessary questions, need you?...You have seen that we have two bedrooms....After the death of our child my wife had my bed removed from her room. I was never prepared to ask her what the reason was. Perhaps that was wrong—possibly so. But I thought and...think still that the joys of having a child did not weigh as heavily with her as the horrors of losing one. You do not know how she took that loss to heart. At no price would she have laid herself open to it a second time...but...you understand...the result was that in recent months I have seen her only between eight in the morning and ten-thirty at night."

"Did you then live together...on...such bad terms?"

I did my best to sound embittered. "Ah, doctor,...there are relationships that do not fall under so general a heading. I do not believe that Anna was ill-disposed toward me. Nor was I ill-disposed toward her...though I have been aware for a long time that it was impossible for me to do anything for her; but..." Suddenly afraid

180

that he might already have heard something from the maids about heated exchanges of words, chair-throwing, and so on, I did not dare proceed.

Now he asked: "So...you believe that sorrow over the death of the child brought her of late to the point of fretting, that consequently she began to suffer from insomnia, and that she took chloral for her insomnia."

"I *have* to believe that; but you must not think I feel certainty about anything! Anna was so reticent that, to put it mildly, I found it most painful."

"It is strange that no one ever advised her to try a less dangerous remedy. After all, there are more harmless sleeping drafts. So you do not either know who prescribed the chloral for her."

I shook my head.

"Was the chloral fetched by one of the maids?"

I shrugged my shoulders, whereupon he asked to be allowed to question the maids. There followed a long interrogation, from which there emerged the following. Only once had the housemaid had to fetch chloral, and then the apothecary had refused to dispense it without a written and signed order from Madame in which she was required to state for what purpose she used the remedy, and that its effects were known to her from experience. So presumably she had fetched the stuff herself the first time, and after these objections from our usual apothecary she had had the chloral sent to the house by another purveyor.

Up to this point everything was going excellently; there was nothing to indicate that I had been acquainted with her use of chloral. However, the case again became more suspect once the maids had been sent away. First the doctor made me relate in detail what had happened since Anna and I had last seen each other the previous night. I dished up my prepared story, and could not detect that he doubted its truth. Then he looked at me again fixedly for a while, and suddenly asked, "Who paid the apothecary's account, your wife or you?"

This question utterly confused me. All kinds of questions, such as, "Have there been apothecaries' accounts?" "Have I paid them?" "Do I remember seeing one?" whirled through my head, and though

181

I knew I should answer without hesitation, I did not know what I could say without danger.

Luckily just the right words slipped out. "Anna saw to all the accounts. I paid without scrutinizing anything."

There was a long pause, till the doctor continued: "There is no doubt about it that your wife took too much chloral; but... did she do so on purpose or by accident? That is the question. Can you shed any light on it?"

"Impossible."

"Your child has been dead for some time.... It is surely strange that only now has she... Did she suffer at all from shortness of breath, difficulty in breathing?"

"As far as I know, no."

"I see.... And have you ever noticed anything abnormal, anything strange in her?"

The question was again a criticism, but fortunately I kept my composure.

"Please listen, doctor. The line between the normal and the abnormal seems to me difficult to draw; but since Anna is dead, I should like to tell you something that you may find illuminating. Anna had conceived an affection for... someone who left the country ten days ago."

There was no trace of sympathy for me on the doctor's face at this confidence. On the contrary, I fancied that he looked at me with stern reproach, almost with rebuke. Then he said, "That is most unfortunate... both for you and for her. But... under these circumstances—that you did not even think of supervising her a little better... of questioning her... if necessary, of warning the maids discreetly—I must say, it is too much, really too much!"

So I had made a mistake after all. How hard it is to lie or equivocate in such a way that something not only appears to be true but also creates the impression one wants.

It seemed best to proceed with as much effrontery as possible. "By Jove, doctor, this is a most fitting moment to reproach me with that! As if I were not in enough of a mess! Should I have had reason for suspecting my wife of plans to do away with herself? She was no longer a child, and as I have already told you—and you know so yourself anyway—she was particularly reticent

182

and secretive. Do you think she would have allowed herself to be lectured by anyone? Do you really think it would have helped me at all if I had warned the maids? How can you say something like that, how can you hurl such reproaches at me!"

The tirade was barely over before I felt that it would have been better to have produced tears and limited myself to the reproach that it was inhumane to intensify my sorrow with such callous remarks.

Now he stood up and replied in a cold, lofty tone: "Mr. Termeer, no matter how unpleasant I find it, duty requires that I notify the law. Without a doubt we are dealing here with a case of poisoning."

I thought that the ground was giving way beneath me and the light of day darkening. Luckily I had not yet stood up, for at this instant I would surely have fallen down. The whole room together with me spun around several times. For a few seconds I felt as if I were about to fall forward and, like a toy acrobat, stand on my head. And when I again found myself sitting in my chair it was as if my temples were being gripped in ice-cold metal pincers which were slowly being pressed tighter and tighter. I could no longer see, I could no longer think, yet I perceived that only perfect self-control could save me. It must have been this sense of danger which in a flash allowed me to find my means of salvation, grasp it, and use it with exceptional composure.

"Doctor ... I was totally unprepared for anything like this. If you say it is your duty ... yes ... good heavens, then ... then I can have no objection. I thought for a moment you meant that it was on me that the blame. ... Oh, only for a moment; but you understand how ... this appalling thought alarmed me. ... Of course there was no question of that. You know me too well for that. ... Heavenly justice! ... But do you know what is most terrifying of all? ... People! If the police or the courts come to have a look ... if the maids are interrogated ... my God, you must surely understand that for the rest of my life I will have to go bowed beneath the unproved ... yes, the unspoken suspicion of having poisoned my wife ... my own wife. Have you really considered how dreadful that would be? You must know how rumors are born! ... And then the parents! ... God in heaven, if they were to come here right now and not only see the corpse of their child but hear that it is suspected...God, God, that cannot be, that simply cannot be allowed! Just ask yourself!...You surely see it will be the death of those poor old people. Mama is a resolute soul—you know her—but the old gentleman...with his weak nerves...oh, my God, my God, it will be the death of him without any question!...Look, I do not even dare tell him that in all likelihood Anna took too much on purpose....I was planning to mention a heart ailment; but the courts, the police—no, no, no, the more I think about it...they would never survive it—neither of them!"

I clearly saw that something serious, something new had occurred to the doctor. There was a changed, more thoughtful, less censorious look in his eyes. After a short silence, he said, "Yes... that is so. What you say there—I cannot deny it. It is truly no small matter...old people...someone with weak nerves...it could be dangerous....On the other hand, you never know...it is not a matter here of a trivial dereliction of duty.... *You* must understand that it is impossible for me to take the responsibility on to myself. I may not do that, nor will I."

"I understand that; but...what has to be done, after all?"·

Again there followed a pause. Then he again stared straight into my eyes and went on: "*This* I can do for you: I will not go to the law myself, but simply hand in at the City Hall my report of suicide caused by chloral hydrate."

It was as if I had emptied a bottle of champagne at a single draft, so bewilderingly did a joyous drunkenness thrill through me at these words. I felt like falling on his neck, and he must surely have read something of this crazy impulse in my eyes, as with a great effort I forced myself to be calm, rather saying nothing at all, rather looking aside in order not to betray myself. However, when he too kept silent I became somewhat more anxious at the thought of the possible consequences, and finally asked, "And then?"

He shrugged his shoulders. "Yes, then...then I do not know what will happen. Without any doubt the people in City Hall will communicate this report to the police. Then...then I think...I am not sure of it, but I think...they will come to me for information. If the court accepts my report, they may still question you; but that will probably—I say probably—be the end of it. If not, then...yes, then you will be faced with the investigation after all."

184

So my joy was tempered just enough to make it easy for me to thank the doctor most earnestly. I added that I understood perfectly the difficulty of his position, that I thoroughly approved of his procedure. In all I thought that I left not a bad impression. Yet he did not offer me his hand when, with a stiff bow, he departed, promising to come again that evening.

Had he suspected me?

My first action was to compose two telegrams to the parents: the first preparatory, the next definitive. The maid who took them received an oral message at the same time for Van Swamelen and Suze. Then followed the chores of seeing to funeral arrangements, the death notice, and the announcements. This kept my attention away from the swift chase of fearful visions flitting constantly through my dark brain like rockets.

The Van Swamelens naturally came before the parents, so it was to them that I had to tell my story. They put a series of questions to me, yet showed more surprise and curiosity than grief and sympathy. It was clear to me from the first that they were relieved, and this did not surprise me in the least. The two sisters could get on quite well together, though they had never been very close. But I, Anna's husband, that dullard, that queer fellow with whom you never knew where you were, with whom no one got on well—I was the stumbling block. Never mind, I thought, we shall lose contact soon enough!

But then came Anna's parents. My brother-in-law had fetched them at the station and told them everything. There was nothing I needed to say.

Ah, how intense one's suffering must be when one no longer shrinks from pulling such ridiculous faces! Never yet had I seen so unseemly and laughable a sight. Both were so beside themselves with grief that I could not understand how they could have left their home and made the journey to The Hague. The old gentleman was almost blind with weeping; in the first half hour his trembling lips did not produce a single comprehensible sound. Mama behaved more calmly, but was still so overwhelmed with tears and so totally immersed in her grief that she did not hear what was said to her. They began by falling on my neck, and before this double eruption of sobs, tears, incoherent words, and cries of pain I did not know what to do or how to comport myself. Everything, particularly the clammy contact of those tear-streaked cheeks and damp lips, struck me as so queer, so repulsive, that what little pity I felt, half genuine, half forced, was soon damped. Luckily the old people noticed none of this. They simply went on lamenting, on and on, conscious of nothing but the fact that their daughter was gone. Mama wept quietly. Papa found it necessary to speak as well.

"Oh God, oh God, can it be! My child, my little girl, my little Anna! Who would ever have thought it! How can it have happened? What carelessness! Come, tell me everything. Her heart, was it? Surely all the sorrow over her child, eh? Ah, yes—she could never get over it! But why did she never say anything about it? Then at least you could have provided her with some diversion, and consulted a doctor—not so? It is true, she was always very reticent. Never once really confiding, eh? But I still don't understand it! I don't understand it! And to think that an apothecary can dispense something so dangerous! There should surely be a law against it. It is frightful—it is appalling! Oh, my child, my daughter, how she must have suffered, my darling little Anna. Or do you think...? Ah yes, you wouldn't know either, of course! Who knows? Who will ever be able to say?"

It escaped them entirely that there was not one word of response to all these exclamations, all these questions. When they had finally become a little more composed, I asked whether they wanted to see Anna again, and then sent them upstairs with the maid, saying that the sight affected me too much.

When I was all alone my fear began to make itself felt more sharply. Every time the bell rang I started up more violently and my nerves grew more taut in shuddering expectation of the noise that would say, "There they are."

Confused by the doctor's declaration, I must have behaved all morning more like one half-crazed than one deeply downcast. Now I even lost the ability to apprehend my condition. It was as if fear turned my soul cataleptic. I felt my mind stiffen, my attention contract till it became like an eye which, looking through a telescope, sees nothing but a narrow grayish circle in which at any moment the object of its terror will appear. And in this painful

186

shriveling together of my nervous life, it was as if my body died off and like an inert mass hung down more and more heavily from my anxiously staring brain.

I no longer understood what was being said to me; I no longer knew where I was; in my mind's eye I saw only the stretch of street before my front door, and watched to see whether it was still empty, empty of strange men.

Aside from the horrifying remembrance of living in this secret fear, almost nothing of the afternoon has remained with me. I see the old people drift around like phantoms, I hear them say incomprehensible things.... Further I remember nothing, nothing at all.

At table I came to myself somewhat. I observed that Bloemendael sat weeping in wordless misery, and that Mama surveyed me steadily with a cold, unblinking gaze. It would not surprise me to find that she had her doubts all along. However, for the moment her unmistakable suspicion was welcome to me as a whiplash to resume my act and persevere in it as well as I could.

As we were having dessert, the doctor came.

Was I imagining it, or was it true that he adopted a much more genial tone toward the parents than he had toward me? How sympathetic he was, how profuse in his praise of Anna!

For a long time—much too long for me—he went on talking. It seemed to me that he was also making attempts to find out from the parents something about my relationship with my wife. Was he perhaps looking for a contradiction between my assertions and theirs? That might well have been the case. But even if he had tried, Bloemendael could not have helped me more than he inadvertently did by simply repeating, "So you also think there was something not quite right about her heart. Yes, that must be it, for otherwise... The loss of that child... yes, that must have affected the heart, for after all she still had her husband. They were fond of each other... they were happy together. She never complained about anything!"

When the doctor finally rose to go upstairs, I followed him closely. He understood with what object, and in the passage he at once turned around.

"You would like to know how it went off, eh?"

187

"That is obvious. The old man is already so upset."

"Well...it went as I expected. I was summoned to the public prosecutor. He made me recount in detail what I found here. He asked whether I had not formed any other suspicions, he asked about the facts of the case, about the names of the apothecaries, and so forth. Whether he is content with my declaration...that I cannot venture to say with certainty; but...I think so."

"Thank God," echoed the words through my head, and again it cost me an astonishing effort not to give vent to my happiness in peals of shouting.

Was I really free of it all? Would no one ever find out anything? Would even the suspicion—if it had existed—remain buried in the brain of this doctor?

No longer did I feel that a bullet was waiting for me! My freedom had returned! Only a suffocating little passage to traverse and I would stand free in the free air! Once more life smiled on me. I had grown older, certainly, but I was not yet *too* old! And money, after all, buys so much, sweetens so much. After such a deed I would surely no longer be a coward! Now I had savoir-faire and experience! Oh, what a glorious moment of triumphant joy! The whole evening I was so full of it that I had to feign a headache and go to bed to hide my nervous excitement.

The next morning I had much less to see to and take care of. Whenever the parents left me alone for a while, I fell into fits of anxious depression alternating with outbursts of joy, the one as irrational as the other. All my arguments about the lack of evidence and the need to keep control over myself were of no avail; only the presence of a third person held me sufficiently in check, forced me to think and talk about other matters. I shuddered at the thought of solitude as at something that would perforce drive me insane, and attached myself to the old gentleman like a frightened child in the dark to a stronger friend whom he does not really like.

Bloemendael's senile whimpering became more unbearable with every passing minute. What reply could I make to his endless repetition of the same questions—"Do you really think that her heart...Did you truly never notice that she was beginning to

188

fret about something or other...?" It upset me quite enough to have to deceive the old man, who had always been so good and friendly toward me. Finally I burst out angrily at him: "I have said no a hundred times!"

"Yes, but then why did she take chloral?"

"Because she could not sleep!"

Then with horrifying calm Mama suddenly asked: "Willem, it is true, is it not, that the two of you got on well together?"

Although I felt as if my head had suddenly become transparent and her clear eyes could see into it through mine and read it like an open book, I fortunately still had the strength to reply, "Of course."

"I was just thinking that in the last while she stopped writing about you. I always asked how you were getting on, but for months your name did not come up in her letters."

It was at this moment that I first felt the terrifying compulsion to tell everything—everything. It wanted to come out, out! The sensation was so unusual and so dizzyingly wretched that it commanded my whole attention. The old people's talk became a soft murmur rolling in from the far distance. I saw them as if through dense gray vapor. Within myself I stared in deathly fear upon the confession that heated my entire soul as if with white-hot writing and shattered its stillness with shrill words. I felt that I might lose consciousness entirely at any moment and, not knowing what I was doing, yell out, "I murdered her!" The discovery of a painless cancer growth could not be more arresting, more revolting, more bewildering than this glimpse into my heart!

Had I spoken at this moment, it would have been out of embitterment, out of a need to reproach this cold, dutiful mother with the coldness and dutifulness of her child. But I felt, oh at once I felt that at the instant I was moved by emotion, by the slightest sentimental softening or by the faintest flicker of misanthropy, the awful words would rise to my lips. So now my fear of the law was drowned in this far deeper fear of my self shuddering through my entire being. The former had been nothing but a single little thought of my brain; the latter was a sickness, a dissolution of my entire personality.

That evening I had myself to get a sleeping draft from the

189

apothecary because I did not have the courage to face the silence of the night with my parents-in-law in the house and my confession on my lips.

During the funeral I bore myself well. The old gentleman made such bizarre grimaces that his performance made me want to laugh, and controlling this urge prevented me from thinking about other things. But whenever my attention returned for a moment to what was going on in my own mind, I saw that dangerous tendency lurking, heard myself call out, "Shall I tell you how she died? I—I murdered her!"

While I was driving through the streets this did not disturb me. I was in a very strange state of mind. Swinging along slowly in this solemn funeral procession through the midst of pedestrians who quietly stepped aside and looked up, I felt at last that I was someone who takes part in communal life and in due time offers his own display of formality. But at the same time I felt that I was deceiving all these people with the secret in my soul, that the deed with which I had defied the laws of society with impunity had placed me above the commonplace surrounding me. For once I enjoyed the illusion of having revenged myself on normal humanity, of having had a chance to triumph over the society that had always confined me and denied me what was mine.

That was how I felt in the teeming city, and that was how I felt too in the quiet cemetery, as I marched decorously behind ridiculously dressed-up undertaker's men and played my part in the tedious theater ceremony around the open grave. It was easy to maintain my indifference there, posing as a steady fellow full of self-control. The thought that I was making a fool of humanity gave me hitherto unknown strength. But afterwards—from our arrival home until the old people left for the station and the Van Swamelens for their residence—for this whole period the terrifying words burned continually on my tongue. And the worst of it was that I could not even, as I had earlier done, down a glass of sherry or gin to put some heart in me. For I know from experience that it is drink most of all that makes me communicative and indiscreet.

It was a true relief to know that at last I was alone in the house
190

with the maids. To make myself feel absolutely safe I went so far as to lock myself into my bedroom.

Thank God, now no one could watch me, no one could speak to me. Here, as if in a medieval fortress, I was separated from mankind by ramparts and passages. I forbade the maid to admit anyone at all, and as soon as she closed the door behind her I turned the key twice in the lock Then I heard her go down the stairs, listened until everything was quiet once more, and called out, "I murdered her ... murdered her ... murdered her!"

Saying these words I felt a nervous chill shudder through me, very much like the chill I had experienced as a boy saying dirty words.

For three whole days I stayed in my room, and during all this time I uttered not one syllable to the maids silently serving me.

The day before yesterday, in the afternoon, I came downstairs again for the first time.

At first I did not dare enter Anna's bedroom. In the room downstairs which the two of us used most, I experienced another distressing sensation: the furniture had eyes and was silently watching me. Every time I wanted to pick up something that had belonged to her, I looked anxiously around to see that nothing was moving and coming toward me. I kept feeling that I was being stared at, as if presently a hand, an invisible hand, would touch me. Then I would scream out, "Yes, yes, it is true, I did it!"

Oh, how frightened I was that someone would hear it!

Gradually some of this irrational fear has worn off, and yesterday I was in the room where the corpse had lain. I opened the cupboard in which she kept various knickknacks, and finally fell to rummaging among them. I did not encounter much of note. But one discovery touched a particularly soft spot. How can it be that I, who did not cry beside her corpse or at her graveside, burst out in sobs at the sight of a portrait of Anna from a time when I did not know her at all? Was it that, because in this faded little picture she already displayed the smile with which she was later to charm me, I felt a compassion for the tender, innocent child still smiling at life which the more powerful woman of experience had no longer inspired in me?

"Poor thing," I muttered: "once you hoped you would enjoy

191

something of life, and what has it given you?" For a long time I sat weeping over this dead photograph. While my sorrow soothed me, as a moonbeam shining through a black storm soothes a lonely wanderer, I could not understand at all what had brought me to my terrible deed.

Why, after all, why?

I told myself that Anna had been my only link with humanity, the only creature who had cared in the least about my fate.

But was it true compassion, true sorrow, or has hypocrisy become so much part of me that I am compelled to make a fool even of myself? I no longer know. Perhaps it is all the result of my fear of the future, of old age.

Who knows how much longer I have to live! Must I go on wandering about lonely among hostile people all this time, shunned like a leper?

Yes, getting her out of the way was an act of madness, her of all people! She hampered my freedom, but what is this freedom worth, what will I do with it?

Caroline?

Whether I will ever find it in me to visit her again is the question. At the present moment I certainly do not have the courage. With her more than anywhere else I shall have to think about Anna, and to her more than to anyone else will I be tempted to confess what I have done. One second of ecstasy in her arms, and with tears in my eyes I will say, "I murdered my wife, murdered her for your sake...for you alone...so that I could possess you utterly, you alone."

What will she do if she hears that?

This morning I went to town again for the first time. A horrible sensation, being among people again without display, without the separating frame of a carriage. I do not think that anyone guesses anything, yet I read in every pair of eyes that seems in the least familiar a suspicion just heard or uttered for the first time. And I feel too as if the whole heartless, milling pack would be prepared to hurl itself upon me as soon as it entered the head of only one of these casual acquaintances to shout, "Here is the mangy cur—throw him in the water!"

No, that is something I will no longer face! Rather break up

192

my household and leave for a country where no one knows me even by sight and where nothing reminds me of the past! Which would anyhow become unavoidable if the old people ask me to take them in and I can find no pretext for refusing.

And what difference does it make where I live? Life is after all the same everywhere.

However...for a whole hour I have walked around Caroline's house without daring to ring the bell and without knowing what I was looking for.

And now, as I write, I feel deep down beneath my fear, right down beneath my gray indifference, the growth of a new question: "If I were to admit everything to her, and at the same time offer her the disposition over my entire fortune—would she not then, for the sake of this deed...for the sake of this misdeed...would she not...not find it in her to...love me?"

QUARTET ENCOUNTERS

The purpose of this new paperback series is to bring together influential and outstanding works of twentieth-century European literature in translation. Each title has an introduction by a distinguished contemporary writer, describing a personal or cultural 'encounter' with the text, as well as placing it within its literary and historical perspective.

Quartet Encounters will concentrate on fiction, although the overall emphasis is upon works of enduring literary merit, whether biography, travel, history or politics. The series will also preserve a balance between new and older works, between new translations and reprints of notable existing translations. Quartet Encounters provides a much-needed forum for prose translation, and makes accessible to a wide readership some of the more unjustly neglected classics of modern European literature.

Aharon Appelfeld · *The Retreat*

Translated from the Hebrew by Dalya Bilu
with an introduction by Gabriel Josipovici
'A small masterpiece . . . the vision of a remarkable poet'
New York Times Book Review

Grazia Deledda · *After the Divorce*

Translated from the Italian by Susan Ashe
with an introduction by Sheila MacLeod
'What [Deledda] does is create the passionate complex
of a primitive populace' D.H. Lawrence

Carlo Emilio Gadda · *That Awful Mess on Via Merulana*

Translated from the Italian by William Weaver
with an introduction by Italo Calvino
'One of the greatest and most original Italian novels
of our time' Alberto Moravia

Gustav Janouch · *Conversations with Kafka*

Translated from the German by Goronwy Rees
with an introduction by Hugh Haughton
'I read it and was stunned by the wealth of new material . . .
which plainly and unmistakably bore the stamp of Kafka's
genius' Max Brod

Henry de Montherlant · *The Bachelors*

Translated from the French and with an introduction
by Terence Kilmartin
'One of those carefully framed, precise and acid
studies on a small canvas in which French writers
again and again excel' V.S. Pritchett

Stanislaw Ignacy Witkiewicz · *Insatiability*

Translated from the Polish by Louis Iribarne
with an introduction by Czeslaw Milosz
'A study of decay: mad, dissonant music; erotic perversion;
. . . and complex psychopathic personalities'
Czeslaw Milosz

Hermann Broch · *The Sleepwalkers*

Translated from the German by Willa and Edwin Muir
with an introduction by Michael Tanner
'One of the greatest European novels . . .
masterful' Milan Kundera

Pär Lagerkvist · *The Dwarf*

Translated from the Swedish by Alexandra Dick
with an introduction by Quentin Crewe
'A considerable imaginative feat'
Times Literary Supplement

Robert Bresson · *Notes on the Cinematographer*

Translated from the French by Jonathan Griffin
with an introduction by J.M.G. Le Clézio
'[Bresson] is the French cinema, as Dostoyevsky
is the Russian novel and Mozart is German music'
Jean-Luc Godard, *Cahiers du Cinéma*

Rainer Maria Rilke · *Rodin and other Prose Pieces*

Translated from the German by G. Craig Houston
with an introduction by William Tucker
'[Rilke's] essay remains the outstanding interpretation
of Rodin's œuvre, anticipating and rendering otoise
almost all subsequent criticism'
William Tucker, *The Language of Sculpture*

Ismaïl Kadaré · *The General of the Dead Army*

Translated from the French by Derek Coltman
with an introduction by David Smiley
'Ismaïl Kadaré is presenting his readers not merely
with a novel of world stature — which is already a
great deal — but also, and even more important, with
a novel that is the voice of ancient Albania herself,
speaking to today's world of her rebirth' Robert Escarpit

Martin A. Hansen · *The Liar*

Translated from the Danish by John Jepson Egglishaw
with an introduction by Eric Christiansen
'[The Liar] is both a vindication of religious truth
and a farewell to the traditional modes of extended
fiction. It is haunted by literary ghosts, and English
readers will recognize the shadowy forms of Hans
Anderson...and Søren Kierkegaard' Eric Christiansen

Stig Dagerman · *The Games of Night*

Translated from the Swedish by Naomi Walford
with an introduction by Michael Meyer
'One is haunted by a secret and uneasy suspicion
that [Dagerman's] private vision, like Strindberg's
and Kafka's, may in fact be nearer the truth of things
than those visions of the great humanists, such as
Tolstoy and Balzac, which people call universal' Michael Meyer

Marcellus Emants · *A Posthumous Confession*

Translated from the Dutch and
with an introduction by J. M. Coetzee
'Since the time of Rousseau we have seen the growth
of the genre of the *confessional novel*, of which
A Posthumous Confession is a singularly pure example.
Termeer [the narrator], claiming to be unable to keep
his dreadful secret, records his confession and leaves it
behind as a monument to himself, thereby turning a
worthless life into art' J. M. Coetzee

THURSDAY
2:00 PM